MISSING—ONE *CORPUS DELICTI*

Item: a black-handled kitchen knife, the blade having a serrated edge and a thin coating of blood. Wrapped in a transparent polythene, the knife lay on the desk of Detective Superintendent Rogers.

Rogers grunted and settled himself in his leather chair. It creaked under his weight like a barn door as he made his points with short stabs of the stem of his pipe.

"Accepting the laboratory test that the blood is human, we must also accept that some person has been wounded or killed. It might be an accident, or it might be suicide." He stabbed his pipe. "If it's suicide, then the disposal of the knife doesn't fit. Any innocent cause would have been reported to us by now, by one of the hospitals if by nobody else. Which leaves," he said, "murder. And I'd feel a bloody sight happier," he snapped, "if I had a body. Something I can get my teeth into," he concluded with unconscious incongruity.

BANTAM BOOKS offers the finest in classic and modern English murder mysteries. Ask your bookseller for the books you have missed.

Agatha Christie

DEATH ON THE NILE
A HOLIDAY FOR MURDER
THE MOUSETRAP AND
  OTHER PLAYS
THE MYSTERIOUS AFFAIR
  AT STYLES
POIROT INVESTIGATES
POSTERN OF FATE
THE SECRET ADVERSARY
THE SEVEN DIALS MYSTERY
SLEEPING MURDER

Carter Dickson

DEATH IN FIVE BOXES

Catherine Aird

HENRIETTA WHO?
HIS BURIAL TOO
A LATE PHOENIX
A MOST CONTAGIOUS GAME
PARTING BREATH
PASSING STRANGE
THE RELIGIOUS BODY
SLIGHT MOURNING
SOME DIE ELOQUENT
THE STATELY HOME
  MURDER

Patricia Wentworth

MISS SILVER COMES TO
  STAY
SHE CAME BACK

Margaret Erskine

CASE WITH THREE
  HUSBANDS
HARRIET FAREWELL
THE WOMAN AT
  BELGUARDO

Margery Allingham

BLACK PLUMES
DANCERS IN MOURNING
FLOWERS FOR THE JUDGE
TETHER'S END
TRAITOR'S PURSE

Elizabeth Daly

AND DANGEROUS TO KNOW
THE BOOK OF THE CRIME
EVIDENCE OF THINGS
  SEEN
THE HOUSE WITHOUT THE
  DOOR
NOTHING CAN RESCUE ME
SOMEWHERE IN THE HOUSE
THE WRONG WAY DOWN

Jonathan Ross

DEATH'S HEAD
DIMINISHED BY DEATH

DIMINISHED BY DEATH

Jonathan Ross

BANTAM BOOKS
TORONTO · NEW YORK · LONDON · SYDNEY · AUCKLAND

DIMINISHED BY DEATH

*A Bantam Book / published by arrangement with
the Author*

PRINTING HISTORY

First published in Great Britain 1968

Bantam edition / October 1984

ISBN 0-553-24439-6

Published simultaneously in the United States and Canada

---

*Bantam Books are published by Bantam Books, Inc. Its trade-
mark, consisting of the words "Bantam Books" and the por-
trayal of a rooster, is Registered in U.S. Patent and Trademark
Office and in other countries. Marca Registrada. Bantam
Books, Inc., 666 Fifth Avenue, New York, New York 10103.*

PRINTED IN THE UNITED STATES OF AMERICA

O   0 9 8 7 6 5 4 3 2 1

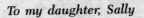

To my daughter, Sally

1

The warmth of the July night was around them like black treacle. Through the openings of the overhanging clouds moving heavily in the humid air, the stars blazed in a brilliance of squandered sapphires and diamonds. It had rained during the past hour and from somewhere within the lushly vegetated banks of the river an unmated frog ballooned air in its throat and ululated its need.

Above the moored dinghy the bridge crouched beastlike, its buttresses and arches concealing in its shadow the two figures in the boat. Squeaking bats wheeled swiftly under the span of the arch and skimmed the stalactites of wet moss as they hawked night-flying insects. From the dark shrouded fringes of the water came the occasional explosion of a disturbed coot.

To Charlie Otter, these things were outside his interest and extraneous to his purpose. His consciousness was narrowed like a beam of light and focused to a single-minded attention on the girl at his side. She—occasionally stirring in protest against the rigid skeleton of the boat— lay quiescent on his jacket, her thickly plastered lashes a darkness on her pale face.

The youth's white shirt glimmered in the inky gloom of the bridge's shadow. The pads of his restless fingers were reading the contours and smoothnesses of her body, much as the fingers of a sightless man would read braille.

She was fourteen years of age and believed she knew precisely what she was doing. Other than smoking (which she had never learned to like) she could conceive of no other means of underlining her grown-upness, her contempt of school and her rebellion against the conventions of the society she thought she despised. She was certain of her ability to contain the passions of the youths she drew to herself with the tartish promise of schoolgirl lubricity.

He was four years older and arrogant in his awareness of his attraction to girls. Older women were drawn to him also, but these frightened him with his imagined inadequacy. His sexual display was the long hair curling over the nape of his neck, the dark trousers tight over his narrow loins and flat stomach. Neither by instinct nor need a lecher, he took girls for the status it gave him. He magpied their favours with the true collector's catholicity.

He had sought by design the concealment offered by the arch of the stone bridge for he still feared his father and dreaded discovery in his intimacies. His mind was now on the two opposing factors of finance and sex. The one of returning the boat before the expiration of the hour for which he had hired and paid; the other, the delicately poised problem of bringing his calculated wooing to a successful conclusion.

He moved himself carefully as the girl's eyelids closed and her body slackened in his arms. As he did so he heard the sounds of approaching footfalls on the bridge above him. He stiffened in apprehension, his finger on the mouth of the girl beneath him, hissing a tobacco-tainted warning to her. The footsteps, hesitant and furtive, echoed their owner's progress along the footpath bordering the parapet.

There was a silence and then a growing whisper of sound from above. A falling object struck the youth on the shoulder, dropping with a sharp rap into the well of the boat. His caution died against this affront to his male aggression and he heaved himself sideways, spluttering his outrage incoherently upwards to the bridge above him.

There was a startled exclamation, the dim shape of head and shoulders peering over the stone parapet and outlined against the star-blazing sky and then the rapid tattoo of running feet.

Unhurt, his aggression mollified by the unequivocal flight, Otter looked briefly in the darkness for the missile that had struck him. Finding nothing, he returned his attention to the girl who was pulling herself upright. She was now all timid schoolgirl and chilly withdrawal and in no mood to prove herself to him.

When he fitted the heavy oars into the brass rowlocks and pulled for the boathouse, he was unsatisfied and angry. Near the second bridge she snapped at his sullenness. He turned the boat into the bank and put her ashore with a silent jerk of his thumb, pulling away before she had completely regained her balance. There was nothing of the schoolgirl in the word she flung at him.

He grudgingly paid the boat owner in the corrugated iron shed that sheltered the few boats and snarled his displeasure at the old man's questions. The significance of the blood on his shirt left him incurious.

Detective Sergeant Coltart, dwarfing the doorframe in which he stood stolidly, watched the boat owner with his small and humourless green eyes. The tiny office in which the two men talked overlooked the mist-smoking river. It was placid now under the growing warmth of the emerging sun, the smooth water a pellucid olive where it combed the flowing tendrils of weed with its currents. Under the protection of the banks, the water supported on its surface a brilliant scum of duckweed, scribbled with the narrow trails of passing water-fowl.

From the awakening town, encroaching its walled alleys and yards to the very edge of the river, came the sounds of moving traffic and echoing early-morning voices.

On the table between the two men lay a knife. The handle was a dull black, the blade slim and wickedly pointed. It was, overall, some six inches in length. The blade, no longer a bright silver, was covered with a transparent varnish of drying blood, still sticky to the touch of a finger.

"Tell me again then," Coltart was growling. "I've had it second hand from the Station Sergeant. Now I want it from you."

The boat owner was an old man with an evil face. He was club-footed and bent. His skin was wrinkled like an ancient grey sock. He was aggressively independent, inherently surly and no man to be pushed around by anyone he considered likely to be exercising any authority. On the other hand, he almost creaked with self-righteous honesty and made a fetish of civic responsibility. None of this, in his opinion, necessitated any obligation to amiability or politeness. Nor did he feel any compulsion to be particularly cleanly in his person for it was self-evident that he neither washed nor bathed himself too often. When he spoke he used his words like fragments of rusty tin, purposeful missiles intended to scratch the skin of a man's esteem and importance.

He owned six paintless, plank-sprung boats and a licence (which he equated with Magna Carta) from the local Authority to permit their hire.

He scratched his aggression now at the impassivity that was Coltart. "I told the young copper about it." His pouched boiled-egg eyes swivelled towards the knife. "It was in the boat. The 'Maid Marion.' The one I let out last night. 'Ow many more bleedin' times 'ave I got to tell you buggers?"

Coltart refused to waste his own verbal weapons on this—in his opinion—contemptible antagonist. He was insultingly bland, his eyes never leaving those of the old man. "Look, dad," he said patiently, "it's not that simple. Who had the boat? Let's start with *him*."

"Don't call me 'dad'," the old man said witheringly. "I wouldn't father you on a camel." His narrow shoulders in the soiled grey cardigan twisted in his annoyance. "My name's Bodger. *Mister* Bodger."

Coltart bobbed his head in mock submissiveness. "Of course, Mr. Bodger. I'm sorry. So shall we start with who had the boat?"

"A young bleeder. 'E 'ad this bird with 'im." Bodger surprisingly jittered his salacity. "A busty bird. I reckon 'e did 'er."

The large man's eyebrows snapped down. "What do you mean?" he demanded. "That he killed her?" He stalked towards Bodger and halted close to him. This near, he could smell the sourness of the old man's uncleanliness.

The seamed and stubbled face looked up at him in astonishment. Then understanding came and one pink-rimmed eyelid closed in a knowing wink. "*You* know," he leered. "*You* know . . . what 'appens with young birds."

"Yes, I do, you dirty-minded old sod," Coltart murmured

inaudibly to himself. Aloud, he said, "Never mind what
you think. Do you know either of them?"

Bodger shook his head. "No. Mind, 'e's been 'ere before. 'Ad the boats I mean. A real randy little 'orror.
Always with the birds. Schoolkids." He turned his head
and hawked his throat in disgust.

Coltart was monumental in his patience. "How old?
Him, I mean."

"Eighteen, nineteen . . . thereabouts. Like I said. A
young bleeder."

"Tall? Short?"

The boat owner measured the large detective with
narrowed eyes. "About up to your Adam's apple and with
'alf of your fat."

"Muscle, Mr. Bodger," he replied without humour.
The old man's malice was too obvious for him to take
umbrage. "His hair. Dark, fair, mousey? Bushy, straight,
greasy? Was it long?"

"'Is 'air was long an' black. Black an' curly. With side
bits down past 'is ears. 'E 'ad pimples too."

"What was he wearing?"

Bodger was beginning to show signs of impatience
and a desire to re-enter the cooked-cabbage smell that
advertised his living quarters. "Clothes!" He paused at the
look in Coltart's eyes. "Oh, *you* know. Skinny trousers an'
a short-arsed coat. A thin tie. It 'ad stripes." He held his
opened hand horizontally across his chest. "Green stripes."
He said it as if it signified putrescence. "Shoes with 'igh
'eels. Pointed toes." His disgust was enormous.

"Are you sure you don't know him?" the detective
growled, suspicion showing from behind the blandless.
"This isn't the time to start being clever. A blood-stained
knife and a missing girl need a good deal of explaining.
And they used *your* boat."

"Ahhh." Spittle wet the distorted lips. "Didn't I tell
you bleeders? I didn't 'ave to. I could 'ave kept it to
meself. I wish I 'ad now," he finished nastily.

"Why not last night?"

The mouth expressed its owner's disgust. "Because
I'm not a bleedin' copper, that's why. Because I ain't being
paid for putting meself out anyway."

Coltart ignored his spit-punctuated outburst. "Do you know him?"

"No." He chopped the answer off with finality.

"What does he look like? I mean . . . what sort of a job do you think he'd do? Could he be a bus conductor, for instance? A clerk? Shop assistant?" He waited while the cross-grained man scratched the stubble of white wire on his chin. His fingernails were black crescents of dirt.

"I dunno why but I got the idea 'e's a garage mechanic. I might 'ave seen 'im in one." He apparently thought this was too helpful and added, "I might not 'ave either. I don't know. I'm jus' sayin' what I think." He challenged Coltart to dispute the rightness and logic of this.

"What about the girl, Mr. Bodger?" This time he allowed his eyes to crease in masculine understanding.

"'Er?" He thought for a moment, his mind almost ticking its processes. "A little girl. She 'ad stuff round 'er eyes though. Black. Like bleedin' soot. An' pale lips. You know . . . white paint stuff. An' she stunk of scent."

"Dressed?"

"Up parsed 'er knees. A striped dress. All colours. Pink an' green an' blue . . . you know?" He shook his head in exasperation at his inability to communicate properly. "An' coloured stockin's . . . they 'ad 'oles in them . . . 'oles. Patterns . . ."

Coltart nodded. "I get what you mean. And I suppose you don't know her either?"

The head wagged. "No, I don't. I 'adn't ever seen 'er before."

"Now go over carefully what he said to you when he got back."

"Again?"

"Yes, again. Exactly what was said to you at the time."

Bodger spat into the river. "I said to 'im, 'Blimey mate, you've cut yourself. There's blood all over your shirt,' an' 'e put 'is 'and up there an' looked surprised. Then 'e said, 'It's spoiled me bleedin' best shirt.' I asked 'im where 'is bird was an' 'e said, 'I dumped the bitch in the river.' 'E then went off."

"Show me the boat, will you."

Bodger shuffled towards the drift of boats roped shoulder to shoulder like tethered steers. He indicated without speaking one of them with the toe of his thick-soled boot.

The detective clambered into it, holding the gunwale with one hand as his weight pressed the hull deeper into the water. He lowered his bulky body on to the seat and scanned closely the well of the boat. Other than a few smears of blood, there was nothing he could equate with the discovery of the knife. Bodger, a congenital early riser at any time, had clumped along the narrow-walled passage leading from the river bank to the main thoroughfare of the borough. To the leisurely striding constable working his early shift the old man, with a sort of bitter satisfaction, reported the finding of the blood-stained knife. Coltart, called from bed by the Station Sergeant and breakfastless, had dismissed the constable back to his beat and prepared to bend his massive persistence to the task of why, who and when.

A blood-stained knife was a simple illustration of violence. But the definition was far too wide and needed narrowing by elimination. The blood might be human. Or not. If animal, its presence on the blade might be due simply to the innocuous cutting of butcher's meat. If human, the cause could be accidental or (and this was the possibility engaging Coltart's attention) by murderous intent.

From Bodger he had obtained the meagre facts that pointed to nothing at all. The youth, accompanied by the girl, had hired the boat for an hour, depositing the sum of one pound against the all too likely probability that, without it, the boat would be abandoned to drift in unpaid aimlessness. At ten-fifteen, within a few minutes of the expiration of the stipulated hour, the boat was returned and the deposit reclaimed. With the difference Bodger had described. The old man, sharp and cunning as a weasel, could be believed in his querulous recital of the facts.

Before he left, Coltart towed the boat to an unoccupied corner of the boathouse and covered it with a tarpaulin supplied ungraciously and with ill-humour by Bodger.

"I'll lose a bleedin' fortune over this," he grumbled into the broad back of the busy Coltart.

The patient detective turned his head over his shoulder, his green eyes direct. "If you hire this boat out against my say-so, Mr. Bodger," he warned him pleasantly, "I'll twist your bloody head off with my bare hands."

The sun was now poised above the serried ranks of slate roofs and squinting brassily between the tall yellow brick chimneys, throwing broad shadows from the bulk of the pottery kilns. An umber smudge of smoke skulked low in a thin disc of discoloration already beginning to stain the clear sky.

Along the otherwise deserted banks of the river— black and muddy underfoot from a splashing of overnight rain—two large and silent men walked, one on each side of the slowly moving water. They wore dark suits and conservative hats. They placed their feet with care and their unblinking eyes scanned both the water and the damp tangle of vegetation through which they pushed. Small swarms of insects rose and scurried before them. Tiny flies settled undisturbed on their perspiring faces.

Like Coltart, who had detailed them this precaution-ary operation, they had not breakfasted and their chins were stubbled with unshaven whiskers.

Item: a black-handled kitchen knife, the blade having a serrated edge and a thin coating of blood. Wrapped in a membranous bladder of transparent polythene, it lay on the desk of Detective Chief Inspector Rogers.

Rogers possessed in abundance the unthinking arro-gances habitual to large men equipped with black eye-brows and thrusting noses. He wore a dark grey suit, a crisp white shirt and an air of earned authority. His occupation was on him like a metal skin; his objective an unwinking eye inside the core of his brain. Despite the pressures of his work, he had found time to graft on to his professionalism a furnishing of graces sufficient—when he bothered—to steer him adeptly enough between the con-trived obstacles of social intercourse. When his need coincided with the occasion, he was, without second thought, hedonistic.

His shoulders were heavy and his arms thick. Beneath the immaculate cuffs of his shirt the wrists were covered with dark hair, curling around the gold band of the steel watch he wore on one. Violence was in him, caged by the dictates of his profession. When necessity compelled him to hit a man he did so without passion, without heat. On the rare occasions he lost control of his temper, his brown eyes darkened to the shiny black of a beetle's wing-cases in a face drained of its swarthiness to a paper white.

He had eaten a breakfast before leaving for his office and was now stuffing shreds of tobacco into the fire-charred bowl of a stubby pipe. He was irritable with indecision and the need for action on an unknown premise.

Detective Inspector Lingard, his newly appointed assistant, sat near him. His hair was straw yellow and an inch or so too long for a policeman. His face was wedge-shaped and saturnine, his build that of a fast three-quarter. He wore light dogtooth check suits with modish waistcoats and consumed powdered tobacco through a narrow, intolerant nose. On this latter, he occasionally perched spectacles with heavy black frames.

Coltart sat opposite Rogers, his haunches overhanging the chair he dwarfed by his size. He had detailed to him his interview with Bodger and the search of the river banks he had initiated. It was not yet nine o'clock.

The sun was throwing yellow brilliance on to the polished chestnut linoleum of the office floor. Within the rays the curlicues of smoke from Rogers's pipe swirled and twisted into a blue haze.

"Is there any chance of it not being human?" The sergeant knew the question was rhetorical. The identification of blood needed only a simple and uncomplicated test. Quandom from the laboratory had been unequivocal in his verbal report. It had taken him but a few twists of the gear wheel of his binocular microscope to bring the disc-like corpuscles into focus. As a bonus, snagged in the irregularities of the serrated blade, the physicist had identified a fragment of lung tissue and a thread of cotton. The thread was blue in colour and three millimetres in length. The blood had not stained it beyond identification. His question to Coltart was no more than a muscle twitch of his built-in scepticism.

"It's human all right," Coltart replied. "Quandom's doing a checking precipitin test but it's more from habit than any need to confirm it."

Rogers grunted and settled himself further down in

his leather chair. It creaked under his weight like a barn door as he made his points with short stabs of the stem of his pipe. Each stab left a small puff of smoke poised in the air in front of his nose.

"Accepting the laboratory test—and I don't see why we should not—we must also accept that some person has been wounded or killed. The wounding or killing might be homicidal in intent. It might be accidental. Although," his mouth turned down, "*that's* extremely unlikely. Or, it might be suicidal." He stabbed his pipe. "If it's suicidal then the disposal of the knife doesn't fit. And I'm sure we should have heard something of it. I don't think we need bother with accident as a hypothesis. Any innocent cause would have been reported to us before now. By one of the hospitals if by nobody else. Which leaves," he said, "murder. Or attempted murder. And I don't think it can be an attempted murder. For much the same reasons which negative the others."

"An outside guess," Lingard offered. "Subject to the qualifications you've mentioned. Quandom *could* be mistaken if he relies solely on his microscopical examination. He isn't a serologist. Corpuscles can be misshapen. There can be confusion. Could the blood, in short, be animal?"

Rogers nodded shortly. "This could be so, David. I wouldn't quarrel with that. Nor, of course, does the lung fragment help at the moment. But what persuades me more than anything else is the thread of cotton. Coupled with the disposal of the knife." He prodded his pipe at Lingard and showed his teeth. "Think about that, David, and you'll agree that your theory is pretty unlikely." He turned to Coltart. "What do *you* think of the girl as a likely victim?"

Coltart, a non-smoker who sublimated any urges he might have had to do so by chewing things, was now splintering the end of a pencil. "If she's in the river she'll be difficult to find," he growled in his bass voice. "It's deep there and stuffed with weeds. It's almost certain she's nowhere on the banks."

"Did Bodger say how much the chap's shirt was stained?"

"Yes. Not much, apparently. A smear more than anything else. He said, though, that it was quite distinct."

"And our pimply friend not explaining it?" Rogers's forefinger seemed impervious to heat as it pressed glowing tobacco more firmly into the pipe bowl.

Coltart wagged his head. "No. Seemed concerned about it spoiling his shirt. Nothing more."

"Not the reaction of a murderer, anyway. What about the girl?"

"That was it. Said he'd dumped her. I suspect he was joking. Or using a colloquialism." He added after a pause, "I hope he was, please the Lord."

"Any line on him?"

"We're doing the garages. It seems our best bet although most of them are only just opening. Anyway, Bodger's seen him somewhere even though he's not disposed to be too helpful." The large sergeant laughed. "I'm not being servile enough to suit him it seems. Still, black face whiskers and acne should narrow the field. Give or take a hundred or so adolescent yobbos." He spat out a fragment of pencil wood. "The lads are out combing now. If old Bodger's right, we'll have him in no time."

"Any ideas on how the knife got into the boat? Accepting again that Quandom's right, the blood is fresh and certainly less than twenty-four hours old."

"Bodger swears it wasn't in the boat when he hired it out to the youngster and the girl. It was daylight then and I think we can accept what he says. After all, he was sharp enough to see it first thing this morning."

"Under a seat? Any concealment there?"

"Not possible. Too high up and too narrow." He grimaced. "About as comfortable to sit on as ladder rungs. And you'd have to be blind or drunk not to see beneath them." His head nodded at the knife between them. "Especially that."

"And I can accept that nobody used the boat after it was brought back?"

"Nobody. Bodger doesn't hire them out after ten o'clock." Coltart sniffed. "You wouldn't believe it to look at him but the old goat's one of these early to bed and up first thing people."

"How far can we rely on his descriptions? We just haven't got any girls of fifteen or so missing. Not locally, anyway."

Coltart looked baffled. "I would imagine old misery guts to be an expert on girls' ages. If he says she was fifteen I'd believe him."

Lingard intervened. "Is there any female missing at all? One that could conceivably be mistaken for a girl of that age?"

Rogers sorted a green form from the thin folder of papers on the desk in front of him. "Not many. A married woman of twenty-seven. Dress: beige jumper, blue skirt, brown shoes, light raincoat and the usual handbag. Quarrelled with her husband over a supposed boy-friend. Her mother has since received a telephone message from her saying she's going for good. I think we can discount her as a victim," he finished dryly. He selected another form. "What about this one? A married woman. Mrs. Doris Stronach. But she's thirty-four. . . ." His brow creased as recollection flicked through the card-index of his mind. "Of course. I thought her name was familiar. She married the doctor of that name."

"Not the Stronach that used to get the drunks-in-charge off the hook?" There was distaste in Coltart's voice.

"That's the man. You name a disease. A physical imperfection. He would swear on a lorry-load of Bibles that it could produce bloodshot eyes, slurred speech and a beery breath. After a run of that sort of quackery he began to be *persona non grata* at Quarter Sessions and Assize Courts. I imagine he saw the light in time and packed it in. The last I heard of him he was doing some kind of hospital work on top of a general practice."

"And who might be the wife who is missing?" Lingard asked. "Do we know her?"

"One of the disadvantages of being transferred from another force, David," Rogers replied, "is that it takes a time before you get to know the minor characters of a town. She's well known to most of the older men here. A woman you used not to see on your own. Not unless you were in need of a very short course on sexual congress without frills. She was a bit of a scourge for shy young men not long away from their mothers. Stronach must be a lot older than she is. And, no doubt, she's a reformed character now. I haven't heard of her for years."

Lingard was asking questions with his eyes. Coltart

was nodding sagely as he made total recall. "Doris something-or-other," he said ambiguously. "I remember her now."

"Couldn't Bodger misremember?" Lingard urged. "Might not Mrs. Stronach be the woman in the boat?"

Coltart challenged him with his green eyes. "I can't imagine him misremembering or believe that Mrs. Stronach would remotely consider getting into one of his stinking little rat traps. And he certainly wouldn't mistake a thirty-four-year-old woman for fifteen. Not even in the dark. Not even a senile old cretin like Bodger." He snickered. "In fact, I'd bet the old goat's a better judge than any of us."

Rogers looked up from the Missing Person form. "Speak for yourself," he said. "When you're as old as he is now, anyone under fifty can look like a schoolgirl." He looked across at Lingard. "I don't think that he could be mistaken that much, David, but you'd better interest yourself in her. I see she's been missing since early last evening. Reported by Stronach some time after midnight. No reason given. Just that she hadn't arrived home. Stronach thought she might have been out with friends. And there's a note added to say that he didn't seem either anxious or very concerned." He passed the form to him. "Probably reverted to type and is tomming around somewhere. Dig into it, will you? She doesn't seem a very likely bet but we can't know until we get some background on her."

Lingard addressed himself to Coltart, to whom he was never less than courteously formal. "Have you checked, sergeant? To see whether she has returned home?"

Coltart shook his head. "No." He did not offer the explanation he would have given unasked to Rogers.

The latter swung around to Lingard. "Hold on, David. He's hardly had time to check missing persons." He softened the rebuke by pulling up the corners of his mouth. "He's been busy on other more important things."

"Of course. I appreciate that. I just do not want to duplicate the work." He unfolded his spectacles and put them on his nose. "Somehow I don't buy that a missing woman of this age . . . from her background . . . poses a question we can answer by saying she's just tomming around."

"Then how would you answer it?" Rogers was prepared, mildly, to scythe his assistant's legs from under him. His self-assurance was sometimes abrading.

"That she isn't missing of her own volition."

"I've already filled in the background for you. What academic bravura convinces you that a doctor's wife doesn't have the potential to live it up with a boy-friend?" He dropped the corners of his mouth. "Not that I disagree with you wholly. But Coltart's missing fifteen-year-old is the major problem at the moment. And you can accept that statistically there are extremely few married women reported missing who don't turn up sound in wind and limb and a dam' sight more satisfied than when they went. Anyway," he added, "the first thing to do is to find out why Mrs. Stronach hasn't come home. The domestic circumstances will probably provide the answer."

The burly sergeant, his eyes dodging from Rogers to Lingard during this exchange, interjected. "I don't think you'll get much change from Stronach. He's a surly uncommunicative bastard at the best of times."

Rogers addressed them both briskly. "All right, leave the bits and pieces to sort themselves out for the time being. This is now a murder-level investigation and I'm setting up an operations room. Sergeant Hagbourne will be organizing the administration and I want all information fed to him. He'll sort and classify it for me. I'll get him to run off a house-to-house questionnaire. So far as hospitals, doctors and the like are concerned, these will be the responsibility of Hannah and a couple of his men. You, David, ensure they don't overlap with your end of it. I'll leave both Stronach and his wife to you. You, sergeant," he said to Coltart, "you'll be left with Bodger's two. The garages first. If he doesn't work in any one of them you'd better toss a coin. It'll be as good as anything else." He showed a momentary gust of irritation. "I'd feel a bloody sight happier if I knew what we were looking for," he snapped. "And a body wouldn't be any hardship. Something I can get my teeth into," he concluded with unconscious incongruity.

In truth, he would have been complainingly happier, far less frustrated, with a body; four-square solid and devoid of life. It would have provided a much more stable basis for an investigation than the ambiguities of the blood-smeared strip of steel, the fragment of lung and the second-hand account of the pimpled youth and his missing companion.

2

The town was a complexity of unplanned blocks of brick, stone and concrete, straggling with unheeded abandon like lumps of grey rubber in a huge bowl. The machinery of its purpose and existence remained, as if by natural gravitation, at the foot of the slopes of the valley containing it. Terraces of narrow-visaged houses followed the ridges of the bowl like huge grey-scaled caterpillars. Below, sapping the strength of the men and women working in them, the disordered convulsions of industry threw up concrete and iron verticalities. Threaded between them were the grey arteries of the town, highways knotted tightly with the thrombus of choking, clogging traffic.

The characterless houses, denied the grace of gardens, faced without protection the thronged footpaths. In the small rectangles of worn-out soil at the rear proliferated pigeon lofts, cabbage stalks, drying washing, dustbins, old cycles, an occasional plaster gnome and rough wooden coal bunkers. Access to these unlovely areas was from narrow alleyways, floored with gritty blue-grey bricks, bisected and made uneven by drainage channels. The alleys were designated The Backs.

In them, over the years since their building, had been perpetrated every crime and obscenity known to civilized man. Within their scabby walls girls had come furtively to viable womanhood and their sons had brawled and bled and fornicated on the unfeeling stones.

At the end of each terrace squatted an unlit block of communal lavatories. Paperless, comfortless and squalid. Too much so for most. But still used by those too insensitive or penurious to have installed their own.

The grey-haired woman with the smeary face who

shuffled towards them was a dirty brown bundle of unwashed decay. She carried a newspaper in one dreadfully filthy fist. She made this journey daily at the same time. She made it unthinkingly and, as a result, often unnecessarily. The one she used was never engaged for no other person knowingly cared to sit in the same soiled cabinet.

Her name was Kitcher and her husband had—gratefully and many years ago—discovered her to be blindly promiscuous after only a token number of purchased gins. He needed no further excuse. She now lived alone in a gaggling, closed-in atmosphere of an unwashed body, putrescent food and stale alcohol.

Her old age and grey hairs could attract unearned, undeserved consideration allied to an entirely baseless assumption that she was kindly and frail. She was neither. She possessed a small and malevolent mind. Her primary emotion was greed. She was as durable and sinewy as she was filthy.

When she opened the green-painted door and saw the body folded within the narrow space her immediate reaction was that the woman was bloody-minded in choosing her lavatory to collapse in. Feeling the flesh of the cheek, her eyes were without compassion. She turned away but halted when her attention was drawn to the handsome leather handbag on the concrete floor.

She looked quickly about her, picked up the bag and wheeled about abruptly, closing the door behind her.

On the way back, hugging the bag beneath the grey pinafore she wore, she decided she would have to suffer the inconvenience of some alternative means within her own house.

The shabby office was as much Rogers's workshop as the laboratory was Quandom's. The latter dealt with largely impersonal materials, his tools the microscope, the spectroscope, chemical solvents and reactors.

Rogers dealt with the products of human chicanery and greed. His tools were mental. The use of logic, his knowledge of the wickedness and predictability of *homo sapiens* and his own refusal to accept anything, at first sight, as it appeared to be.

Structurally, the office was a large one. From the

second floor of the headquarters building it overlooked a small, open yard which served as a car park for members of the public calling there. On those uncommon occasions when Rogers had both the time and wish to stand idly at the window, he could look down over the yard and into the bowl of the town. From it by day came an orchestration of industrial noises; the clash of impacting metals subjugating by their sharper dissonance the animal-like growling of petrol and diesel engines.

Even on the brightest day, light bulbs burned in the tiny-windowed room. The dun yellow walls served as a neutral backcloth for the green and brown ordnance maps and the street plans; each pinned, chinagraphed and battle-flagged against the advancing striking-forces of crime. A calendar, advertising steel and showing a furnace in full blast, provided a garish splash of scarlet on the wall behind him.

The wooden desk was overloaded with regimented parades of law and instruction books, paper-loaded wire baskets and glass jars of ballpens and coloured pencils. A red telephone handset was used as a weight on a sheaf of manilla files. A chunky green glass ashtray was littered with used matchsticks and grey cones of tapped-out tobacco ash.

On the white windowsills were terracotta pots of scarlet geraniums.

Otter, seated on the hard edge of a chair on the wrong side of Rogers's desk, was justifiably nervous. Coltart had ferreted him out (in the short time he had predicted) from the inspection pit in the garage employing him. The sergeant had offered no explanation for his peremptory invitation to go with him. Nor had Otter asked for one.

In silence, Coltart had driven him to his home—Otter breathing a heartfelt prayer of thanks that his hardfisted father was out—and collected from inside a curtained recess in his bedroom and blood-smeared shirt. This had provoked an incoherent, untenable explanation from him for no other reason than that he lied by instinct at the best of times. And this was not one of his better moments.

"Cut meself shaving," he babbled at the frowning detective. His giggle had an edge of hysteria to it as he realized, too late, he must now produce a scar. "Dun' show . . . bled a lot. . . ." He had dribbled into feeble silence, staring mutely at the policeman. The enormity of his troubles appalled him. "You don' believe me, do you." It was a statement, not a question. His oafish mind grappled unsuccessfully with events moving too fast for his comprehension.

He made no audible protest when Coltart's enormous fist clamped—not unkindly—on his shoulder and guided him out of the room and into the waiting car.

To both Rogers and Coltart, he was physically and psychologically everything the cantankerous boat owner had described. Obviously a man of razor-sharp perceptivity, Bodger had limned him with a searching tongue.

Otter's head was adorned with a growth of contrived overlapping ridges of hair and his face—pitted with the eruptions of acne. His chest was exceeded in narrowness only by his blue-jeaned loins.

The seated, unsmiling Rogers added fear to his discomfort. He was reading rapidly through a file of papers. The office was a breathing silence of waiting. When at last he looked upwards at Otter his eyes were dark and unfriendly. Speaking, his words were clipped to severity.

"I've read these reports," he said, "and Sergeant Coltart's told me about your shirt. It would seem that there are a few questions needing satisfactory answers. I hope you have them."

Otter opened his mouth to reassure the men present of his innocence of whatever it was. He closed it promptly when Rogers turned the palm of his hand against him and halted him peremptorily. "Wait!" he said sharply. "I haven't yet said anything requiring an answer." He started again. "You hired a boat last evening. From Mr. Bodger at nine o'clock. You were accompanied by a girl. A very young girl. After an hour or so you brought the boat back." He paused, his eyes hard on Otter. "Alone." He paused again and the youth stirred restlessly on his hard chair, restraining his natural volubility only at the insistence of the eyes holding him.

"You had bloodstains on your clothing." His head nodded towards the crumpled shirt prominently displayed on the desk and immured in polythene. "You told Sergeant Coltart you had cut yourself shaving." The terrifying regard dropped and scrutinized the unmarked jowls. "A lie, of course." He spaced the rasping words carefully. "This morning—in the boat you had used—we found a knife. A blood-stained knife!"

Behind the seated youth the framework of Coltart's chair groaned as he changed his position on it. Otherwise, the office was again silent. From outside (to Otter, a sunlit unattainability) came the noises of passing traffic, the tapping and scuffle of the footwear of free men. From somewhere in the morning radiance the whining of a flying jet scratched itself against the milky blue bowl of the sky.

Otter's chin dropped. Then, closing his mouth, he swallowed the dryness of panic. Rogers waited. Then he said, "All right, lad." The words were precise. "Get it out. We're waiting."

His tongue under control, Otter babbled his innocence, his purity of thought and deed. He was oddly believable. "Christ," he protested, after his first gushing of incoherence. "A knife . . . not in the boat I 'ad. A mistake, per'aps. This Bodger bloke. Couldn' 'e 'ave made a mistake?"

"Your shirt. What about your shirt?"

His eyes hunted frantically around the office. Somewhere, somehow, he found his answer. He was eager to be believed. "Blimey. I remember now. A bloke. Up on the bridge 'e was. Dropped somethin' on me. It 'it me on the shoulder. She'll tell you . . ."

Rogers interrupted him. "She? Who is 'she'?"

Otter was all despairing impotence as he groaned, "Oh God. Shirley. Shirley . . . she din' tell me."

"Leave it. We'll come back to her. Your memory might improve before we're finished. Tell me more about the man on the bridge."

"Well . . . I was there. With this bird. Shirley she said 'er name was." He swallowed. "I met 'er in the Dungeon caff. When we was under the bridge we stopped for a bit, sort of." He looked unsuccessfully for understanding in Rogers's face and continued. "We was . . . we was snoggin'. Then I 'eard these footsteps an' they stopped on the bridge. This man looked over an' dropped this . . . this thing on me. 'It me on the shoulder like I said. I couldn' fin' it. Not in the dark.' He groped again for masculine sympathy. 'I din' look real 'ard. Bein' busy with this bird. She was breathing 'ard by this time. So I couldn' really.'

"Describe the man." The voice was a hairsbreadth less implacable.

He sought inspiration once again in the drab yellowness of the office walls. 'Sort of medium. I only saw 'is 'ead an' shoulders.'

"A hat?"

A shake of the head. "I don' think so. I didn' really see."

"Are you sure it was a man?"

"Well . . . yes. I suppose so. I thought it was." He was still anxious to convince.

"What do you mean by 'sort of medium'?"

A baffled wave of the hands. "'E looked ordinary. Nothin' different. You know?"

"No, I don't. Did he speak?"

"No." Regretfully.

"How do you know he dropped whatever it was on you?"

"'E was there. Nobody else." His face brightened. "I remember. I shouted out to 'em. 'E said somethin' like 'e was startled. Then 'e ran for it."

"You say it must have been the knife he dropped on you?"

An eager nod of the head. "It must 'ave been."

Rogers reached in a drawer by his side and withdrew the polythene-covered weapon. He placed it carefully on the blotting pad, between himself and Otter.

"Look at it," he ordered. His hands were palm down on the desk on either side of the knife. "Look at the blood on it."

The youth's eyes were fastened hypnotically on its dark-red nastiness. He said nothing.

Rogers continued, his voice even and expressionless. "That's human blood. So far as I know, that knife has killed someone. A woman? Perhaps you know more than I do." He raised his hands as Otter started to protest. "Listen to me first," he snapped. "It's the easiest thing in the world to say "no" and I want you to think hard before you say it.

You went out with a girl. You returned alone. Now tell me why."

"I put 'er off at 'Atts Wharf. Honest, I did."

"Why?"

The youth's face reflected hs continued discomfort. "She changed 'er mind. We 'ad a bit of a barney."

"So you told Bodger you'd dumped her in the river." His voice was cold and metallic. "Is that what you said? Is it?" he finished harshly.

Otter suddenly leaned forward and buried his face in cupped hands. It was a juvenile and theatrical gesture. "Honest, Mr. Rogers," he said, his voice muffled. "I din' do anything. I know it looks bad." He straightened his back, clasping one narrow wrist with his fingers, twisting his wristlet watch in his agitation. "I mean . . . I did say to the ol' man that I 'ad dumped 'er. I admit that. I said it all right. But . . . I *mean*. Say I 'ad done somethin' to 'er. Would I 'ave told 'im that? That I 'ad dumped 'er in the river? I wouldn', would I, Mr. Rogers? Blimey," he said with inescapable logic, "I'm not *that* stupid."

"Whose idea was it? To get her off at Hatts Wharf?"

"Mine, I suppose."

"What happened?"

Otter fingered the knot of his blue knitted tie. It was already greasy with continual handling. The grimace he essayed was meant to embrace both police officers in a man-to-man fellowship. "Like I said. We 'ad a barney. About what we din' do." He almost, not quite, leered at Rogers. The latter's expression was as receptive as hard rock. "She changed 'er mind and I got grotty. So I pulled into the wharf an' she got out." He made a noise in his throat. "The trouble is, I don' even know where she lives. I only see 'er in the caff." He smiled weakly. "'Er mum, you understand."

"Why did you tell Sergeant Coltart you had cut yourself shaving?"

His head hung down. "I was frightened."

"Of what?"

He shrugged his shoulders apologetically.

"It was a lie."

"Yes."

"What were you frightened of?"

Otter hesitated. "I wasn't sure. I only knew Mr. Coltart was after me for somethin'. The blood on me shirt scared me. I 'adn' given it any thought before. When 'e asked about it . . . well, it seemed I 'ad trouble."

Rogers indicated the knife. "You've never seen this before then?"

He shook his head violently.

"I'm asking you because I shall be checking it with your parents."

Otter winced. "Do you 'ave to, Mr. Rogers?" His words were a plea. "My dad'll murder me. Honest."

"Why?"

The absence of an immediate answer suggested a raw area for exploration. "I said 'why?'"

"Do I 'ave to?"

"Yes, you do."

"I got a bird into trouble." The admission came reluctantly, without pride.

Rogers repressed a smile. "A very young "bird," I imagine?"

"Yes."

"Has she had it?"

"Yes."

"Adopted?"

"Yes."

"Your father had to pay out, of course?"

"Yes."

Rogers now attacked from his consolidated position; but casually, almost disinterestedly. "What school does Shirley go to?"

"I don' know."

"She does go to school, then?"

He bit at his bottom lip. He had no ready answer to this.

"How old is she?"

"I don' know . . ." He looked into Rogers's eyes and decided to be more specific. "Fifteen . . . per'aps a bit under."

"Is that the reason she's so conveniently anonymous? Because of her age?"

"I . . . honest, Mr. Rogers, no. I jus' don' know." He made a half-hearted defence of his association. "I never really asked 'er 'ow old she was. She uses eye shadow an' stuff."

Rogers shrugged comfortably. "Doesn't matter. If what you say is true we'll find her easily enough. If it isn't," he said ominously, "life will begin to be a little more than difficult for you." He held out one hand. "Now turn out your pockets, there's a good lad."

Otter was appalled. He rose in his chair and Coltart, behind him, rose with him. "You can't," he cried in despair. "You 'aven't got a warrant."

"I know I haven't. Neither do I need one." Rogers, his hand remaining outstretched, flicked finger and thumb. "What have you got to hide? Another knife? Come on," he said with a touch of impatience. "Either turn them out yourself or I'll have Sergeant Coltart do it for you."

None of the commonplace articles Otter placed so reluctantly on the desk appeared any reason for his vehement protest. An oil-stained handkerchief, a red plastic wallet, a few silver and copper coins, a door key, a screwdriver and a sparking-plug gauge; a partially flattened packet of cigarettes and a box of matches.

A deft check of a now unprotesting Otter's pockets by Coltart produced only a cinema ticket stub and a hard grey pellet of used chewing gum.

"Something embarrassing in the wallet?" Rogers asked, opening it and pulling its contents on to his blotting pad. A ten-shilling note, two photographs of two very ordinary people posing stiffly in a back yard, a card advertising the Dungeon Café, a bill from a local trader apparently incautious enough to have allowed him credit, a newspaper cutting showing a photograph of a younger Otter in a school football team and a small curl of sulphur-yellow hair.

Rogers poked disappointedly at the small pile of personal rubbish with his forefinger. "Why, lad? Why the big protest act?"

Otter seemed to be having difficulty with his breathing but was working hard at maintaining a semblance of nonchalance.

"Ah . . . ah, it's the principle of the thing. I 'aven't got anything to 'ide, you see. It's the principle . . ." His voice died abruptly as Rogers picked up the cigarette packet, pushed a thumb inside the base and slid it open. The detective knew, without looking, that this was the jackpot. Otter's face was tallow-coloured, his eyes haggard.

With the four remaining cigarettes was a small cylinder of tan paper, sealed by twisting at each end. Unfastening the paper, Rogers carefully spilled the contents on to his blotter. There was a tiny pyramid of ochre leaf fragments. Among them, like insect eggs, were the brown seeds of Indian Hemp.

"Sit down, Otter, for God's sake," he said crisply. "You aren't going anywhere now. Blood-stained knives, missing girls," he exaggerated deliberately, "and now peddling drugs. Have you any more at home?"

Otter pulled dumbly at his sidewhiskers and collapsed slowly into the chair pushed against the backs of his calves by Coltart. He was incapable of speech, wagging his head in mute protest.

Rogers grunted his irritation. "Don't start saying 'No' again," he said, a little unfairly, "I haven't finished with you yet. Not by a long chalk. Do you have a toolbox or similar at the garage?" He read the answer in the flickering eyes and spoke to Coltart. "Get hold of Hannah, sergeant, and have him check." He turned to Otter. "All right, what is he going to find? You'd just as well tell me now."

"Nothing . . . nothing at all, Mr. Rogers." He nodded at his scattered belongings on the desk top. "They're in the matchbox."

Coltart paused on his way to the door and waited while Rogers pushed open the yellow and green box. Among the matches tumbled on to the desk were three pale cobalt tablets. "French blues?" he asked.

"Yes."

"From?"

"The Dungeon."

Rogers looked at Coltart. "Get Hannah cracking will you? And bring back Inspector Lingard from wherever he is." If Otter thought this was anything more than a temporary reprieve he was soon disillusioned. "From whom did you get them?"

He seemed now without resistance although his replies were almost monosyllabic and wholly reluctant. "A man."

"His name!" Rogers glared at him and he winced.

"We call 'im The Dropper."

"His real name?"

A gesture, indicative of his impotence. "I dunno. None of us knows."

"Us? You know the others?"

"Yes."

"We'll have their names later," he promised grimly. "For the moment, how do I contact this man?"

"We 'ave to look for 'im. In the caffs . . . usually The Dungeon."

"Does he carry them on him?"

A shake of the head. "No. We ask for what we want in advance. We pay 'im an' 'e tells us later where to pick it up . . . in the toilet, 'idden in different places."

"How much?"

"The pills?"

Rogers nodded.

"Two bob each."

"The marijuana?"

"Five bob. Five bob a stick."

"From the same man?"

"No. One of my mates."

"The girl. Did she have any?"

"No. Not so far as I know. *I* never gave 'er any," he added virtuously.

"I suppose you smoke the stuff . . . take the pills?"

Otter hung his head.

Rogers's prominent nose wrinkled its owner's disgust. "You bloody stupid little twit," he said harshly. "Can't you see what you're heading for? Is it too much to stand on your own two feet without stuffing yourself full of filth? Are you *that* much of a weakling?" He looked as if he were about to spit in the metal paper bin. "Why should I bother?" he growled. "You won't take any notice."

The facts of Otter's utterances were now recorded by Rogers in his careful script; his pipe hard between his teeth, his attention full on the process of recall. Otter sat silent, his expression part anxiety, part resignation. Rogers had tossed him a cigarette and he smoked this in short, greedy gulps.

When Coltart re-entered the office, the air in it was a blue haze. "Inspector Lingard's still out," he rumbled, his voice like the base notes from a cello. "Hannah's on his way."

Rogers closed the small notebook with a slap of his hand. "Good," he said briskly, "Otter here wants to make a statement. When he's done so, put him in with the Station Sergeant until we decide what's next for him."

The youth stood. "Am I being lifted?"

"Not at the moment. You are helping us with our inquiries." He looked at him levelly, measuring him. "Don't push too hard on your luck, laddie. We can always charge you with possessing drugs. In fact we might still do so. It depends largely on whether you are a small fish or a big fish. If you are small enough I might be disposed to chuck you back."

"Will my father be told?" He scrubbed the glowing end from his cigarette, placing the half stub behind one ear. He had little faith in an early release.

"Most certainly he will. We shall be searching your room for one thing."

"There isn't anything there. Take my word for it, Mr. Rogers."

The detective dismissed his appeal. "Don't be silly," he said tartly. "I might be a lot of things. I'm not a bloody fool!"

3

The old woman kept to the back ways in her passage to the shop on the corner of the street. Her fawn slippered feet scuffed the displaced flagstones of the pavement. Her mouth moved soundlessly; rehearsing, it seemed, the mechanics of her proposed purchases.

Her disgusting flesh was cocooned in malodorous

linen, elasticated wool and wrinkled grey stockings. Over one arm hung the handbag she had stolen; its leather flanks a glossy chestnut, its fitments dully gleaming and patently expensive.

Inside the vinegar- and cheese-smelling shop she waited impatiently behind the woman receiving the attention of the aproned proprietor. She ground her toothless gums together while her eyes scanned greedily the packed shelves and the untidy scattering of goods on the wooden floor.

When the other woman had left the shop, she ordered her needs in a strident voice. The foods she demanded were strong cheeses, tinned meats and fish, sweet biscuits and pungent sauces and pickles.

The shopkeeper made no effort to conceal his dislike of the old crone; keeping as far from her as he decently could, removing uncovered foods she might handle from the counter. When the pile of provisions reached what he obviously considered excessive proportions, he paused in his reaching and stacking and flattened both hands on the polished wood. He looked pointedly at the handbag.

"A new bag, Mrs. Kitcher?" he asked.

She pressed it against herself. "A present," she snapped. "My birthday."

He nodded at the pile of groceries. "A bit more than you usually have?" He left the implication of his words hanging between them.

She was sharp with outrage. "I can pay. You jus' serve me and mind your own business. I ain't a pauper." Her dreadful fingers twisted open the clasp of the bag and a knotted hand withdrew from it a purse. Holding the bag under her arm, she opened the purse and showed him a small wadge of green notes.

The man said nothing for a moment. Then, "What else can I get you?" He said it evenly, his eyes thoughtful and never for long leaving the bag.

Lingard inserted the thumb and forefinger of his right hand into the pocket of his pale lemon waistcoat and lifted out a small ivory box. He transferred it to his left hand, tapping the lid with the nail of his forefinger. Opening it, he pinched up a few grains of the powder it contained and inhaled it into his left nostril, repeating the operation for the right. With a red silk handkerchief he then dabbed elegantly along the line of his upper lip.

The taking of snuff was for him a tribute to the eighteenth-century elegance he so much admired, the passing of which he so deplored.

His clothing reflected subtly a similar pattern of dandyism. Away from the exercise of his profession, he drawled his polished witticisms and used his Paisley handkerchiefs with flair.

Now, hinged on a bar stool with panache, he placed his elbows on the counter and pulled his shirt cuffs out to an acceptable two-and-a-half inches. In front of him waited a glass of watered Pernod and a dish of salted peanuts. To one side, his tweed hat shrouded a syphon of soda water. It matched precisely the immaculate suit he graced by wearing. His shirt was a cadmium and sepia check with a high modish collar. The maroon tie he wore was identical in shade to the silk socks showing above the glossy calf shoes.

The morning was still a cool freshness and the sun had not yet entered the deepset windows of the lounge bar. The barman, white-coated and blue-jowled, was holding a beer the detective had paid for. He had refused politely and unhesitatingly the proffered snuff and was answering questions around the fuming cigarette between his lips. Occasionally, he coughed, not removing the cigarette to do so.

"Yes," he said, "I certainly know Mrs. Stronach. I'm sorry she's missing," he added conventionally.

"I'm sure you are. A regular visitor?" The two men knew each other well.

"Most evenings." He sipped at his beer then held it to the light, squinting at it. "You might even say every evening."

"With her husband, of course."

The barman smiled. "You're joking."

Lingard lifted his blond eyebrows. "I am?"

"You have to be."

"A friend?"

"Several." He took a gulp of beer and wiped his mouth with his index finger. "She wasn't very selective about them. Their ages, I mean." He sniggered. "But they all followed a pattern. They had just sufficient control to wait until they got outside. She could set fire to a deep-frozen polar bear."

"You think so?"

"I'm sure." He adjusted his bow tie and smirked. "She tried for me once."

"She's blind as well?" He sipped at his Pernod and smiled gently at his own humour. "Was she in last night?"

"Until closing time."

"With a girl-friend, I imagine." He said it dryly. It was his turn to feed the other's wit.

"Yes. One with hair on her chest."

"Know him?"

"A lout called Mike something or other. A woolly bastard from Low Moor way. Bottle fighter, I'd say. Has a long scar down to his kisser. Pity it never reached his throat." He didn't say it as a joke. "Looks like an Italian. I heard his name once. A foreign one although he's no foreigner." He made a moue with his mouth. "Trouble is he's tough with it. Otherwise I'd have belted him with my bungstarter long ago."

"I'm glad you didn't. I'd have missed you. Has she been in with him before?"

"Several times. She dribbles over him like he was a luscious cream cake." He shredded his cigarette in an ashtray, his eyes thoughtful.

"Did she leave with him? Last night?"

"No. This might fit it. He left first. I couldn't hear what was said. Not across a crowded bar. But she was livid about something." He indicated one of the small circular tables on the far side of the low-ceilinged bar. "They were sitting over there. He stood up suddenly. Left his gin and just went. She was flabbergasted. Looked a bit of a fool, naturally. She came over to the bar. Full of the old I-don't-give-a-bloody-damn spirit and ordered another Bacardi. She'd had a fair few by then, mind you. Glassy eyes and a thick tongue. Staggering a bit. She had a few more before the gov'nor called 'time.' She left quietly enough, though. No trouble."

"Did she say anything? To you or anyone else?"

"No. Not a word." He heaved a short mirthless laugh.

"She was . . . what's the word? . . . smouldering. I wouldn't have dared say anything to her. She'd have clobbered me with a bar stool. I don't get paid enough to risk that."

"Describe her to me, will you?"

The barman finished his beer, swilled the glass in a sink of water and upended it on a draining slab. "About thirty-five. Name's Doris, by the way. Well fleshed, intense type. Dyed black hair, nice smooth skin; doesn't use makeup. Fabulous sexy legs. I'm not a leg man myself but I'm prepared to concede she's got something pretty special under her skirts."

Lingard sniffed. "You wouldn't last long preparing wanted notices for the Police Gazette."

He adopted a look of injury. "I'm trying to introduce some colour into your life. Is that a crime?" His blue jowls quivered with silent laughter as he pumped beer into a fresh tankard. "Another Pernod for you?"

The blond detective shook his head. "Not this early, thanks. I'm only a beginner. What height is she?"

"Five feet six. Round about that."

"Dress?"

"Sometimes trousers and woollen things. Sometimes cotton dresses. I don't know much about women's clothes."

"You know her husband?"

He was definite. "Never been in. You know he's a doctor?"

"I have heard. What about Mrs. Stronach's boy-friend?"

"God! You jump around like a blue-arsed fly," the barman complained. "Why don't you stick tight for just one minute."

Lingard laughed. "I don't want to give you time to be devious. How old would you say he was?"

"Twenty . . . twenty-five. You know. A young strapper the married women go for."

"And what does he do? Apart from making married women happy."

"He works in one of the furnaces. Strong back and a weak mind kind of stuff. Nothing intellectual," he said with heavy irony. "He'd make a good policeman."

Lingard smiled tightly. "Do you know from which mill?"

The barman was an old enough acquaintance to risk

a final witticism. "Would you like me to call in at the office?"

The detective exaggerated the shudder of distaste. "God forbid. But why?"

"I thought you'd like me to knock out a progress report for you. I've done just about everything else."

He tapped the lid of his snuffbox, opened it and charged his sinuses with Attar of Roses. "All you've done is to gossip. To twitter like an old fanny, my dear chap," he said smoothly. "You wouldn't have missed it for worlds."

The leather seat of his open Bentley was warm against his shoulder blades as he changed gear and pulled away fast from The Falcon.

4

Rogers stood on the bridge, feeling its parapet hard against his thighs, contemplating the scene below him. The sun, hot on his back, reflected its brilliance in splinters of blinding light in the clear water, casting sharp-edged shadows of the bridge on the yellow gravel of the river bed. To each side, above the folding green spears of the reeds and flags, the darting blue damsels hawked tiny insects. Hidden grasshoppers rasped their desire with their legs and over all was the soporific hum of bees. The flowing silver of the river glittered between the overhanging foliage of willow and elm. Small gobbets of white cloud drifted slowly against the cerulean blue of the sky. Only below was the brown stain of industrial exhalation polluting the air.

Behind Rogers was the grey tarmac of the road and along it moved the opposing streams of two almost unceasing processions of vehicles. Adjacent to the bridge were tidy rows of detached houses, their green gardens sloping down to the paths bordering the water. Beyond them were allotments, gasometers and white-lined playing fields.

From this spot, Otter had alleged the knife had been

dropped. Rogers was accepting this. Apart from possessing the ring of probable truth, it was the only explanation he had concerning the introduction of the knife into the boat.

Although he conceded that the strand of cotton could have come from the clothing of a man, he did not believe it had.

So far, no girl justifying honest comparison with Otter's companion had been reported missing. With each passing hour, Rogers knew that the likelihood of her being the victim was becoming more remote. As a corollary, he had to accept that Mrs. Stronach was fast assuming a greater significance in the investigation.

Climbing the iron gate at the end of the parapet, he descended the stone steps to the earth path. Walking was pleasant in the summer warmth and conducive to ordered thought. He wondered, egotistically, whether any other investigator had been saddled with a similar case of either attempted or accomplished murder with no body: nor, indeed, with any real conception of who had died. With only his logic and intuition giving any indication of the sex of the victim, he could be so wrong; concentrating wholly erroneously on either Mrs. Stronach or Otter's unknown girl.

The river and its immediate environs had been combed clean of probabilities under the close regard paid to it by the team of detectives detailed by Coltart. An underwater scrutiny of the river bed adjacent to the bridge was in the planning stage. Rogers expected it to produce nothing more useful than the casual rubbish thrown into it at different times.

The path he was following became civilized; flagstoned and circumscribed by white-painted posts and rails. It led to a large rectangle of compacted black ash, contained and supported by concrete blocks. This was Hatts Wharf; a disused unloading area for ore barges that no longer came. Embedded in the concrete at each end of the huge rectangle was a rusted iron winch. A short drop of stone steps—a leftover from Victorian industrialism—afforded access to the river.

Across the stretch of water was a lock, separating the flowing water of the river from the gravy-brown stagnation of the abandoned canal. The wharf was used now only as a park for cars and lorries. Access to the town was by a narrow walled lane leading from it.

Nothing in the wharf's gritty dinginess could support the thesis that Otter was lying. Or, conversely, telling the truth. It was unhelpfully mute, bearing only indecipherable tyre marks and oil stains on its surface.

Rogers pressed tobacco into the bowl of his pipe, his eyes not watching the movements of his fingers. The flame of the match was invisible in the bright sunlight; only the curling blackness of the charring wood showing it to be there.

Trailing blue smoke, he walked through the lane from the wharf, following in what he conceived to be the path of the unknown girl. It was a predictable waste of time. The lane debouched into the main artery of the town, now growling and fuming with the thickening traffic of mid-morning. He quickened his pace as he pointed himself in the direction of his office.

The man was slumped loosely on the seat of the bright yellow forklift, an insolent rider on a mustard horse. Lingard stood facing him. The engine of the loader was running and the elegant detective was raising his voice, trying to make himself heard.

The backdrop to his questioning was the gloom-shrouded structure of a mill shed. From the hissing metallic monster in the background glowed the intermittent spitting brilliance of spilled white-hot slag. There was a constantly shifting disorderliness of activity by overalled men dancing attendance on the furnace.

Behind Lingard and the man on the forklift, a bright rectangle of sunlight threw solid shadows on the harsh stone floor. Skips of ore banged and rattled hollowly in the caverns leading from the shed.

It hadn't proved difficult for Lingard to trace a scarred furnace worker living at Low Moor and frequenting The Flacon. He had asked the Plant Superintendent to fetch Drazek from the shed. The Superintendent had returned, his expression non-committal. There was a message. Watered down by his disinclination to become involved, it was to the effect that Drazek was occupied with matters more interesting than talking to Lingard promised to be; that he could imagine no occasion when he would not be.

The spruce detective possessed his fair share of bloody-mindedness and resource. He had, his eyebrows down and eyes ice-blue, exercised it by brushing aside both the protests and the interposed body of the Superintendent and seeking out Drazek in the cacophony of the furnace shed.

The English-born Pole was a hard-muscled animal of a man, arrogant and ignorant in his indestructible youth. His hair was a bristling of black gloosiness, long sidewhiskers reaching down his cheeks like rats' pelts. A long pink leach of a scar bisected the left of his handsome face, curling the corner of his mouth into a deceptive, lopsided smile. His bared forearms were thick and hairy, his fists hard-knuckled and scarred.

His uncouthness nettled Lingard. "Switch your engine off and get down," he ordered.

Drazek did neither. He sneered his disregard. "I'm busy." He pushed a gear lever and hauled at the control wheel.

As the machine lurched forward, Lingard leaned over and deftly removed the ignition key. Drazek turned his head in astonishment, pointed a prognathous jaw at him and leapt lithely from the now motionless and silent forklift.

He thrust his face to within inches of the detective's. "I ought to push your bloody face in," he growled, his insolent good humour lost. He held out a huge paw. "Give me that key or I will."

Lingard regarded him coolly and dropped the key behind the silk handkerchief showing itself from his breast pocket. "When you've the courtesy to answer my questions. And," he added stiffly, "don't threaten me."

Drazek looked at Lingard incredulously from the top of his tweed hat to the neat gloss of his shoes. He hawked in his throat and spat accurately to miss narrowly on one side. "You're a bit away from your home patch, aren't you? To talk like you're talking, I mean."

The red patches staining his high cheekbones were the only indications of Lingard's anger. "Mrs. Stronach might not agree with you," he said evenly.

The man's head snapped to full attention. "What's that? What's that?" His voice was harsh. "What's she got to do with you?"

"If you'd listen instead of bellowing like a cretinous calf, you might be told," he said. "Mrs. Stronach never arrived home last night."

Drazek's eyes flicked away from those of his inquisitor. "So?"

"So you were the last man to be with her."

"So *you* say."

"Weren't you?"

The scar twitched. "Get stuffed. Say what you mean."

"I mean you were quarrelling with her in The Falcon. Since when—significantly—she's been missing. I mean finally you might have some explaining to do."

The silence that followed was comparative only. The backdrop was still wallpapered with violent light and clanging movement.

Lingard continued. "So why don't you stop acting like a thickheaded hooligan?"

"I've nothing to say." The scarred lip curled still further. "I don't want to talk to you bastards on principle. And I don't have to. If you think you've got some sort of charge try and arrest me. If you haven't, give me back my key and——off." He again held out his hand.

Lingard regarded him attentively for a long moment then, without comment, took the key from his pocket. He looked at it in the palm of his hand and then tossed it suddenly towards Drazek. "I'll see you. When you aren't surrounded by machinery," he promised. "Don't start chucking your weight around. Not then. Not unless you're prepared to back it up." His voice was mild although his eyes were not. "I don't like being threatened by ignorant thugs." He smiled, tapping his snuffbox and recharging his sinuses with powdered tobacco.

Drazek was unimpressed. He turned on his heel and mounted his machine. "Get stuffed." His contemptuous repartee was limited.

"I will," Lingard said agreeable. "I will."

Back in his office, Rogers dialled a number on the telephone handset at his side. He slouched back in his chair, the receiver to his ear. "Joanne?" he asked when the call tone ceased.

The woman answering had a warm voice. "George? How nice. I thought I'd lost you."

"Temporarily mislaid," he excused himself. "The dishonesties and bloodlettings are outnumbering the hours we have to investigate them."

"And now?" She said it lightly.

"Now I've decided you've been neglected. I love you enough to even consider forswearing my duty."

Her interjecting laugh was pure derision.

He laughed with her. "All right. Not quite but nearly. I wondered if we could eat this evening. It'll be no longer than that, I'm afraid," he said regretfully. "Paradoxically, I'm asking you at my busiest. We've a likely murder on our hands."

"But just a meal?" She was disappointed.

"Just that," he replied firmly. "I've got to eat and that's my only opportunity." His voice was affectionate. "I'm sorry if I'm so unsatisfactory a bargain. You should have known better than to have had anything to do with a policeman."

She sniffed. "I shouldn't have started smoking, either."

"Where would you like to eat? The Bar Grill?"

"At eight?"

With his spare hand he slid open the matchbox on his desk, removed a match and scratched it to flame. The wooden shaft snapped and the burning head dropped on the white of his blotting pad. "Blast!" he cursed.

"Darling?"

"I'm sorry," he said. "I'm incinerating myself. Eight o'clock it is."

"Bring lots of money," she cooed at him. "I've a terribly expensive thirst on me that won't be easily quenched."

Replacing the handset he flipped sheets of paper, underlining with pencil odd words, recording brief notes in the margins.

When Coltart clumped into his office, the air in it was thick with tobacco smoke. The burly sergeant's nose wrinkled, his eyes creasing their distaste. "Shall I leave the door open?" he inquired pointedly.

Rogers looked astonished and grunted through the haze. "What the hell for? The window's open. And this isn't a two-acre field. Sit down and tell me what progress we've made."

The chair settled under Coltart's bulk as he sat himself in it. "I think we are going to identify the girl." He looked at his wrist-watch, his pale face smug. "If I don't get her name and address in thirty minutes flat you can measure me up for a uniform."

Rogers's eyebrows raised. "You sound pretty certain, don't you? It's not like you to put yourself so far out on a limb." He smiled sardonically. "I don't know, anyway, that the uniform branch would particularly want you. So don't think you'd be doing them a favour." He drew the mouthpiece of his pipe across his teeth like a stick across railings. "I shall be most surprised if she's missing when we check. Everything we know adds up to her going off home in a huff."

Coltart nodded. "I'm with you there. I think our spotty friend Charlie's going to prove a blind alley."

"So far as the girl's concerned, I gree with you. But finding her doesn't cancel out the knife. We'll probably discover she's only one of the blind alleys before we're through."

"Have we anything further about Mrs. Stronach?"

"Lingard has some sort of a line on a boy-friend of hers. A chap called Drazek." He looked sour. "One of a long line of stud bulls stretching back to when she wore blue bloomers and had mottled legs. I've had second thoughts about her, too. She's much more likely to be our victim than anyone else. Married women with well-upholstered homes and fat wallets don't chuck them away for the sort of man they can pick up in a boozer. Why should they? There's always somebody like Drazek to keep them satisfied. They all have much the same equipment. And it's not difficult to hire. A few free drinks and whatever attraction their own marital experiences have for a younger man." His eyes were thoughtful. "But there's often the occupational risk. One day she meets up with a man who either wants a lot more than she's prepared to give or who won't accept that she's got her eye on a successor. And we know Mrs. Stronach's predilection for frequent changes."

"Do we know this Drazek? The name seems familiar."

Rogers tossed a yellow card across the desk. "A rough-neck. Previous convictions for G.B.H. and drunk and disorderly. He was also the injured person in a pub brawl. Someone sliced his face with a razor blade. He wouldn't say who. He probably sorted him out in his own way and a brutal sort of justice was done." He was astringent with disapproval. "He was drinking with the Stronach woman in The Falcon last night. Left before she did after they'd had some sort of a quarrel."

"What about her?" Coltart uncrossed his thighs and put the end of a blue pencil between his teeth. He began tearing at the wood with his strong teeth.

"She left after a few more drinks. On her own and in a poisonous temper. Wobbly on her legs, I understand. The barman said she was about as amiable as a tarantula with a migraine. So that was the last anyone saw of her. At least," he corrected himself, "anyone we know. Somebody must have seen her afterwards. If she's gone off with someone, then *he* knows. If she's dead..." The words trailed into silence and he shrugged. "I refuse to anticipate the worst. It might turn out to be something very much less than murder." His voice lacked any belief in this hopeful state-ment. "How did Hannah get on?"

"Nothing startling. Found a few names on odd papers and letters. I had to dig Charlie's father out of his boozer. He'd been on a night shift and wasn't very lovable about his son. Said, 'keep the little bleeder in.'" Coltart showed his teeth. It wasn't anywhere near a smile. "He's going to take Charlie apart at the seams when he gets hold of him."

Rogers prodded a thin pad of papers in front of him. "His statement seems fairly comprehensive. But nothing new in it."

"Nothing except the names of the mates he's dropping in the dirt with him. I thought Hannah might follow up the drug side of it."

Rogers nodded. "Yes. You stick to the girl. We don't want to confuse the issue. And if he's telling the truth I want that part of the inquiry out of the way. We can then concentrate on Mrs. Stronach."

5

High Moor was a green and ordered peace, aloofly overlooking the ugly and gritty confusion of the town below. Here lived men who drew dividends or earned salaries and fees; men who drank wine with their meals and whose wives played bridge, committing occasional and discreet adultery *en passant*. It was a wholly conventional community; open only to those who conformed to its unwritten but rigid rules.

It had large cars, a sprinkling of small second cars (usually of continental marque), motorized lawnmowers, summerhouses and odd-job gardeners. The males were community-minded, belonging only to those organizations and clubs associated with charity and providing, as a reward for giving or doing, *entrée* to the otherwise closed shop of business directorships.

The women were, on the whole, pleasant place grabbers; for ever jostling courteously for position in a social pecking order decided by the business or professional status of their husbands.

As a medical man, Stronach rested securely on this contrived social structure of High Moor. Rogers and Lingard, seated in his study in soft grey leather chairs, saw him as a scrubbed-pink fat man with frozen unco-operative eyes, enthroned at his roll-top desk. His hair was white and worn thick on the nape of his fleshy neck. His vast waistcoated belly—a wobbly cloth-covered pudding—hung between his high thighs. When he spoke it was in a chesty rumble and he showed small seedlike teeth, incongruous in his round face.

Despite this fatness, Rogers was certain there was nothing soft about the doctor. In his experience, fat men were generally self-designated buffoons. When they were not, they had eyes that chilled and were as dangerous to cross as mad water buffalo. Stronach, he thought, must be considered doubly dangerous because of his background, his intelligence and his knowledge of the body's frailties. With this consideration of the man's potentiality, he was endeavouring to prise from him information about his missing wife.

"We are anxious to trace Mrs. Stronach's friends, doctor." He was being discreet with the knowledge he possessed of her association with Drazek. "And where she spent last evening."

The cold eyes were, if anything, colder. "My wife's friends are her own, inspector. As mine are mine. I saw her last at dinner. At about eight o'clock. I had no surgery and we ate early."

"I take it she went out alone?" Rogers was formal, his words clipped. He did not like this man. Lingard sat elegantly and silently, watching Stronach with intent interest.

"I left the house after dinner. My wife was still here."

"And you returned when?"

"Midnight. Near enough then."

"And that's when you reported her missing?"

"Later. About twelve-thirty."

"I assume that this was unusual?" Rogers was patient with the uncommunicative man.

"Yes. She was usually in before then."

"You said you weren't worried. That she could have stayed over with friends."

The pink and white head nodded. "I did."

"I don't understand why you then reported her missing."

The glistening skin of the fat face grew pinker. "I did so because she was."

"Now, yes. But not necessarily when you telephoned."

"Don't talk nonsense, man." The blue eyes were hostile.

Rogers flushed. "An offensive attitude, doctor," he said severely, "won't get you very far. I'm not asking you questions for my own amusement. In fact, I don't find you amusing at all. If you aren't interested in having your wife found, say so."

There was a long and thoughtful silence. Somewhere

in the tree-lined road a gardener was shaving a lawn, his mower buzzing like a well-bred bee.

Stronach cleared his throat. "Don't be so touchy, inspector." It seemed the nearest he would ever get to apologizing. "I reported her missing as a precaution. Because I thought she could be with friends was no reason for ignoring the possibility that she had met with an accident."

"Such as?"

The huge bulk shifted in the swivel chair. "My wife has an unfortunate predisposition to alcohol. Even in the smallest quantities it can upset her." He was looking away from the two policemen, his face expressionless. "You may imagine that under these circumstances an accident, a misadventure, may occur. Which is why I telephoned. That she is still missing supports my original fears."

"Does she drive?"

"No. She has never had a licence. She normally travels by taxi."

"Had you any particular friends in mind when you mentioned the possibility of her staying with them?"

"No." The answer was crisp and final. "Her friends are her own. I have said this. We have few, if any, in common."

"Have you checked whether she has taken any luggage?"

His head swivelled round, his eyes glaring. "You mean, has my wife left me?"

"Not necessarily, doctor," Rogers equivocated smoothly. "But she may well have left on an extended visit." It sounded weak as he said it.

"Without my knowing of it?"

"How would *I* know?" Rogers snapped angrily. "All right. So she hasn't gone on a visit and she hasn't taken away any luggage." He swallowed his bile with an effort and tried again. "We know she was in The Falcon until closing time."

"She was?" His voice was indifferent. "You appear to know more of her movements than I."

Rogers waited for something more. When it didn't come he asked disapprovingly, "Doesn't it mean anything?" He raised an eyebrow at Lingard.

"No. As a matter of fact it doesn't."

"She was with a man. A man called Drazek."

"She was?" His lips were thinned to a colourless scar. If Rogers's flat statement had jolted him he wasn't showing it.

"She was. Don't you know him?"

The face turned pink again. "What does he do? For a living, I mean."

"He's a furnace worker. A truck operator of kinds." He knew he was being cruel but there seemed no future in concealing the truth. And Stronach's manner sandpapered his good humour.

"Then I'm hardly likely to know him. Which, in fact, I do not."

"Not as a patient?"

In the silence that followed, Rogers regarded the man's belly and pondered on it. Its obtrusive sphericity must, he knew, be an almost insuperable barrier to physical love. A disability certain to provoke extra-marital activity in the least promiscuous of women. And Stronach's wife had never aspired to that status.

"So, inspector . . . you know that my wife drinks to excess. You also know she has . . . she has friends I do not share. Or approve. However," his voice hardened, "despite these matters of difference between us, I am fond of my wife. She *is* my wife and I expect you to find her. This is your responsibility."

"Responsibility is a two-way traffic, Doctor Stronach, and please don't forget it. It isn't solely ours. You have to do your part." He was curt. "Such as giving us whatever relevant information—"

The telephone bell, ringing with sharp abruptness, cut him off in mid-sentence. Stronach lifted the handset, turned his back on the two men and spoke into it. "Yes?" From it, they could hear a metallic monologue, Stronach confining himself to guarded and monosyllabic grunts.

While this was continuing, Rogers scanned the study, reading from its furnishings and belongings his interpretation of the man's character. One wall was papered a drab moss green. On it hung framed prints of iridescent swallowtail butterflies and hawk moths. Running the full length of the far wall was a glass-fronted bookcase. There were—apparently additional to his main interests—a set of Handbooks of British Birds, Bechyne's *Guide to Beetles* and

Keble Martin's *Concise British Flora*. Straining his eyes, Rogers could see also a few copies of the *Entomologist's Gazette* and the *British Museum's Instruction Book for Collectors of Insects*.

The midday sun struck through the linen-draped windows and brightened the seaweed-brown carpet in rectangular patches. On a small table was a silver tray, a syphon of soda water, a tantalus of decanters of whisky and four cut-glass tumblers. Neither detective was given the opportunity of refusing a drink.

An Afghan wolfhound with blonde ears lay in the patch of sunlight watching Stronach. She occasionally showed her teeth and curling tongue in a wide pink yawn.

Stronach replaced the handset and returned his attention to his visitors. "You were saying?" he asked with pointed indifference.

"I was seeking your co-operation, doctor," Rogers said blandly. "Which, I said, I was certain I could count on."

He received no reply to this and continued. "We cannot find anyone who will admit to seeing your wife after she left The Falcon." He waited, his eyes calculating the probability of an explosion. "Where were *you* between then and midnight?"

Stronach turned a port wine pink. "I hope you've a good reason for asking that." He was a buffalo, head down and poised to charge.

"I don't need a reason. I'm just asking. You, of course, may please yourself whether you answer." He was relaxed but watchful.

"Tell me why I should."

"If you don't, you cannot blame me for thinking you might have something to hide."

Stronach was patently astonished. "Something to hide?"

"Yes."

"Because my wife is missing? You must be mad!" he said contemptuously.

"Mad I might be, doctor, but not stupid," Rogers said comfortably. "There are good precedents for me casting my net widely. Perhaps you'll now tell me where you were."

The fat man regarded his brocaded belly stonily. Half-closed, his eyes were reptilian. When he spoke it was with

a voice as soft and treacherous as spider's silk. He was
more dangerous than when charging with his head down.
"All right, inspector, so be it. I won't quarrel with you. I
was working at the hospital. You may check if you wish."

"Until midnight?"

"Yes." The eyes were cutting out Rogers's viscera
without anesthetics.

"You had no idea with whom your wife was?"

"That is implicit in what I have said."

"Has she been missing on any previous occasion?"

"No."

"Have you any reason to suppose she might be in
trouble? That she might have come to some harm?"

"Other than an accident, no. Of course not."

Rogers's eyebrows went up. "Why 'of course not?' You
have a reason for saying that?"

The fat man was impatient, his eyes seeking—without
concealment and as an indication of his wish to be done—
some other point of interest in the room. "No, I haven't.
But things of that sort are impossible to imagine or accept
in broad daylight."

Rogers could not accept this from a doctor but he
forbore saying so. "They happen to people all the time,"
he said without elaboration.

Stronach stood up. "I'm a busy man, inspector, and I
have a surgery after lunch."

As Rogers pushed back his chair, he said sharply, "As
you wish. But we will talk again, Doctor Stronach. Telephone me if you hear anything of your wife."

He saw them out to the door. The furnishings of the
hall were a further reflection of his character and interests.
A pair of buttoned foils were crossed on a wall and, above
them, a faded blue cap with a tarnished gold tassel. A
younger, slimmer Stronach was pictured in photographs of
groups and teams of fencers and rugby players. In the tall
coat stand, festooned with leather dog leads and chains,
was an assortment of walking sticks; the accumulation of a
once active walker. Among them, a sober crow in black
livery, was a lonely umbrella. It had, Rogers noticed, a
handle fashioned from a boar's tusk. With it was a shooting
stick with leather loop handles. In the corner behind the

stand was slung a bag of golfing-clubs and irons and an aluminium bag trolley.

They did not shake hands on leaving, although Lingard unbent himself to reach down and scratch the hound's ears.

Roger's office was beginning to assume some of the characteristics of a Turkish bath. He found a note from Coltart on his desk. A surly voice from the Dungeon Café had telephoned Hagbourne and had given him the name and address of a girl. Coltart was now out checking.

"If this is Otter's Shirley, it'll put him in the clear," Rogers observed to Lingard. He pulled his mouth down. "And it makes Stronach's wife a that much more possible victim. I'm beginning to smell blood in the wind."

Lingard charged his nose with snuff. "What do you think of her fat spouse, George?"

"Cold, callous and indifferent. He isn't going to weep tears of blood for her. Whatever has happened. She must be an embarrassment to his standing in the community."

"If she's our victim he could very easily be the man with the knife."

"I've thought that one out. A bit crude for a doctor, don't you think? I always associate their violences with subtle poisons or methodical dismemberment."

Lingard shrugged. "If he was in a passion? Wife discovered *flagrante delicto*? Taunts about his fat belly? His white hairs? She'd do that from what you've told me." He was cynical. "Not exactly the occasion for dinner jackets and subtle poisons."

"We could have checked his knife drawer." Rogers wasn't being serious.

Lingard laughed with him. "I can imagine his reaction to that. You were probably wise not to bring the subject up."

"I certainly will if his wife turns up dead with a hole in her bosom," he promised. "I'm gentling him along only because I'd look a bloody fool if she walked in safe and sound."

"I'll push on with it. This afternoon. Are we lunching?"

Rogers nodded and yawned into his fist. "Sorry," he apologized. "Up much too early. Let's eat in the canteen. I've yet to check on the progress of the other inquiries."

He paused in the act of locking the drawers of his desk. "I'll tell you something for nothing, David," he said. "If ever I saw in a man the potential for murder, I saw it in Stronach today."

6

To question a man is to know him. Despite his attitude to interrogation he reveals, consciously or otherwise, something of his character. He exudes an aura; sometimes as a warm red glow, sometimes an emanation of chilling ice or, occasionally, a twisting rope of knotted darkness.

This is the solid core of any investigation. What people say and how they say it.

Rogers, deep in his consideration of the collated words of sought-out witnesses (most of whom were witnesses of nothing), grunted irritably as his door was tapped from outside. A constable entered in answer to his peremptory invitation.

"There's a man called Otter downstairs, sir," he said. "Wants to see his son."

"Well?" he replied impatiently. "And so he can. Isn't there an inspector on the Station?"

"No, sir. And the Station Sergeant's dealing with something else."

Rogers banged his pipe on the desk top and swore. "All right," he said. "Bring him up here. Then fetch his son."

Otter senior was not more than five feet in his heavy metal-shod boots but he made up for his shortness in the bulky breadth of his body. His soiled overalls strained across the gorilla-sized pectorals of his chest. The planes of his face were rough hewn and meaty. About him—like a yellow nimbus—was the sweetness of exhaled beer fumes. Although he swayed on his gross legs like a tree buffeted by strong winds, he was in apparent control of his faculties. Ignoring Rogers's request that he be seated, he placed his fists on the desk and pushed his chin towards the seated detective.

"Wheresh'e?" Rogers flinched from the wafting beer fumes. "Where'sh that lil bleeder of a son of mine?"

A flap of an intolerant hand. "Sit down, Mr. Otter, for God's sake. He'll be here in a minute." He scowled at the man.

Otter turned away and lowered himself with exaggerated caution into the chair behind him. As he did so he was muttering hoarsely to himself. While largely unintelligible to Rogers it was patently invective and directed against his expected son.

"What are you bitching about?" Rogers was being patient. Otter was no more than forty and in the full power of his rough manhood. The detective had no particular wish to scratch at the man's obvious potential for unthinking violence, exacerbated as it now was by alcohol. It was not that he had any particular fear of the outcome but he had spoiled too many suits in past scrabblings and threshings to go out of his way to meet trouble.

"Lil bleeder," he hiccoughed, his eyes glassy and unfocused. "I'll screw the bastard's head off."

Rogers sighed and stood. Trouble was co-existent in the air with the smell of beer. He chopped down his eyebrows. "Suppose you behave yourself," he snapped. "While your son is in this station you'll not touch him."

Otter looked astonished. "Wash the blurry matter with you?" he asked. "Wha' you on about? Eh?" He pulled, with some difficulty of co-ordination, a packet from a pocket and put a cigarette in his mouth. He struck a match, aiming the wavering flame unsteadily at the end of the cigarette. The match dropped to the floor and he fumbled out another one, lighting the tobacco at his second attempt. Receiving no answer, he regarded Rogers with baffled anger.

When the young Otter appeared in the doorway, the constable looming behind him, he looked frightened, his face the colour of cheese. "All right, Brewer," Rogers said. "Leave him with me."

The youth swallowed, his throat working convulsively. "Dad . . .'ullo, dad." He waited.

His father lurched out of his chair and stood, arms hanging and belligerent. He looked at Rogers, undecided at whom to direct his growing rage. "Whash he in for? Whaffor?" He dropped his cigarette on to the floor and ground it and the top layer of linoleum to extinction with his boot.

Rogers moved towards him. "Nothing very serious. In fact, he's doing his best to help us."

Otter ignored this and addressed himself to his son. "You bin getting girls into trouble again." His blunt chin was outthrust, his pig eyes narrowed. "Eh?"

"No, dad." The youth looked at Rogers appealingly. "Not girls."

Otter shuffled a pace or two nearer, a menacing animal. "What then?" he demanded. "Stealing?"

The son was in a condition of painful indecision. He looked from Rogers to his father and back again. The detective said nothing. "Pot, dad," he babbled. "Jus' a bit of pot." He grinned ingratiatingly.

"Pot? Pot? Wha' you mean, you blurry silly lil bastard."

Rogers intervened. "He means drugs. Marijuana, cannabis, whatever you choose to call it . . ." A thick arm brushed him roughly to one side and he staggered backwards in astonished anger to crash against his desk.

Young Otter gave a shrill whinny of terror as his father closed with him, slamming him into the door with a blow to his narrow chest. Rogers, propelling himself forwards, encircled the massive neck with his arms, endeavouring to unstick him from the dazed youth. "Stop it, you bloody maniac!" he snarled. "*Stop it!*"

The three struggling figures—Rogers and the youth being swung helplessly around the sturdy body of Otter—fell crashing through the door on to the landing outside. Young Otter, detaching himself from the bolus of straining bodies, ran with a groan of despair back into the office. His father, shaking his shoulders like a wet dog, his eyes seeking wildly his slippery son, freed himself from Rogers's arms. In doing so, he threw him tottering backwards off balance. Stepping forward, his mouth open in a fury of frustration, he hit the helpless detective a cruel blow under the heart bouncing him, blank faced with pain, off the wooden banisters and tumbling down the stairs.

Sprawled on the polished linoleum below, Rogers beat a fist on the floor as his leg, twisted beneath him, grated its agony from the broken bone.

Coltart, bursting from his own office at the commotion of Rogers's descent, looked down into the well of the staircase. Needing no explanation for the tableau beneath him, he leapt forward and towards Otter. From below, Rogers could see only the two pairs of trousered legs, truncated at the waist by the ceiling of the stairway, moving towards each other, eager and purposeful. Then the sounds of smacking flesh and angry gruntings. The moving backwards of the overalled legs, the grey trousers following. Then a heavy groan and the forced exhalation of breath, followed by a hingeing of the overalled legs as Otter slid abruptly down the wall to a sitting position, his meaty astonished face coming into view.

The huge sergeant, the angry flush under one eye not disguising his solicitous expression, ran down the stairs. "You all right, sir?" He held Rogers's arm, preparing to assist him to his feet.

"I'm wonderful," he snarled. "Apart from breaking a bloody leg." His eyes were dark with pain and he grunted. Then he grimaced a twisted smile. "Sorry," he said penitently. "It's not too bad but don't practise your first aid on me. Be a good chap and fetch a vet." He looked up the stairs. Otter was still in a sitting position, making snuffling noises and staunching a bloody nose with his handkerchief. "I don't know who needs him most," he said.

7

With Rogers submitting ungraciously to the attentions of the hospital casualty officer and Otter senior being charged with conducting himself in a drunken and disorderly manner, Lingard took over the leadership of the department.

He had no illusions that his tenure of office would be

anything more than brief. It might last only until the return of Rogers from the hospital. But he hoped not. Rogers's chair had an attraction for him he could not wholly conceal. The older man had said often—not always humorously—that only amputation or clinical death excused a detective from reporting for duty. A broken limb, he conceded, would relieve the sufferer from carrying out normal activities. But, he would point out, there were clerical duties that could be efficiently undertaken by willing cripples. So, the department, carrying on its multifarious investigations, awaited with interest Rogers's reaction to a fractured leg bone.

Lingard was ambitious and purposive in his single-minded resolve to achieve the summit of his personal mountain. As a corollary to this, he demonstrated unknowingly the flaw in the smooth exterior he presented to the beholder. The tilt of his head, the architecture of his mouth, suggested a moiety more than allowable self-esteem.

Despite his apeing of elegance—sometimes he approached a caricature of it—he was otherwise as sound and as solid as the leather of his bespoke shoes. Too many men had been delivered to prison because of his acuity for any to claim him either a buffoon or an incompetent.

Slim as he was, fragile as he may have appeared, he was tempered steel and hard rubber. His bookish foppery was misleading if it suggested any lack of physical or moral strength. Violence he despised as a weakness. To combat it, to make it possible for him to remain aloof from it, he had acquired for himself an expertise in a simple, horribly efficient, form of judo.

He was pondering the fact of Stronach as he sat in his green Bentley outside the huge glass and aluminum aquarium of a hospital. A telephone call from his friend, the barman of The Falcon, had produced the surprising information that Stronach had entered the lounge bar at a time which must have been only ten minutes or so after Rogers and Lingard had left him.

He had (so the barman said) been blunt in his approach, demanding rather than asking an account of his wife's visits to the premises. In between his consumption of whiskies, he had forced from the barman much of what Lingard himself had obtained. The barman had clearly been intimidated by the fat doctor. He made no attempt to conceal from Lingard that he had been. The superimposition of cultured arrogance on Stronach's frightening physique was sufficient to cow men more aggressive than the barman claimed to be.

Lingard tapped the nails of his slim fingers impatiently on the wooden rim of the steering wheel. His check on Stronach's presence or otherwise at the hospital had resulted in nothing more positive than another imponderable. It had neither confirmed Stronach's claim to be working nor refuted it. The medical staff, professionally uncommunicative to the point of mutism, had finally and reluctantly ignored the Hippocratic oath sufficiently to inform a hardpressing Lingard that Dr. Stronach could have—subject to human fallibility in the field of recall—been working in his office. Or not. No man had actually seen him, no man had spoken to him or had any other evidence of his presence.

So, Lingard concluded, he could—as he had claimed—have been in his office during the previous evening. He could, equally, have been elsewhere. Plunging a knife into his wife's brisket. None of which helped very much. Lingard was, however, concerned about the doctor's visit to The Falcon. This seemed grossly out of character and could mean something or other. Perhaps to someone else. Certainly not to Lingard. His narrow face frowned his irritation at this other imponderable.

When Rogers appeared at the hospital door, supported at each elbow by a nurse, he creased his eyes in a sympathetic smile, swung nimbly from the car without opening the door and went to meet him.

In the car, Rogers was disposed to be more expansive now that the unpleasant medical side of the broken leg had been suffered and done with. The fracture had been more painful than serious, less disabling than a pulled ligament. None the less, the Casualty Officer had plastered his knee to a confining rigidity and recommended a few days at home with an improving book. Knowing Rogers, he said it tongue-in-cheek. Rogers had cursed him briefly with the privilege of a long-standing friendship, stumping towards the door and accepting the assistance of the nurses only when his knee brought him to an ignominious halt, his forehead pimpled with globules of sweat.

"I can get about," he said smugly in answer to Lingard's query. "Just aim me in the direction of the office and I shall be perfectly able. I need only a walking stick and I'll be as mobile as a starving flea."

"I'm sorry I helped you into the car," Lingard said dryly. "It goes to show, doesn't it? I thought they'd put you down. Like a spavined horse."

Rogers smiled comfortably. "A fractured tibia," he exaggerated, "isn't going to stop me from putting in my usual twelve hours a day."

Lingard looked pointedly at the plaster-stiff leg. "You're joking," he said. "Aren't you going sick?"

"Going sick? In the middle of a murder inquiry? Are you bloody barmy, David?" He was plainly affronted.

The blond man persisted. "I think you should," he said stubbornly, "This is the eventuality for which a second-in-command is provided."

"I said 'no'," Rogers snapped. "I'm not an old woman to be tucked into bed and fussed over. I am," he said with emphasis, "remaining in charge of the investigation. I don't think with my leg," he added sardonically.

"I'm sorry, George," Lingard said placatingly. "I was thinking only of you."

Rogers grunted. "No offence, David, but if you don't mind I'll do my own bleeding. I don't need you or anyone else to do it for me."

The late afternoon sun shone brightly, filling the open cockpit of the car with a golden warmth. The airstream, gently flowing over the rectangle of thick glass windscreen, cooled them as the Bentley hummed quietly down the long drop into the dehydrating heat of the town.

Hagbourne was waiting for him as Rogers dragged the weight of his plastered leg into his office. He grimaced as he shrugged off the sergeant's offer of assistance. In the background, Lingard grinned crookedly. He had endured the profanity of Rogers's determined and unaided ascent of the stairs.

"What is it, sergeant?" he panted. "Some good news? It'll be a change," he added sourly. "So far it's been all death and disaster."

Hagbourne looked apologetic. "I'm a bit diffident about mentioning it," he said. "Call me an idiot if you like, but I've a snippet of something from a statement that could be connected. One of Hannah's men filled out a questionnaire for a shopkeeper in Deburgh Road. It seems he added a footnote that a dirty old biddy—Mrs. Kitchen or similar—did a bit of shopping this morning." Hagbourne's brown eyes were gauging the measure of Rogers's patience. So far, the level was encouraging. "It seems also she had a very expensive handbag with her. Quite out of character, he says." He paused. "She also had a roll of notes big enough to choke a donkey to death."

Rogers looked perceptibly happier. "I'm right with you. Go on," he said.

The sergeant nodded. "It could be coincidental. I'm not denying that. It might be a simple larceny by finding. But a woman rarely goes out without her handbag. If she's murdered, or has an accident, there's always the possibility that the bag could be floating around. Ownerless, so to speak." He flicked a finger and thumb together, making a small snapping sound. To himself, this theory was gaining credibility as he expounded it. "So this old woman finds it. Hangs on to it."

"By the lord, it could be!" Rogers exclaimed. "If it is, it'll tell us who our dead woman is. Perhaps even where." He turned to Lingard. "Take the car and get the old lady up here . . ." He swung his head round to Hagbourne as the sergeant interrupted him. "Yes, what is it?" he said impatiently.

"It's already being done." Hagbourne's face was wooden. "I hope you don't mind. You were both at the hospital and I couldn't get hold of Coltart. I also," he continued, "sent Hannah to The Falcon to check with the barman. To see whether he can remember Mrs. Stronach carrying a similar bag."

Rogers grunted his approval. "Good for you. It might have been preferable if we'd stayed at the hospital. You seem to have got on better without us." He spoke to Lingard. "When she arrives, David, hump her up the stairs, will you. And," he concluded acidly, "watch her closely. She'll probably have a go at breaking my other leg."

With the departure of Lingard and Hagbourne, he lifted the handset and dialled Joanne's number. His humour was sunny with optimism as he recounted to the warm-voiced woman at the other end of the connection a picturesque account of his misfortunes. "I'm afraid our dinner is off, Joanne," he finished. "I can't see myself hopping about like an arthritic stork. At least, not in the Bar Grill."

She was brisk. "You've got to eat, George, and I can't see you doing it in the canteen." She was coaxing him. "I'll pick you up in the car and you can have a meal at my place."

"What! In that motorized matchbox of yours!" he scoffed. "What am I supposed to do with my leg? Stick it out of the window?"

"You've been glad enough to ride in it before," she said witheringly. "It's your head that may not fit in. What time shall I call?"

He looked at his watch. It was a little after five-thirty. "Say about eight. But depending very much on the next hour or so."

Replacing the handset and hitching his plastered leg to a more comfortable position, he removed and unfolded a letter from the envelope addressed to him in Coltart's hand. It said, with a typical economy of words, that inquiries had turned up a chemist on the far outskirts of the sprawling suburbs who had that morning received a request from a customer for attention to a badly cut hand. The wounds had needed urgent medical dressing and the chemist had said so. He had sold the man some rolls of bandaging and an antiseptic dusting powder, advising him strongly to seek immediate treatment. The man had refused further advice and his attitude had aroused the chemist's suspicion.

Rogers knew, for Coltart to deal with this apparently unconnected triviality himself, that the large detective was following his nose. This, together with a monumental persistence, was his highly efficient stock-in-trade. On the whole, it was successful. It was largely so because its practice stirred the depths of unknown and unsuspected abysses of human behaviour, disturbing things believed long buried, probing forgotten emotions, promoting revealing activity. And truths bubbled up from the concealing strata for Coltart to examine and act upon. He was a comforting man for society to have on its side.

*   *   *

Mrs. Kitcher—her eyes no less venomous for the fear present in them—sat crouched on a chair in her kitchen. Standing over her, their heads an inch or so from the room's web-festooned ceiling, were Rogers and Lingard.

The detective sent by Hagbourne to bring Mrs. Kitcher to the station had baulked at the old woman's implacability and her threat of screaming violence. He had explained miserably over the telephone that he would, without quibble, accept and execute any order to arrest a dozen drunken Irish steel erectors but not, please God, this grim-visaged, filthy old hellcat.

So Rogers and Lingard had come to the woman, Rogers cursing malevolently Lingard's alleged inability to drive his car over anything but lumpy boneshaking rubble. Dragging his plaster-weighted leg into the malodorous house did nothing to amend his preconceived dislike of Mrs. Kitcher.

"All right, madam," he snapped, banging the glossy handbag on the table before him and sending up a mist of dust. "Where did you get it?"

If he thought Mrs. Kitcher an unworthy adversary or unequal to his ill temper, he was immediately disabused. It was well for Lingard and the unsmotherable smile on his face that he was behind Rogers. With small gobbets of froth spattering from the mouth shouting backstreet abuse at them, she rose from her chair, pulled open to the door and pointed dramatically with a shaking hand. "Out! Out!" she spluttered. "Get out of me 'ouse before I call a policeman!"

The two men stood stolidly, looking at her in surprise. Rogers then scowled. "Would you mind not making an exhibition of yourself, Mrs. Kitcher," he said frostily. "We *are* the police. As well you know." He changed his voice to a softer, more friendly tone. "Come on back into the room. This isn't doing you a bit of good." He withdrew a letter from the handbag. "This belongs to a Mrs. Stronach. A doctor's wife." He waited as the old woman, reluctantly and fearfully, stepped back from the door, closing it against the warm clear air from outside.

Inside, the atmosphere was an amalgam of the smells of dust, stale food, pickled onions, unwashed bed linen and the woman herself. Lingard armed his sinuses against its unpleasantness with repeated chargings of Attar of Roses; Rogers, equally on the defensive, maintained a steady fire in the bowl of his pipe. Occasionally he twitched with discomfort and ate a pain-killing tablet.

The heat in the room had a steam-laundry humidity to it and the men felt the start of dampness between their shoulder-blades. Sweat began to trickle between the plaster and flesh of Rogers's damaged leg.

When she had resumed her seat, he continued. "Mrs. Stronach is missing... perhaps dead." He paused to allow his words to have the effect intended. He thought he could detect a glint of a recognition of something in the watery eyes.

Mrs. Kitcher, malevolence having failed, was regrouping her defences and allowing herself to snivel. She was old and lonely and frightened. She looked at Rogers as she thought a mother might regard a cruel and neglectful son. "I'm sorry, mister," she quavered humbly. "I found it outside in the alley." Her face brightened. "I was just goin' to take it along to the police station when your young man came. A nice, polite young man 'e was," she added obsequiously.

"So nice that you frightened him half to death," Rogers said, poker-faced. "Have you looked inside it?"

Outrage was in the grimed creases of her face. "*Look inside!* Someone else's 'andbag?" she snarled. "Let me tell you I'm an honest woman...." She trailed into silence as the recollection of her spending intruded into her protest. She looked down and scratched vigorously at one of the grey stockings covering her legs. When she finally looked up, Rogers's eyes were still on her in accusatorial silence. She blinked and twisted her parchment-shiny fingers together. Despite the season of the year, the knuckles were misshapen and red as if with chilblains.

"So honest that you spent some of the money in the shop at the corner?" He jerked his head in its general direction. "So honest that you told the shopkeeper the bag was a present?" His voice roughened. "Come on, Mrs. Kitcher, *please!* Where *did* you get it?" A tear, any significance it may have had being lost on Rogers, trickled jerkily down the crease between her nostril and mouth. He continued. "If you lie in one thing, you will lie in another."

She swallowed. "Is she dead? I didn't know. I didn't think she was . . . I mean . . . she didn't look . . ."

He glared at her and exploded. "For Christ's sake, woman, out with it." He limped swiftly across to her, catching hold of one thin arm and pulling her to her feet. "Now," he barked. "*Quick*! Tell me."

She swung back and lifted her free arm. "You wouldn't hit an old lady," she snarled up at him.

Rogers made a derisory noise in his throat. "God, but you tempt me, madam." He paused and then spoke slowly and distinctly to her. "You must tell me where she is. She may not be dead. She may need help. Medical attention." He lowered his head to within biting distance of her. "Have you no single spark of humanity in you?" he hissed.

She made no reply but, taking a rusty woollen shawl from a hook, opened the door and stepped out into the alley. The sun had been blanketed by dark hanging clouds and there was a hush over the town, a waiting for the summer storm to discharge its cooling benison.

With the two detectives flanking her, she stopped several feet from the quiet green door. Both men shared a sensation that the door emanated a brooding balefulness. Suggested as it might have been by a pre-knowledge, they none the less believed they could sense death waiting (and death has a characteristic and distinctive aura of its own) behind the concealing wood.

Rogers nodded and Lingard stepped forward, lifting the iron catch slowly and pulling the door open towards himself.

Even before he saw the body, Rogers observed its unpleasantness reflected in the spasm of distaste on his assistant's features and in his involuntary inhalation of breath. Swinging his rigid leg and pushing Mrs. Kitcher away, he stepped towards the shadowed interior.

She was a collapsed and twisted flaccidity. Jammed between the pedestal and the lime-washed bricks of the walls, she was doubled in suffocating distortion, her head downwards and under the white curve of the china bowl.

The flesh at the back of her neck was chill to Rogers's touch and mottled livid and mauve. Her face was not visible. There was, so far as he could see, no wound in the upper aspect of the trunk and no blood. There was a sharp, sour reek of alcohol about the body and she had vomited over her legs.

Rogers turned his head around and spoke to Mrs. Kitcher. His voice was not pleasant. "Go home," he said. "Go home and stay there. I'll see you later."

8

Coltart mopped his moist red face with a handkerchief and scowled his discomfort. Where his clothing touched against his large frame it stuck. Although the clouds screened the sun, the heat was no less oppressive. He slammed shut the door of his car, leaving the chassis and body to shudder from the impact. He strode across the soft tar of the footpath and entered the door of the chemist's shop.

On the way to it he had disposed of the last reason for supposing Otter to be involved in the use of the knife.

Shirley, as accurately described by Bodger as had been Otter, was a highly perfumed, rankly sexual child. Her fat mother, over-protective and stupid as a cow, blind to her daughter's development, had flatly refused to believe her connection with anything so male and dangerous as Otter.

Coltart, brusque in his impatience to close the door on this abortive aspect of the investigation, quickly disabused the mother and reduced the girl to a sullen admission of the association. Before he was done, there was little to choose between them in both wishing him gone, both rejecting the destructive truth he had shown them. He was not the first policeman by many thousands to discover that the face of truth is an ugly crone more often than not; that you cannot wed her to the simpering blindness of stupidity.

To Coltart, the Otter affair was now a bolted warren

and the smell of blood in his nose drew him away from the rabbit to the unknown wounded tiger.

The chemist, a tiny rosy man swathed to mid-calf in starched white overalls, chattered his anxiety to help the large sergeant. He was equally anxious to emphasize that he had not given medical treatment or advice to his uncommunicative customer.

The man had not entered the shop with the confidence of indifference. He had, initially, examined from outside the displayed contents of the two windows. The chemist, not being busy at that early hour, noticed his pale hovering, one arm behind him, his eyes anonymous behind dark glasses. He had, he said, been wrong in assessing the man's need.

He was tempted strongly—he turned slightly more rosy—to go outside and refer him to the nearest hairdressing establishment. ("I don't stock the things," he said primly, his rimless glasses glinting at Coltart. "It embarrasses my girls to be asked for them.")

When the man eventually entered it was when only he, the chemist, was in the shop. He had been initially alarmed, thinking the time had been specifically chosen to push a gun into his face and demand the contents of the till. But when he held out his hand, it was heavily bandaged. He noted the extreme pallor of the face, looking as if it had been bled white. The chemist had spoken halting words about "was it an accident?" The man said "yes." That was all. Uncompromising with no explanation. The bandage was loosely, amateurishly coiled about the hand. When it was unrolled some bloody cotton-wool had come away with it.

The rosy face wrinkled in remembered distress. "The hand was *sliced*," he said. "Not cut, you understand, in the ordinary way of such things but gashed across the palm several times. It wasn't bleeding then but the gashes needed stitching. Badly. The wounds would never heal without first closing them. In one gash I could see the bone." He licked his lips. "A horrible mess. I said to him, 'Good God, my dear chap, you need a doctor . . . probably hospital!' I asked him why he hadn't been to a doctor. He just shook his head. Then said no, he didn't want to. Didn't believe in them. Then he came up with an explana-

tion about being a Christian Scientist. He obviously said it
on the spur, so to speak. Didn't care whether I believed
him or not. That was his attitude. So I said, 'What do you
want from me? I can't do anything useful for you.' 'Ban-
dages,' he said, 'and antiseptic.' I told him I wasn't allowed
to treat people. That I could only give first aid and supply
medicaments and drugs. He said, 'All right, all right, spare
me the lecture. Give me what you think right.' He threw a
screwed-up pound note on the counter. He was a very
impatient and contemptuous man," he commented. "*And*
a very sick one. God Himself knows how he stopped the
bleeding. From the look of his hand, he could have used a
tourniquet of some sort. Anyway, to get to the point. I let
him have some bandaging and a drum of dusting powder."
He looked apologetic. "I *couldn't* let him have anything
stronger. He'd have done holy murder to his hand. He was
so clumsy about it I helped put the bandage on for him.
Anyway, he was anxious to get away from the shop and I
had to call out for him to come back for his change. He
didn't hear me, though. Or wouldn't." He pointed to a
small pile of coins on the top of the till. "It's waiting there
for him."

"So which hand was it?" Coltart asked.

The chemist closed his eyes the better to visualize the
man. "His left," he said with certainty. "Yes, I'm positive it
was."

"Did you see which way he went?"

"I did. I followed him to the door—his change, you
understand—and saw him turn the corner."

"To where?"

"Not to anywhere. It's just a street."

"It must lead somewhere," Coltart said patiently.
"Even if only into a brick wall."

"Yes, of course. I'm sorry, sergeant. I meant, it's just a
street. Running into other streets. And that one runs into
another. All residential, you understand?" His kindly little
face brightened. "He had a car with him. Or," he qualified
cautiously, "I think he did."

"Ah!" Coltart was eager. "How was this?"

"After he turned the corner. I heard an engine start
and a car drive away. A big car, I should say. It didn't come
out into this road so it obviously went in the opposite

direction," he finished apologetically as if it had been some fault of his.

Coltart looked dubious. "*Could* he drive a car with his hand?"

"I think you can do anything when the need is pressing enough," the Chemist countered shrewdly.

The detective knew him to be right. He, himself, had known a man to shoot himself twice in the heart, both wounds proving fatal, the gun being reloaded between shots. He had seen the body of a man who had walked several hundreds of yards after severing his own trachea with a completeness that denied a single further breath. A gashed palm need not prove so at his house.

Vouchsafing no acknowledgement, no recognition, he ignored Lingard; speaking only to the waiting Dr. Hunter. Lingard had watched him—remembering Rogers's final assessment of him—closely and with intense curiosity, trying to pierce the man's inscrutability. Stronach's undisguised hostility was the rapping of a sponge on the plating of Lingard's self-sufficiency. The slim detective was armoured with a belief that the doctor would be his eventual prey; that their roles had already been cast by fate.

He had noted the formality of Stronach's dress: the dark grey suit, the stiff white collar and black tie, the bowler hat and the tightly-furled umbrella.

Dr. Hunter—the examination completed—stripped the pale yellow rubber gloves from her slim hands. They made ugly sucking noises and left her wrists covered with talc powder. She regarded Lingard with her serious intense eyes. They were the colour and texture of orange wallflower petals.

"I detected a sub-zero temperature between you and my departed colleague," she said. "I didn't realize you knew each other."

"We're sweethearts," he said lightly. "Having a bit of a tiff."

"In other words—mind my own business." Bridget Hunter rarely smiled. When she did there was an exciting warmth about her. Her expression now remained serious. The two knew each other well. They were only a pinch of recklessness away from being lovers.

"Not really. It's my policeman's reflexes." From the table, he picked up the springclip board of papers on which he had been making notes. "You're sold on asphyxia, I take it?"

She put a foot on the pedal of a white enamelled disposal bin and dropped the gloves into it. "Suffocation by pressure. Assisted by regurgitation. It's all yours how it happened." She looked at him curiously. "You were getting all ulcerated over a knife."

"I was. It doesn't come into the context of that." He gestured towards the dead woman. He did not look at all happy. "But she still poses a problem. Why, for instance, she should choose—if she did choose—to be in such a distressingly foul hole. Despite her sexual licence . . . the company she kept . . . she was a woman of some refinement."

"If she was breaking her neck she possibly wouldn't be too particular," the girl murmured. "We women can be very basic when necessity pushes." She looked directly at him. "And don't forget that necessity often disregards convention."

Lingard twitched his shoulders uncomfortably. "I'll ignore that," he said. "It sounds as if it means something indelicate." She was stripping off her white surgical overall. It was fouled with ugly red blotches. "Have you finished?" he asked, "because if you have I'll buy you a drink." He pushed back the cuff of his shirt-sleeve and looked at the watch on his wrist. "It's nearly eight."

Elbowing the long curved handle of the tap, she washed her hands and forearms, performing this with meticulous care, using a large brush for the cleaning of her unpolished nails. Before wiping her hands dry, she replenished the water, adding an antiseptic to it. During this ritual she neither spoke nor looked up. Lingard remained silent also, watching her intently.

The streets outside were quiet with lifeless air; the sky heavy with black, solid cloud. From within the depths of their mighty canyons came an occasional faraway rumble of sound. The humidity in the atmosphere clarified perspective, foreshortening middle and far distances to a telescoped huddle of encroaching buildings. There was an inky-blueness about the roof tops and the horizons were a clearly defined indigo.

The Spanish Bar, into which they entered, was an adequately contrived reproduction of a Costa Brava bodega. Purple and green cellophane grapes, vast barrel ends sunk into white limewashed walls and bullfight posters were the main properties of its staging. The beamed ceiling had been artificially smoked to a golden brown and from it hung a profusion of long sausages resembling dusty red and bronze stalactites. The wooden chairs and tables were chunky, processed with straw cord and woven matting. The sherry, served direct from small polished kegs on the shelves at the back of the bar, was worth drinking.

The people in the bar were jacketless or limp in thin dresses. Most of them had dark patches under the armpits or down the ridge of the spine. They were lethargic with the heat and without the energy to string words together.

Lingard and Bridget sat beneath a reproduction Picasso, a schooner each of iced lager before them. The bar was not the usual choice of either. The heat made its contiguity to the mortuary a convenience and its only recommendation.

"How is the Lord High Executioner?" she was asking him.

"Rogers?" He laughed. "Poor George. He's cracked a patella or tibia. I don't suppose he cares which. Otherwise he's his usual carping self."

"Don't be feline, David. An accident?"

"No. A very purposeful act. Some thug he was trying to stop committing bloody mayhem. Chucked him down his office stairs. George, I mean. All a bit tiresome, really." He took out the ivory box and pinched snuff into his nose. "He's far from being *hors de combat*, you know." He dusted away a few loose grains with his large silk handkerchief. "When I left him he was hopping around his office. In a rare old stew. He took it personally that Mrs. Stronach wasn't bleeding from every pore."

"You've a mean spirit," she reproved him. "I like George. He's a very direct man." Even in the humid closeness of the small bar she was smooth-fleshed and cool.

"He was very direct about your findings, I recollect," Lingard smiled. "When I telephoned him he was anything but pleased."

She made a moue with her mouth. It was decidedly

kissable. "It isn't always possible to be unequivocally, unblushingly definite. I have to qualify my findings. If you consider asphyxia, you'll find that everyone dies of it in one form or another. It's the causation that's important. A stab wound in the heart, a cut throat, pneumonia: all in their different ways a forced cessation of breathing." She took a flat case from her handbag, slid from it a cigarette and flicked her lighter to its tip. She breathed deeply at it and blew smoke from her nostrils. "As, of course," she said, "is advanced carcinoma of the lung." She shook her head sorrowfully. "Physician, heal thyself."

"Dangerous habit," he observed smugly. "As, indeed, a graduate in morbid anatomy should well know."

"Your own isn't so much better," she countered. "You appreciate, I suppose, that you will most likely finish up with a couple of sinusoidal papillae as big as walnuts?"

He gave an exaggerated shudder. "You see death and decay in everything about you." He showed his square white teeth in a laugh, looking at her whimsically. "Don't sidetrack me by appealing to my hypochondria. I know enough about fatal dyspnoea. It'll happen to all of us. as you say. But—as you well know—I have to discover the way in which it happened to Mrs. Stronach." He dipped a finger in his beer and drew strokes on the table top as he made his points. "Stabbed? That's one thing we can be certain she was not. Manual or ligature strangulation? No bruising, hyoid bone unfractured . . ."

She interrupted him. "Glaister quotes an instance," she said, "where asphyxial signs were so slight as to be practically non-existent. Vaso-vagal inhibition leaves very little but a dead body."

His eyebrows questioned this. "Nothing?"

"Quite possible." She was brisk with certainty. "If there has been pressure applied exactly over the carotid sinus then you may get this sudden cardiac arrest and stoppage of breathing. It just doesn't come on again. This is a possibility in any death from asphyxiation where the more obvious symptoms are absent."

"As easy as that?"

"It would be common enough," she said carelessly, "if karate was taken to its ultimate." She eyed his throat. "I could kill you easily, David. One day I think I shall."

He fingered his tie and smirked. "I cannot imagine a more delightful executioner." He returned to his main theme. "What about some other means? Her, I mean. Not me."

"Well..." She was doubtful. "There was certainly potechial haemorrhaging from the eyes and on the face. This is a usual enough symptom of asphyxia anyway. The complexion was livid and we had some congestion." Her straight hair, glossy brown and reflecting the overhead lighting, swung from side to side in negation. "I just cannot pin it down. She had those marks on the lips. They *could* have been caused by biting. But not necessarily."

"Probably kissing Drazek goodnight," he said disconsolately. "He looks the type to chew on his conquests."

"It could be what it appears to be. Neither of us has to be too clever. Reading into it what isn't there."

"An accident?"

She had a direct and disconcerting way of regarding him, forcing her femininity into the exchange of words. "Tell me why it needn't be."

"Say she was pushed down forcibly? Between pan and podium, so to speak."

"With no serious grazing? No abrasion? Morbid anatomy and common sense says 'not very likely.'"

"But possible?"

"Possible, yes. Probable, no."

"And 'possible' won't be enough for George. Not with his broken leg... this heat." He sighed. "I'll almost certainly get posted to Siberia."

She slapped at a fly on her bar arm. "About the same degree of probability we're discussing. And, at the moment, it sounds Elysian."

"George's equivalent of it isn't." He dropped his flippancy. "So it's no go?"

"Just a strong likelihood one way. Not absolutely eliminating the unfriendly assistance of a second party." She squashed her cigarette out. "Giving evidence, I would lean heavily on it being an accident. The regurgitation could certainly follow a collapse from an overdose of alcohol." Her nose wrinkled. "She had a wagon-load of *that*. In the position she was found she could quite easily compress her respiratory system sufficiently to suffocate herself. And now, David," she said, "I'm afraid it's all yours. I've given you my all." She emptied the schooner of beer in a final flourish.

He grimaced. "What the hell am I so concerned about. I mean, I *want* it to be an accident. But I want also to be one hundred and ten per cent certain it was." For a moment his blue eyes were frosty. "I wouldn't like to think a murderer was escaping justice."

9

Rogers, his leg supported horizontally on an adjacent chair, sat askew at his desk. He had taken the constricting links from the cuffs of his shirt, the sleeves were not rolled.

When finally he lifted a sweaty hand from the paper on which he had been writing it left a damp grey blotch. He cursed pointlessly and threw his pen onto the desk. His pipe tasted bitter and was a hot irritation to his tongue.

Outside, it was still light and the stored heat of the day pressed down on the town like a heavy blanket.

His necessarily cursory examination of the grotesqueries of Mrs. Stronach's body at the scene of her death had convinced him that he had to seek further for the victim of the knife. Lingard's call, informing him of the ambiguities resulting from the post-mortem examination, was what he expected. Coltart's information had now taken over the running. The bandaging and cottonwool brought back by him had been quickly tested in the laboratory. The blood grouping was different from that on the knife. This was of no immediate assistance other than eliminating the possibility that the weapon had caused the gashes in the unknown man's hand.

Rogers had prepared and circulated information.

In connection with the finding of a knife, believed used to wound or murder some person unknown, it is desired to establish the identity of the following described man: gave name of WILLIAM COLLINS (believed false); approximately 30 years of age; 6'0" to 6'2" tall; slim build. Brown hair (worn long), clean shaven, pale complexion, clusters of hairs on ear lobes. Speaks in educated voice; well-dressed in fawn linen trilby hat, light-weight suit (brown with faint red line), fawn shirt, brown shoes. Called at local chemist's shop asking treatment for badly cut left hand which needed stitching. Wearing sun glasses and carrying gold-capped pen and pencil in breast pocket. Suggestions as to identity to Detective Chief Inspector Rogers.

It wasn't a lot, thought Rogers, and a town of 300,000 population was probably eaves-deep in tall, slim men with educated accents. It was only too apparent from his caution in obtaining some sort of relief that the chemist's taciturn customer was not going to draw careless attention to his only identifying feature. Any man walking the streets with a bandaged left hand was but a brief instant from a forced visit to Rogers's office.

He was hoping that the disseminated blueprint of the man might prod the recollection of someone to the point of recognition. That, and a further dogged round of hospitals, doctors and chemists.

Somewhere, he suspected, a man waited in apprehension, his mind a sweat of terror for the knock of the door, his soul shrivelling in self-defeating despair.

He was not overlooking the improbable likelihood that the man had given his correct name. The vast complex of criminal records had been examined, together with voters' lists and telephone and street directories. All were being searched or scrutinized by tenacious men.

All this, and—as Rogers knew—it might be yet another unconnected incident. A phantasmagoria of unreality leading them on to yet further purposeless and barren effort.

Beneath the shielding plaster, sweat trickled down his leg and he groaned his discomfort. He felt void of intelligent thought, his mental processes an unhappy stumbling through cold grey porridge. He read the notes he had written, scowled irritably at their incomprehensibility and screwed the paper into a small ball. This he flung venomously to the far corner of the office, flinching as he twisted his leg in doing so.

When he heard the tiny car purr into the yard below his office window, he locked the drawers of his desk and kicked the supporting chair away with his plastered leg.

His irritability was not lessened by the vexation difficulty he was having in manouevring his leg and himself into the passenger seat of Joanne's car. Experienced in the handling of this often intractable man, she made no effort to assist him. Neither did she offer encouragement. Ignoring his cross-grained awkwardness, she busied herself removing a bottle of wine and some packages from the front seat to the back. Only when he had grunted himself into an apparently suitable posture did she seat herself and speak to him.

"Now that you're settled," she said sweetly, "perhaps you'll stop behaving like a fractious rhinoceros and tell me whether you want to go anywhere first."

He looked sideways at her, started to snarl, changed his mind and laughed sheepishly. "Good grief," he said, "it's not like me, is it."

"It is," she assured him. "Quite typical."

"I'm sorry, but I've had a dreadful day. I feel as if I've been up since the beginning of time. I've been chucked down my own stairs by a blood . . . by a raving lunatic. I've been devilled by two women—one Methuselah's grandmother, the other *rigor mortis* in her lavatory—and I'm back to where I started from this morning."

She didn't smile at this catalogue of his misfortunes. Her silver-grey eyes were soft as she touched his cheek with the back of her hand. "Poor darling," she said. "Does it hurt?"

"I'm probably crippled for life."

She twisted the ignition key, dragged the lever into gear and drove out from the yard. "I'm sure you are. How many nurses did it require to hold you down for the plastering?"

He looked superior. "I wasn't a woman giving birth to

some puny infant. Anyone else would have been given a general anaesthetic." He humped the leg to another position. "Actually," he said, "it isn't anything but a hairline fracture in the upper shinbone and some bad bruising. It isn't even painful unless I twist it about or walk too much. It's just that it's so dam' inconvenient and uncomfortable."

"Are you going sick?"

He snorted. "Not you too. Lingard can't wait to get me off duty and into bed. I don't suppose there's any ill-feeling about it but he's an uncommonly ambitious man for my chair."

Above the humming of the wheels, they could hear the premonitory muttering of thunder. The parked cars lining the street seemed to crouch animal-like in fear of the storm to come. Occasionally, a rapid flicker of luminosity reflected itself as a lurid scarlet splash on the bonnet of the moving car.

They were silent until they reached the door to her flat. Then he stretched and said, "Thank God for little girls with comfortable apartments. Help me out of this sardine can you misname a car, will you please."

Inside, there was a cool haven of air conditioning and insulated quiet and Rogers fell gratefully on to the long, dropsical sofa. He was barely conscious of gentle hands removing his shoes before he dropped suddenly into oblivion.

When he awoke it was to the intolerably fragrant smell of grilling kidneys. He yawned and squinted at his watch. "How long?" he asked the ash-blonde woman looking down at him.

"About an hour, you idle loafer." She rumpled his hair. "Dinner will be ready by the time you've washed and combed your hair." She had changed into a black fringe-knit top with red linen trousers. Her body was slim and straight-limbed. Around her throat she wore a double-stranded rope of pearls.

He reached for her hand and touched the back of it with his mouth. "You are getting dreadfully bossy, Joanne," he said, "and you're brainwashing me into liking it."

The dining-room was small and elegant. The suntan canvas-covered walls supported a chartreuse ceiling. Slim teak furniture, low and functional in design, stood on honey carpeting. The room was illuminated by four

geranium-red candles on the table. The cutlery glittered
in the light-winking dimness.

Seated at the table, replete and content not to move,
they loved one another with their eyes. With the falling
down of the dying sun, the purples and blues outside
deepened to darkness and the earth lay quietly breathing.
There was a welcome coolness in the air, whispering along
the streets in gentle gusts. From the interior of the
overhanging cloud masses the rumbling was louder. One
could imagine its vast impatience.

Flickering light illuminated the towering columns of
cumulonimbus. Occasionally, a spiteful jagged streak of
fire thrust down through the floor of the cloud mass as if
seeking to splinter itself on the waiting earth below.

The room was a small golden cave in the elemental
disorder without. She pushed the decanter of cognac over
the polished surface towards him. "How much longer,
George?"

He pursed his lips and shook his head. "Only God
and the judicature would know that. She's not contesting it
and that's something I should be grateful for."

"She's not contesting it only because she has no case."
She looked at him curiously. "Do you ever see her?"

"Very occasionally. Not to speak to. We've nothing left
to say to each other." He made a gesture of distaste. "I'm
sorry, Joanne. I've tried hard enough, pulled a few strings.
It adds up in the end to waiting your turn."

"She is still living in town?"

"Yes. You've not seen her yourself?"

"Not that I know of. I've seen her only once. The
time you pointed her out to me. I'm not even sure I'd
recognize her if I fell over her in the gutter. Nor," she said
nastily, "would I particularly wish to."

"I don't think she goes out much for anyone to see,"
he said patiently. "Be fair. She isn't flaunting herself. It
could be downright embarrassing for me if she did."

"She doesn't work?"

"No."

"So I suppose you still maintain her?" She was bitter.

He twisted his mouth. "I'm still liable at law. Even
had I no moral obligations."

"She's no more your wife than a hole in the road

outside is. Why doesn't she get off her fat backside and work?"

"Her backside isn't fat," he grinned, "and she doesn't work because she suffers from female disorders."

Her grey eyes glinted. "She's an idle cow, George, and as fit as I am."

"All right, if you say so. But let's not worry about her. A few months from now and I'll be free to enter into holy wedlock with the bossiest woman in existence."

"Come into the other room," she commanded.

On the oversize sofa she was a sweet-smelling laxness in his arms. He kissed her. "Why is it that kissing with overtones of cognac in it always raises the beast in me?" he asked rhetorically. "And under these particularly unfortunate circumstances."

"Circumstances?" she questioned blankly.

"I mean being loaded down with a half-a-hundredweight of plaster." He slapped it impatiently with the flat of his hand. "Look at it. I might as well be handcuffed to an incubus for all the use I am."

She kissed him. "*I'm* not encumbered, darling, so just lie still and don't be irritable."

She was gentle with an affection he had never received from the woman still legally his wife.

Outside, unheeded, large spots of rain splashed down like molten silver coins.

In a house far away at High Moor a man cried.

The room in which he sat was in darkness. The drapes were undrawn and the windows open to the oppressing sky, breathing in recurring gusts of cooling air. He hunched in the chair, not seeing the shimmer of light on the walls of his study.

One hand supported his stricken face, the other fondled the blonde ears of the Afghan hound stretched at his side.

He had been crying as a man cries: bitter, racking tears that dragged holes of pain from his chest. When he had finished he continued to sit in the darkness, eyeless and without conscious thought.

The lightning, when it came, bleached the blackness of the room to a non-dimensional electric blue. The crack-

ing rumble of thunder that followed sent the dog twitching
with fear to crouch beneath the desk.

After a while he went to the bathroom where he
bathed his swollen red eyelids in cold water. When he
returned to his study he drew the drapes and selected a
book from the wall shelves before him.

10

The storm had ripped open the swollen udders of the
hanging clouds and the world was a turmoil of lancing
rain. The streets and roofs were a wet darkness as they
reflected the increasing frequency of the forking of cold
flame through the falling water. The coolness was now a
reality, no longer a promise.

Sergeant Mogg drove the black car through the turbulence of water with an unconscious brutality towards its
insentient metal structure and the thrashing pistons forcing it up the steep terraced hillside of Low Moor. At his
side Lingard sat quietly, peering through the segments of
watery visibility left by the sweeping wiper blades.

The wheels hissed through the surface water, throwing up plumed sprays on each side of the vehicle. Occasional drops of rain entered the open side windows, spotting
the intent faces of the two silent men. Overhead, the radio
antenna thrummed in sympathy with the vibrating engine.

Although Sergeant Mogg was accounted to be a
frighteningly hard man in a fight, it was entirely fortuitous
that Lingard was using him to drive him to The Bessemer
Arms. He had happened to be on duty and available.
Lingard anticipated trouble but was unconcerned either
about his ability to deal with it or its outcome.

He entered the uncurtained austerity of the premises,
leaving Mogg in the car outside. No customer of the house
would ever be accused of using superlatives in describing
its interior furnishings. If, in fact, they ever noticed them.

The woodwork and walls were shinily varnished an

umber brown, made more dingy by the smoke of countless pounds of tobacco burned within the bar. The high ceiling was supported by painted iron pillars placed with no apparent regard for free movement from door to bar and for no obvious structural reason. The floor was covered with a rind of dun brown linoleum; scuffed, scratched and pock-marked by the feet of drinkers and tables alike. These latter, naked of comfort, were graceless with marble tops and ornamental iron legs.

To the men frequenting the bar, the accoutrements of drinking were of minimal importance. Drinking in The Bessemer Arms was not accounted an adjunct to social intercourse. It fulfilled a physical need, the bitter satisfying liquid replenishing body fluids expended in the man-made solar flares of the furnaces.

The alcohol was drunk in quantities producing huge paunches and explosive humours. The fists that clamped themselves around tankard handles were not by any means scarred wholly from the exigencies and hazards of their work. They were hard and rough men. Men who would maim or disable without the saving grace of uncontrolled passion.

The women they married knew better than to expect to enter this all-male province. On those occasions when alcohol conceded second place to sex, the men changed their overalls and boots for suits and shoes, taking their potential for unthinking brutality to the curtained and carpeted snugs of other premises.

When Lingard stepped into the bar, his neat person an insult to their dirty overalls and stained shirts, the head-turned silence was palpable. The eyes that waited for him were hostile. It was as he had expected. He knew also that his profession was as clear to them as if the word had been embroidered on his tie.

Drazek, standing in a small knot of men at the far end of the bar, smiled. Not at Lingard but patently at some secretly anticipated pleasure he could foresee for himself. He put his beer glass down on the counter, shouldering his way through the men about him and facing the detective. He belched deliberately and offensively, smacking his flat hand hard against the tightness of his belly.

"Is it me you want, mate?" he asked, his scarred lips

sneering his antagonism. He was standing legs astride, solid meat and bone in his aggressiveness.

Lingard stared at him, his blue eyes insulting in the curiosity they revealed. He was looking through an invisible quizzing glass. "As a matter of fact, it is," he drawled. "I want to talk to you. At the station."

Drazek gave an incredulous laugh. "At the . . . ? You must be bloody stupid! Who's going to take me there?"

"The general idea is that I am." He said it calmly, almost mildly.

"On your own?" The steelworker, uncertain in his incredulity, looked around at his friends for the moral support of laughter.

"I have a car outside, of course." Lingard walked the remaining few feet towards him and stood, facing him squarely. "Don't play about, Drazek." His voice was now clipped and official. "This is serious business."

The other men in the bar had gathered around the two, forming a human amphitheatre as a setting for the anticipated violence. The barman, caught between two forces, dissociated himself from both by absorbing his interest in the washing and re-washing of glasses already cleaned.

Lingard let his cold eyes travel the ring of unfriendly faces. "Listen to me," he said. "I am a police officer on duty. My business is with that man." He nodded his tweed hat at Drazek. "If any one of you interferes with me, assists him in any action against me, I promise you that you'll occupy a cell before the night ends." His eyes dominated them with his disdain. "Sergeant Mogg"—the ensuing exhalation of breath was clearly audible and he smiled contemptuously—"Sergeant Mogg is outside and only too anxious to have an excuse to come in. Don't give it to him," he warned.

Mogg of the rib-cracking punches was known to them all. In a fight he was metal-clad in absolute fearlessness and in his desire to meet brawlers and disturbers of the peace on their own terms. They, for their part, knew they were on a bet of nothing against the painful exchange of blows and the certainty of a month in gaol. While a few may have accepted either alternative with a brutal fortitude, the two together were odds that only the most drunken local or ignorant stranger cared to take on for a matter of principle.

For Drazek, however, there was no room for such niceties of manoeuvre. His status as a man was irretrievably involved. To go quietly with the detective like a haltered sheep with the butcher was to be relegated to the level of a clown; to be ridiculed by his congeners with savage, unforgetting contempt. Not that he would have gone without a fight in any other circumstances. Not disliking Lingard as he did.

For Lingard, this was written on the wall in large letters and he had been preparing the arena; watching the man's eyes for the first warning flicker of intended movement. He was not, however, to be taken by surprise for the handsome and contemptuous steelworker put his two fists forward in Corinthian style and said, "Come on! Come and take me, you toffee-nosed bastard!"

The detective shrugged. "I don't want to brawl with you, Drazek. Put your fists down and walk through that door. I'm not arresting you. I want only to talk to you."

Drazek laughed scornfully at Lingard's apparent mildness, his confidence a distended bladder. He sauntered by him, still laughing as he bundled him heavily with his hard body in passing.

The laugh died abruptly as two firm hands grabbed him from behind; one by the bicep of an arm, the other by a wrist, pushing the arm against the fulcrum of the shoulder. With Lingard enforcing this painful armlock, he necessarily stood still, his bull's head twisting from one side to another in an endeavour to see the enemy at his rear. When his sluggish brain got organized and he attempted to kick backwards, the arm was tweaked upwards with an agonizing wrenching of muscles and tendons. "Are you going to behave yourself?" The voice was menacing, no longer polite.

"Let me go!" He was white with anger and mortification. The whole of his conscious world was a desire to macerate this taunting man to a crimson, jammy pulp. He kept his voice under control. Without it, he knew that he would scream his impotence to his watching fellows. Already he had lost much of their respect for the childish way he had fallen victim to Lingard's skill. Retrieve it here and now he must. "Let me go," he repeated in the same furious monotone.

The arm tweaked its pain again and, involuntarily, he ejaculated his agony. "Are you going to behave yourself?" the hateful, arrogant voice breathed in his ear.

Sweat was on his forehead and his eyes moved in desperate entreaty from side to side. He saw nothing in the watching eyes to give him comfort. After a while his dark, glossy head bobbed agreement. He was panting his distress.

Lingard released him, stepped back and indicated the door. "Come on," he said, not unkindly.

Drazek spread wide his arms and opened his mouth, showing the white crescents of teeth against pink tongue and gums. A small runnel of saliva was on his chin. He made a shrill noise like a wounded horse and charged.

Even a skilfully wielded foil cannot parry the full impact of a bludgeon and the slim detective went down before Drazek's rush, taking with him a splintered chair and table. Pulling himself to an upright position he threw a delaying chair at the legs of his opponent, manoeuvring himself between the scattered furniture until his senses returned to him. With blood welling from a split over a cheekbone, his hat gone and his blond hair disordered, he faced his approaching adversary with regathered aplomb. From the corner of his eye he saw an anxious Mogg in the doorway and signalled him to keep out.

He advanced his right foot and held his two open hands forward, palms downward and fingers crooked. Drazek, showing his teeth again, leapt with an athletic bound at him, his hard fists cutting the air with murderous resolve. Lingard seemed to melt before him like a boneless wraith and for a moment, still moving forward, the scarred face showed bewilderment.

Then there were the two hands again, grasping simultaneously the lapels of his overalls and the crutch of his trousers. For the bewildered Drazek there was an ignominious whirling around in a bruising cartwheel with ceiling and walls in a turmoil of motion. Then, taking two of the slower-moving spectators with him in a skittle-like tumble, his head struck the iron leg of an overturned table with a final thud.

Flat on his back, his head ringing and his lungs heaving at the air they so desperately needed, he felt himself hauled forward and upward by his sorely stressed lapels. The two huge knuckled fists, pulling at the cloth under his nose, led his wobbling eyes along the blue serge arms to the grim face of Sergeant Mogg. It was a kind of satisfaction to him that the final humiliation of being dragged outside was to be at the hands of Mogg and not Lingard.

"Put him in the car, sergeant," the latter instructed, brushing himself down with his hands and retrieving his hat from the floor. He did not look at the silent men waiting his departure.

Neither did he vouch anything to them but a courteous, unanswered "goodnight" as he left.

The rain was still hammering down as he ran to the car outside. Mogg was seated stolidly in the rear seat, his bulk pinning the dazed and wit-scattered Drazek securely in the corner. The windows were beginning to steam over from the warm humidity within the car.

Mogg nodded as Lingard took the driver's seat. "He'll be all right. He's not going to give any more trouble." His voice, rumbling out from the huge frame, reverberated in the confined space.

Drazek looked neither left nor right as Lingard led the way from the car and into the station, through the dark passages and up the stairs to his office. The detective did not bother to look around to ensure that his prisoner was following. When Drazek was seated, he nodded at Mogg. "Thank you, sergeant," he said. "Leave him with me."

He sat himself at his desk and took a packet of cigarettes from a drawer. He opened it and held it out to Drazek. "Have one of these."

Drazek shook his head once. He was curt with the detective, hating him in his humiliation. Lingard tossed the packet back into the drawer, closed it and then pinched snuff into his nose. His chin was thrusting, his eyes steady and overbearing. "Just so that you know exactly where you stand, Drazek," he said, his voice nasal with contempt. "Don't think that what happened to you was fortuitous. Just a run of undeserved bad luck. Something you might reverse on a more auspicious occasion."

Drazek, his mouth beginning to shape itself to a

bellicosity, flinched when Lingard brought his palm down on the surface of the desk with a loud smack. "You've already got yourself into trouble by shooting your big mouth off. Talking instead of listening," he snapped. "So shut up now and and listen." His eyes were hard and held down the man opposite him. "How long have you known Mrs. Stronach?"

Drazek was studying his fingernails with an insolent obduracy. He lifted his heavy shoulders. "Does it matter?"

Lingard's lips thinned with anger and he moved swiftly from his chair. He stood over the still lounging man. "Come on," he rapped. "I've had enough of you."

"I prefer to stay here." Lingard could see that the man's eyes did not support his arrogance.

"Get on your feet. I'm putting you in the cells."

The glossy head jerked, the expression startled. "What for? What've I done?"

"For a start you've assaulted a police officer. The fact you've come out of it a poor loser doesn't alter that fact." He held the other with his steady gaze. "More important is that you were the last person to have been with Mrs. Stronach."

Drazek's forehead creased. "Is that a bloody crime?"

"Assaulting a policeman . . ."

He cut him short. "——you," he said. "That doesn't worry me. I mean, who hasn't?" Indeed, in Drazek's world such a conviction was analogous to being mentioned in dispatches. "Mrs. Stronach. Is she still missing?"

"No." Lingard was deliberately unforthcoming. He returned to his side of the desk and sat again.

Drazek flushed red in the face. "For Christ's sake get to the point," he snarled. "Say what you have to say and let me go. Or," his voice rose, "put me in your bloody cell."

"I want to know what you did last night."

The steelworker opened and closed the fists resting on his thighs, allowing his rage to cool. Finally, he straightened himself in the chair, making an obvious effort to control himself. "I was in The Falcon. With Mrs. Stronach."

"Was it the first time?"

"No."

"You've been with her before?"

"Yes."

"Often?"

"A few times."

"What was your relationship with her?"

Drazek looked puzzled. "Relationship? You mean like she was my...like she was my aunt or something?" He drew his black eyebrows down. "You want to watch it, mate. You can't say things like that."

The detective grimaced his disgust. "For God's sake. I mean, were you her boy-friend? Or did you collect pressed leaves together?"

"Don't be bloody sarcastic, mate. We were..you know."

"You mean you were sleeping together."

"Not much sleeping about it. I never went to bed with her. It was usually the canal bank. But you've got the idea."

Lingard smiled gently. "A little out of your age group, weren't you?"

Drazek was contemptuous. "*She* didn't think so. Her husband wouldn't...or couldn't. So I did. We're both over twenty-one."

"The occasional cigarette-case, I suppose?" He looked pointedly at the man's wrist. "Or watch?"

He flushed a dull red, the scar by contrast livid on his cheek. "You make it sound like a crime. It was all for free and as often as I liked."

"I'm sure it was," Lingard murmured. "Anyway, came the rift in the lute. You quarrelled."

"So you say."

"So someone at The Falcon says."

A long silence. "Can I have that cigarette?" He added a grudging, "please."

Lingard flipped one to him and waited while he lit it. "So? You quarrelled. What about?"

Drazek drew deeply at the cigarette, his cheeks sucking in. Then he released the smoke through his nostrils, not blowing it out, allowing it to trickle and to gain time for his explanation. "I'm a married man. My wife's having a kid soon. I told her I'd got to lay off for a bit because the wife was getting in a bit of a state." He sucked in again from the cigarette. "She got nasty. Said she could always get someone else. Someone probably better." He brooded on this for a moment. "So I told her to get stuffed. And that's the last I saw her. I got up and left her in there."

"What did she call you?" There was a quirk of amusement on his mouth.

"She didn't call me anything."

"I'd bet a pound note she did," he said confidently. "They always do. Still, not that it matters." He shot the next question at him. "Where did you go from there?"

"I went home."

"And you've got your wife to say so."

"It's the truth." He said it belligerently.

"Bless my soul, of course it is. Who would dare impugn it. What time?"

"Ask *her* if you don't believe me."

"I'll ask you first. What time?"

"——you." The obscenity was without rancour. "I got home about half-past ten."

"Walking?"

"I didn't fly."

"No buses?"

"——the buses."

"All right——the buses. But why?"

"I got done once for sorting out a conductor."

"Now *persona non grata*, I presume?" This went unanswered. "Did you see anyone en route?"

"Not to speak to." His face brightened. "Yes, I did. I dropped in at The Goat for a last drink. I left my gin on the table at the other place."

"All right. Who did you see there?"

"The landlord. He served me."

"As he hasn't a barman I'd supposed he had. Does he know you?"

"I don't know."

Lingard grunted. "A big help. You won't get much of an alibi from *him*."

"Why should I need an alibi? Are you having me on about something?" He was showing his belligerency again.

"Simmer down, Drazek," Lingard said casually. "All in the full of time. Did you see Mrs. Stronach on any other occasion? After you left The Falcon?"

"No. And I don't know where she is now."

"She's dead." He dropped the words like heavy stones on to a wooden floor.

Drazek's mouth opened and his eyes exposed the whites. Although his tongue moistened his lips for speech, no sound came. He closed his mouth and swallowed hard. Then he tried again. "No," he finally croaked. "You're having me on. You don't bloody well mean it." He rose from his chair, his shoulders hunched, his eyes dangerous.

Lingard also stood, his lips thin. "I've told you once, Drazek. Next time I'll really hurt you. *Sit down*," he barked at him. Drazek sat unwillingly, still razor-edged in his hostility. "Lingard re-seated himself and continued. "She was found dead. In one of the backs off Deburgh Road." He watched him closely. "Asphyxiated."

"Asphyxiated!" Drazek groaned and covered his face with cupped hands. Lingard thought he was going to cry and he waited. The cigarette between the man's fingers was now a stub and it suddenly burned the flesh. Drazek swore violently and flung it from him. He then looked squarely at Lingard and when he spoke his voice was mild. "Was she killed?"

"She might have been. It's difficult to tell. She certainly didn't commit suicide."

"I didn't do it. You believe that, don't you?"

"Give me a reason why I should. You quarrelled with her. You were the last person to be seen in her company."

"You think I should see a solicitor?"

Lingard shrugged. "A matter for you, of course. Do you think you need one?" He said it with apparent indifference, watching carefully just the same.

"You make it sound as if I do."

"No, not I. Only you do that."

"Well, I'm not worried." The voice carried no conviction. "I didn't see her after I left The Falcon and that's that. Whatever happened to her wasn't by me." He looked sombrely at Lingard and added inconsequentially. "I wish you'd clobbered me properly up at the boozer. My mates won't think much of this wrestling caper. I'll have to sort out a couple of them to prove I'm not a patsy."

"You're sticking to your story, then? I mean about when you last saw her."

His expression was completely unconcerned. "I don't

care what you think. I didn't see her after I left the place and all the coppers in the world can't prove I did. And," he said, looking at Lingard challengingly, "I don't care much for you. You rub me up the wrong way. Don't think I'm such a bloody ignorant layabout that I don't know what you're saying."

"I have a very high opinion of you, old chap," the detective smiled. He lifted the telephone. "I'm sure you won't mind if, in the meantime, we see about charging you. And locking you up."

Before he had time to put the threat into operation, there was a thunderous rap on the door and Coltart entered. The sergeant glanced at Drazek and then at Lingard. "Will you telephone Mr. Rogers," he asked. "He wants words with you."

11

It was an hour from midnight and the rain was lessening to an intermittent drizzle. The storm had passed on to the dark horizon, only the faint querulous rumbling of thunder and a fitful flickering of light on the far cloud base serving to remind the town of the power that had lashed it.

Rogers had been returned to his bachelor flat by Joanne, his leg arranged comfortably on the sofa on which he lay, his cheek brushed lightly with her lips and left to himself.

The flat was functional with the minimum of upholstered comfort. It was neither intended nor furnished for prolonged indolence. Rogers used it as an instrument for the necessary processes of cleansing and resting his body.

He was a man who chose to spend his leisure time in the company of his fellow humans. The violent hurt his wife had done him was only thus anaesthetized. It became an unbearable nostalgia when supported by darkness and prolonged solitude.

Eileen was a physical woman and he had been drawn to her by an uncomplicated need. Her own needs were more complex and their satisfying beyond either his willingness or capacity. Towards the end she had asked nothing from him but an undemanding neutrality. He had suffered badly, his frustration running riot in imagery and fantasy.

He had not endured without retaliation but his liaisons had in them always the ashes of further despair. The exorcizing of her witchery over him necessitated unending immersion in his work and a cultivated regard for women he would otherwise not have sought.

He had finally—with a self-destructive obstinacy—driven her to leave him for the man employing her as his secretary. She came back finally, too proud to accept the abortion by which she could remove the reason for her lover's sudden shying away from the relationship.

Rogers had (with masculine logic) rejected her in his turn. And so she lived, his unforgiving shadow athwart her life, too obstinate to leave the town he wanted free of her. She made no pretence of the morality she had been required to assume as his wife and from time to time the ripples of her growing promiscuity reached him.

Reaching out from his position on the sofa, he pulled the telephone handset on to his chest and dialled a number. "I'm glad I caught you, sergeant," he said to Coltart who had answered his call. "I've an idea that might result in running our Collins man to earth. I think we must accept your chemist chap's assessment that he's an engineer of some sort. It's only a straw but it's all we have. Now, get cracking with Hannah and his men in the morning. Cover every mill, every engineering concern, every toolmaker's establishment. I don't care how grandiose or fleabitten the firm is. Check them all. The Trades Directory'll help. So will the Telephone Book. And don't forget the Borough Engineer's Office, the Technical Colleges and the Naval Establishment. What we want is a list of every man in engineering—concentrate on the managerial and executive side—who wasn't at work today. Then," he commanded, "go to their homes. If you don't have him before the morning's over you can come up here and break my other leg." He paused. "And what do I infer from those non-committal grunts of yours? Disapproval?"

"I was making notes, sir." The sergeant sounded immoderately cheerful. "I think you've got something with this. I'll get on to it right away."

"You'll get to bed, sergeant," Rogers growled. "Get some sleep as I propose to. You'll be useless tomorrow if you don't. And don't argue," he said sharply. "Get one of the night men to draw up the schedule for you. And before you go, perhaps you'll ask Lingard to telephone me here."

He was pouring himself a very large undiluted whisky when the call came. "Wait a moment, David," he said into the telephone, "while I hitch my leg back on the sofa." He settled himself and drank half the whisky. "Right. Fill me in with the details."

When Lingard had finished his narrative, Rogers frowned. "Where's Drazek now?"

"In my office. He's all right. There's a constable with him. I'm telephoning from the sergeant's office."

"Not charged?"

"No. Not yet."

"Not at all, David." He was giving an order.

"Christ!" He was outraged. "We can hold him on an assault charge. In the meantime, we might get something more on Mrs. Stronach."

"I don't believe there's any more to get. I didn't see anything that wasn't different from other asphyxiations I've dealt with. Until your pathologist friend says differently—categorically and not hypothetically—then I'm accepting that it's accidental." He waited a moment. "*Is* she going to say differently?"

"She isn't sure, George. You can't expect her to be. Not one hundred per cent certain."

"I can in this instance." His peremptory voice softened. "I'm sorry, David. I know Drazek committed—or tried to commit—an assault on you but I'm not going to have you hold him. If he'd really clouted you, yes. As it is, you'll only give him an importance he doesn't warrant. Charge him and, in his own eyes, he's done something meriting our serious attention. Kick his backside out of it and you are showing your contempt. He won't like it at all. Not when he's had time to reflect on it."

Apart from the hissing and clicking of the connection, there was silence. When he spoke his voice was carefully neutral. "Of course, George. I see your point. I'll get rid of him."

"Good chap. Now, what do you really feel about Mrs. Stronach?"

"Deathwise?"

"Yes. You haven't anything to suggest it was other than accidental?"

"I've a buzzing noise up near my pineal eye. I've learned to respect its warning."

Rogers laughed. "I get one in the back of my neck. But," he added, "not on this occasion. No, David. Unless you have something else it remains misadventure. Have you seen Stronach?"

"Not since he identified her. No very cogent reason for doing so." He sounded regretful.

"He knows the cause of death?"

"Bridget told him."

"No comment?"

"Not a word. Barely polite. Thanked for her telephoning. That was all."

Rogers did some complicated manoeuvring with pipe, tobacco pouch, matches and the telephone handset and finished up with a smoking pipe between his teeth. "Sorry, David, I must have suffered a good twenty minutes without a smoke and I was approaching breaking point. Where were we? Ah, yes. Perhaps you'd better see our doctor tomorrow. Yes?"

"I mean to. I hope you agree, George, but I have to have some sort of a go at him. I don't know anyone with a better reason for knocking off his wife. I accept your opinion," he assured him hastily, "but you wouldn't expect me not to?"

"No, I don't suppose I would." Rogers was guarded. "But be careful. He isn't a man who'd be backward in pushing you into trouble. Nothing more on his movements during the evening?"

"No. I have to concede his story has all the inconsistencies and ambiguities of the truth."

"Or a first-class alibi?"

"That too. I don't underestimate him."

"I still hold it's accidental, David. In which event an alibi is a *non sequitur*."

"I'll bear your admonition in mind. But somehow I think you are going to be wrong."

"I'll be the first to put on a hair shirt if I am. By the way . . . better check with the landlord of The Goat."

Lingard was sour, although wise enough not to allow it to show. "Betting each way, George?"

"No. Back to first principles. Never accept anything without checking. Particularly the obvious."

Released from the telephone, Lingard returned to his office. After the escorting constable had been dismissed, he spoke to Drazek. "I've been thinking about you. I've come to the conclusion it's all a bit too trivial to bother with." He smiled sardonically. "I mean, it wasn't much of an assault was it? Not on your part. I've been hit harder by a wet sponge."

He noted Drazek's growing anger and became brisk. "Right. On your way, Prince Charming." He hooked a thumb at the door. "Out!"

The burly steelworker showed his teeth and snarled at him. "Why don't you get stuffed?"

"You have a distressing sameness of invective," the detective chided. "But just buzz off like a good chap, will you?"

"I shall be bloody glad to." He stumped to the door and then stopped. "How am I going to get home? Walk?"

Lingard passed by him and went through the door. "I'll get you some transport. I didn't appreciate you were a crippled old lady."

Outside, the rain had ceased and there were clear patches of steel-blue sky between the scurrying clouds. A gibbous moon slid silently across the open gaps, flooding the shining wet town with a moving phosphoric light and making by contrast the dark shadows a deeper blackness.

Lingard waited with Drazek until the patrol car turned into the yard and took on board the glowering man.

Neither knew it but Drazek had no reason to be grateful to Rogers.

The morning burned under the threat of a scorching afternoon. The sky was a dimensionless vault of milky-blue porphyry and no winds disturbed its timelessness. The sun, an orange flare of light, had dried the previous night's rain and already the town appeared devoid of strong colour.

Foliage hung leaden on trees and the river flowed slowly like liquid silver. Away on the far horizon there was a thin livid streak, the promise of a further, possibly more violent, storm.

A few birds dribbled their pastorales into minor hesitancies in the shelter of the trees and quarrelsome sparrows scrabbled in the hot dust. Dogs lay in the shade and panted, their pink tongues hanging like strips of wet flannel.

Rogers, refreshed by a night's undisturbed sleep, sat at his desk, attacking with renewed interest the documented information on the matter of the knife. As yet his office, the low windows denying the sun access, was shaded and cool, his shirt still crisp. Despite the difficulties he had encountered in struggling his trouser leg over the sleeve of plaster, he was unruffled and the injury was causing him little discomfort. The upper reaches of the room were a grey haze of tobacco smoke and, as he consumed pipe after pipe of the fragrant shreds, so it grew in density.

Coltart and Hannah, organizing their teams of men, were assembling a considerable list of absentees in the higher grades of the engineering and mechanical industries. Coltart had reduced them to convenient dimensions by eliciting from managements the age and general appearance of each medically-excused employee. As a precaution, he prepared a second list of all those absent on holiday. When he had winnowed the pages of names to his satisfaction, he divided them into equal numbers and gave each man his immediate task. For himself, he chose those few having the forename "William."

It was close on one o'clock when he rapped on the door of the house in Spye Green Crescent. The sun was at its zenith and shadows were hard-edged and foreshortened. Leaves hung motionless and the heat drew up perfumed exhalations from the herbaceous plants in the garden borders.

The woman who opened the door to his knocking was of a pleasing plumpness. She was small and soft-skinned and her eyes were a sparkling chestnut brown with clear whites. The plain gold dress she wore graced her roundnesses. He guessed her age as thirty.

She read the inscription on his warrant card gravely and with care. Then she smiled. "Yes, Mr. Coltart? I hope there's no trouble."

Seeing the inquiry in his lifted eyebrows, she added, "My son, Timothy. He's only ten but it's not often he isn't in some trouble or another. Getting into it, not causing it."

He smiled. "I'll keep an eye peeled for him, Mrs. Dyson. However, it's not young Timothy I'm after. I'd like to see your husband if I may. Not a serious matter," he hastened to assure her, for her pleasant face had taken on a look of worried concern. "We're searching for a man who called at a local chemist yesterday for treatment to his hand. If Mr. Dyson . . ." He halted as he read his answer in the perplexity of her eyes. "Has he an injured hand?" He asked it gently.

She nodded dumbly.

"His left?"

Again the nod. Then, "He cut it at the laboratory. Was there anything wrong?"

"I honestly don't know." He was feeling acutely uncomfortable at the increasing distress of this pleasant little woman. "Is he in?"

She looked backwards through the partly open door. "He's eating his lunch." She looked pleadingly at him. "I've a dreadful feeling that something's wrong."

He shook his head regretfully. "I'm sorry I'm upsetting you. It'll probably be all right. All of them have been so far." He looked into the doorway. "Would you get him, please?"

She pushed the white door open with her tiny plump hand. "Please come in," she said. "I'll call him." He caught a flicker of movement from the far end of the hall, an almost subliminal impression of a hand grasping at an object.

After she had left him for the inner depths of the house, Coltart looked around him. The funishings of the hall were in gold and green. There was a copper-framed mirror on a wall and a jar of branches in one corner. None of it told him anything of the occupants.

From the rear of the house he heard the sound of a car engine being started and the noise of wheels moving rapidly over gravel. His scalp tingled with apprehension as he heard the woman calling "Bill! Bill!" her voice coming from outside and with overtones of panic to it.

He cursed explosively and leapt along the hall, flinging open the door screening from him a passage leading to a large straw-matted kitchen. Entering this, he saw through the open french windows a green expanse of sunlit lawn. On the yellow gravel bisecting the bright grass the woman stood motionless, her back to him, her arm held upwards in mute supplication.

He ran to her. "Quick!" he snapped brusquely. "The number. Give it to me."

She looked at him vacantly. "He's gone," she said. "He was eating his lunch and just went."

Grasping her arms—even in his urgent endeavour he felt the softness of them—he shook her. Not violently, but enough to jerk black strands of hair across her forehead and to focus her attention on him. "The number of your car, Mrs. Dyson," he repeated urgently. "Give it to me, please."

She bit her bottom lip. "Should I?" she wailed. "Must I?"

"Yes, you must. It'll do nobody any good for him to go off like this."

"Is it serious?" Her plump face was white.

He regarded her for a very long moment. "It could be," he said at last. "For why should he go like this if it were not?"

She hesitated and then gave him the number. "Don't hurt him," she pleaded.

He shook his head impatiently. "We shan't hurt him, Mrs. Dyson. What make and colour?"

"A Citroën DS." She was still reluctant and the words came hesitatingly. "Blue . . . dark blue. With a white roof."

"The telephone. Where is it?"

She gestured vaguely. "In the drawing-room." She was still stunned.

He took her arm gently and led her into the house. "May I use it, please?"

"Use it?" She looked blank and then laughed without

humour. "Oh, the telephone. I thought for a moment you meant the loo. Why not," she said bitterly. "I don't suppose I could stop you."

"Please sit down," he urged. "I would like to ask you more questions when I've made my call."

With the woman seated numbed in the kitchen, he sought for and found the telephone. Contacting Rogers as he was about to leave his office for a meal, he gave him the details he had obtained, requesting a Search and Stop for the fleeing man. "When I get something from her," he said, "I'll ring you again. In the meantime, would you send a policewoman in plain clothes. I'm on my own and she could go into hysteria when she gets over the shock."

When he returned to the kitchen she was still seated, her eyes unseeing and directed at the bright rectangle of sunlit window. Her face was paper-white. He took a tumbler from a dresser and filled it at the tap, holding it to her lips while he pressed one sympathetic hand on her shoulders. "Drink some of this," he ordered. She took the tumbler from him and held it with shaking hands, drinking it in obedient gulps as it rattled against her teeth.

"Is there anything else I can get you?" he asked. For such a huge and powerful man, he was curiously gentle with this tiny woman.

She looked up at his anxious face and smiled briefly. Some of the colour was returning to her flesh. "I'm sorry, Mr. Coltart."

He flapped a protesting hand. "It's I who should be sorry. And I am. Barging in here and frightening you to death." He looked contrite. "I really had to get moving. I hope you appreciate that." She nodded. "Can I help you into a more comfortable seat?"

She stood. "I'm quite all right now. I'll make a cup of tea for the three of us." She dimpled her cheeks wanly at his surprise. "I'm sure your policewoman will want a cup when she gets here. And I promise you I won't get hysterical."

He flushed a dull red. "I'm sorry, Mrs. Dyson. I had no idea..."

She put a tiny hand on his sleeve. "Please don't apologize any more," she said. "You didn't say anything that embarrassed me. But you do have such a booming voice."

While she gathered together the cups and saucers and spoons, Coltart perched his bulk on the edge of the table and continued his inquisition. He could not but admit to himself that his probing was somewhat blunted by her pleasantness towards him and his own sympathy for her. When he essayed a smile, it reached his eyes and softened their uncompromising greenness. She, for her part, had obviously decided to answer his questions without quibble.

"They were nasty cuts," she was saying as she placed the cups in the saucers. She did it gently, without noise. "He wouldn't show them to me. I saw them when he was putting powder on. He said he'd gashed his hand on the sharp edge of some metal he was using in an experiment. I suppose that wasn't the truth?" she added quietly.

"He told the management he'd a gastric infection," Coltart said without inflexion. "By telephone. They told him to rest it up for a couple of days."

"Bill . . . that's his name . . . said he'd had treatment at the plant surgery. I couldn't understand why he was doing the bandaging himself. Why he wouldn't see Parker. He's our doctor," she explained. "He got very angry with me." She was visibly embarrassed and her bottom lip trembled. "He shouted at me. Said I was making a fuss. Anyway, he stamped out of the house and was out most of yesterday. When he came back I was in bed. So I didn't see him."

She flushed at the question in his eyes. "I sleep ḍly," she said awkwardly, "and we find it convenient. I mean, he needs his sleep so much."

"He's an aerodynamics man, isn't he?"

"Yes. On wind-tunnel experimentation and research. It's an exacting job. It needs a knowledge and differential calculus and things. Yards above my head, I'm afraid."

He returned to his main theme. "So he was out last evening. Do you know where?"

She put a cup and saucer on the table at his side and he moved to an adjacent chair. "No," she murmured. "I assumed he'd gone to his club."

"Oh?"

"The Junior Executives," she replied.

"I know the place," he said. "Park Lane. Was he out the evening before?"

"Yes, he was. He was working that evening. That's when he gashed his hand."

"A special job? Or does he work evenings often?"

"He does so regularly." She paused and considered her reply. "Bill's very ambitious, you know. He works most evenings on the calculus for an experiment of his own. He's doing a paper for some scientific society."

"Is the plant surgery open during the evening?"

Her eyes searched his face. "You must think me incredibly naïve, Mr. Coltart. I'm pretty sure it isn't but the point hadn't occurred to me until you asked. They don't do shift work at the plant. Bill has often said he's the only one there on any evening that he works."

A knock at the door interrupted them. "Shall I answer it?" she asked.

"I will, if you don't mind. It's probably the policewoman and I can tell her to wait in the car." He looked discomfited. "I don't suppose you'll need her, will you?"

"I don't think so, Mr. Coltart. I am quite all right now." She smoothed her dress tight across her thighs. "Please do what you have to do."

When he returned she was already putting the cups and saucers into a dish-washing machine. She turned her head to him. "Is it another woman?"

He was nonplussed. "The policewoman?"

"No, of course not. Is Bill concerned . . . mixed up with another woman?" She seemed wholly calm, although Coltart was not deceived. She switched the machine on and resumed her seat near him.

"Do you think he could be?" he countered.

"Please don't play with me," she pleaded, her eyes hurt. "I'm entitled to know why you are seeking him."

"You are," he admitted, "but I must admit it's not easy to say. In fact, in fairness to your husband I shouldn't anyway. If he chooses to explain his injuries to our satisfaction then he's not the man we are specifically interested in." He cocked his head to one side. "Does that make sense to you?"

She creased her eyebrows. They were precise semicircles of brown on the smooth skin. "Not really . . ."

"Look," he said patiently. "We're checking on all kinds of people; injured, sick and plain bone idle. Anyone absent from his place of employment. It just happens that your husband has an injury similar to the one we are seeking. Even so, it may have a quite innocent cause."

"Which would explain why he ran away when you called, I suppose?"

He didn't answer this. "You asked me a minute ago about a woman. Please don't take offence . . . but could that be a possibility?"

Her dark eyes were liquid hurt. "I've sometimes thought . . ." She trailed off miserably.

Coltart made clucking noises and combed his hair with his fingers, visibly embarrassed at the prospect of tears. "I'm sorry," he said. "These things have to be asked. You don't know?"

She shook her head. "I'm just not sure."

"Have you a photograph of your husband I can borrow?"

Her mouth was crooked. "To help you to catch him?"

"It has to be, Mrs. Dyson. Perhaps the sooner the better. He could get into worse trouble."

She inclined her head. "I'll get it," she said. "It doesn't matter now."

The photograph, retrieved audible from a pulled-out drawer in another room, was handed to Coltart in silence. It was postcard sized and, after looking at it cursorily, he slid it into his jacket pocket. "What was he wearing?" he asked.

"A blazer . . . navy-blue. And whipcord trousers."

"Is there a badge on the pocket?"

"No. Nothing like that."

"Has he a lightweight brown suit?"

She was surprised. "Yes, he has."

"A fawn trilby hat?"

She nodded.

"Does he wear a wristlet watch?"

"Yes, he does."

"Sunglasses?"

She knitted her brows. "He keeps a pair in the car. Usually on the ledge near the windscreen." Her fingers twined together. "This means he *is* the man you are looking for, doesn't it?"

Coltart cleared his throat in embarrassment. He put a paw out and patted her shoulder. Tiny women had this effect on him. She reached up and held his hand in her own. It was an odd, childish gesture. "Poor Mr. Coltart. You aren't enjoying this a bit, are you?" she said.

He released his hand and stood. "I'm sorry," he said again. "I won't bother you further. We'll let you know immediately we hear of anything." He looked at her with compassion. "Please telephone me if you hear from him or if he returns. He's got to stop running sometime."

He followed her along the hall to the door and frowned when she stopped suddenly and looked with concern at a small recess to the side of the door leading into the dining-room. He stood by her. "What is it, Mrs. Dyson?" he demanded.

She was worried and he detected overtones of approaching panic. "Oh Bill," she breathed. "What are you doing?"

He stepped in front of her, a large figure blocking out the light from the glass-panelled door behind him. There was nothing lumbering or slow about him now and his voice was authoritative. "Come on," he snapped. "You know something important and it's obviously serious."

"Oh, it is," she said. Her eyes were dark like moist liquorice. "He's taken his gun with him."

Coltart was startled. He remembered the glimpse he had of the quickly moving hand, cursing himself for forgetting. "His gun?"

She pointed to the empty recess. "It's always kept there. In a leather box."

"A revolver?"

"No. A shotgun."

"A 12-bore?"

"I think so. I've heard him say that."

"Ammunition?"

"In the car. He keeps the gun and cartridges separated because of Timmy." Her eyes filled with tears when she spoke her son's name. "And the case is always locked."

"It couldn't be elsewhere?"

She was miserable, unhappy in her fear. "No. I saw it there just before lunch."

He pushed hard at the facts because he had to. He mistrusted women in any case and he accepted as a matter of faith that Mrs. Dyson might not be as wholly forthcoming about her husband as she appeared. Not, he admitted, that he could blame her.

"What sort of a man is he? Temperamentally? Is he violent? Highly strung?"

She was shaking her head in negation as he put his points. "Please, *please*, Mr. Coltart."

"Why does he have a shotgun anyway?"

"He belongs to a shooting club. Clay pigeons and things."

He regarded her for a long time without speaking and then turned away from her. "I must go now," he said, his face expressionless. "I'll keep in touch."

When he stepped from the coolness of the house into the thudding sunlight, the heat hit him brutally and he began to sweat.

12

It mattered little to Dr. Hunter the manner of their going; it was the causation that mattered. Within limits, sex and age were of no account. Similarly, she was not swayed by any grotesqueries of physical development or beauty of face or body their cadavers might still possess in death. When she approached the upward-facing, floodlit nakedness of a corpse she saw only the dead tissue, inanimate organs and inert fluids from which she had to wrest the cause which triggered off the act of death. The triggering could be as obvious as a shattered skull or as subtle as senility. With scalpel and probe she traced the lonely wanderings of embolisms and the haemorrhaging of blood vessels.

She donned her squeaking rubber gloves as a housewife would don hers to wash dishes. She chose as impersonally the flat-bladed knives with which she sliced

so carefully the brains and organs, searching for the fatal
malfunctioning, the disruption of the vital force. Often she
removed suspect parts and bloody snippets that interested
her, to place them to float in glass-stoppered jars of
formaldehyde and saline, there to blanch slowly over the
years to a livid white.

She operated in two fields. One was the small mortuary at the rear of the hospital. It was a small room,
made smaller by being divided into two parts by a thick
blue plastic curtain hung on sliding runners. In the
larger part, the central feature was a white enamelled
examination table; rounded at one end, square at the
other. On it stood a small wooden block, a U cut into it to
hold the head of the table's occupant steady. A metal
cabinet held glittering instruments on plate-glass racks.
On a wall shelf were a pair of rusty household scales, a
telephone and an aerosol air freshener for weak-stomached
visitors. A deep sink occupied a corner and over it were
long swan-necked taps.

The smaller section of the room contained two iron
coffin stands and a large refrigerating cabinet. On the wall
was a large notice—in epitaphial black and white—sternly
instructing undertakers not to remove bodies from the
mortuary without first signing for them.

Dr. Hunter's secondary field of operations was her
office. In it she maintained her regimented records of
death. Death by design, accident or inevitability. No
death was so commonplace that she refused it room on a
card.

Death by violence was of no specific importance to
her. Unlike death from disease, it posed no absorbing
problems in diagnosis and was rarely subtle enough to
exercise her skill. Already the fact of Mrs. Stronach's
decease was boring her. It had been tabulated and
relegated to the anonymity of a statistic. Lingard was
asking for conclusions where none could be given; asking
for presumptions where presumptions could only be tenta-
tive.

He was doing so now in her office. He was earnest
and, despite the afternoon's heat, coolly immaculate in a
suit the brown of a deep sun tan. A strip of plaster covered
the cheekbone split by Drazek.

"Have you considered, Bridget," he was saying, "that the marks on her lips could have been caused by a hand being pressed over the mouth?"

She regarded him with thoughtful eyes. "I thought we'd been over all this? That we'd scotched any suggestion of foul play."

"I suppose we had more or less," he said uncomfortably. "But I've this feeling that Drazek is pulling a fast one on us."

"On you," she corrected, "if anyone."

"All right, on me," he agreed. "What sticks in my craw is the unlikelihood of Mrs. Stronach voluntarily entering that cesspit of a place where we found her."

"I've already told you it's not such an improbability. Not when you've the choice between that and doing it in the street like a horse." She was deliberately coarse with him. "I wish you'd understand that I'm not going to be able to help on this, David. Much as I want to. That must be my answer to your question about the marks on her lips." She gestured her impotence with her hands. "You know as well as I how many imponderables there are in pathology. You, yourself, are always saying that medicine's an art and not a science. So it's the same for pathology. If you get a better operator you might get better results." She brushed aside his protests. "That is what, in effect, you are saying, David. However, to illustrate what I mean in simple terms I'll use the analogy of a man sustaining fatal injuries in falling from a height. It's for you to say whether from an aircraft, a cliff or the Eiffel Tower. And it's for you to decide whether he fell or was pushed. So, in this case, I'm telling you Mrs. Stronach was asphyxiated. The rest is all yours. I'm sorry," she added, "there isn't anything more I can do."

He pulled his bottom lip with his fingers. "But you can't say she *wasn't* asphyxiated by external force?"

"Of course not." She was patient with him. "It's a matter of probabilities. The position in which she was found and her intoxication could, in my opinion, have caused her death."

Taking his ivory box out, he took snuff. "I'm not disheartened, Bridget," he said cheerfully. "If it *is* Drazek, I shall have him."

She stared at him curiously. "Forgive me asking, but I thought the husband occupied more than a passing interest from you?"

"He does indeed and I've been doing a fair amount of hithering and thithering on him." He was a little wary. "I have to have *something* to justify putting pointed questions to him. And this was the purport of my visit to you."

"So you've wasted your time?"

"Not entirely," he said. "I've given myself the opportunity of seeing you. A lovesome sight on a hot day. All cool and clinical."

Bridget walked towards him, dropping the folder of cards she was carrying on to the desk. She kissed him lightly on his damaged cheek. "You smell nice," she said. "Like embalming fluid."

Hoggart drank his wine in lip-smacking gulps as if he hated the stuff and wanted to destroy it. On his desk, by the wine bottle, was a plate of cheese cubes and a knot of purple grapes. To Rogers, seated near by, the cheese had the smell of a wet dog.

"I hope you don't mind," Hoggart had said. "I've just finished a late lunch." A cigarette was wedged between two stiff fingers.

The detective was again being shown the obverse side of the coin of truth. Hoggart, planning supervisor of the Research and Experimental Laboratory, had seen Dyson casting a quite different shadow than had Mrs. Dyson. "The man's changed during the past few months," he was telling him. Through the pebbled glass walls of his office could be seen mistily the assembled metal frames and sheets of aluminium of the laboratory mock-ups; the blurring of moving mechanisms on steel benches. There was a sharp smell of fabric dope in Rogers's nostrils. It was evocative of aircraft and hangars. "To be frank with you, Mr. Rogers, I thought he was cracking up."

Rogers, his leg stuck out from him like a trousered signpost, was sweating gently and steadily in the sound-proofed office. A small rubber fan whirling silently in one corner did no more than riffle the lifeless air. "By what symptoms?" he asked.

"He confided in me on one or two occasions. About his domestic difficulties, mainly. It seemed he was a bit irrational about her." He smiled introspectively and dribbled more wine into his glass.

"His wife?"

"Yes. My wife and I know her well. Very well. Although," he added guardedly, "not Dyson himself. He isn't easy to get along with. Nor is he particularly sociable."

"But his wife is?"

"Most certainly, yes."

"So why was he irrational about her?"

"He reckoned she was...how shall I put it?... promiscuous." He shifted in his chair. He was slim and silver haired with black eyebrows and sunken cheeks. His skin was translucent, a tinted polythene film. He seemed a dry man; shedding the particles of hair and dried skin scales of middle age as a fine dust. Withal, he was a vital man with dark bird-bright eyes. His thin paper-dry fingers were stained golden from the smoke of cigarettes. He was cool and appeared not to suffer from the heat.

"Does that make him irrational?"

"If you knew Anne as I...as we do, you would think so."

"You consider this present business of the injury and so on to be all of a piece with it?"

"Yes, I must. For him to tell her that he used the laboratory in his spare time is nonsense. The whole of the power is disconnected at six and the security systems we employ militate against any entry until the morning."

"Anything else, Mr. Hoggart?"

He mashed his cigarette into a black glass bowl. "Yes. Dyson isn't normally a talkative man. At best, he's morose. But lately he's been even less communicative than usual. Almost to the point of being sullen." He lit himself another cigarette. They were oval and gold-tipped and smelt of incense. "Also, he absents himself occasionally. It is true we do not keep the checks on our scientific staff we keep on others. But we expect some rationality about this. Dyson was popping out at all sorts of odd times. Rarely for more than half-an-hour but with increasing frequency." He grimaced his displeasure. "It was all rather disturbing."

Rogers was thoughtful. "You think he was checking on his wife?"

"He could have been."

"That might mean trouble."

The silver head nodded. "I think it could. Taking the gun was an additional stupidity."

Rogers brought his head up with a jerk, his eyes angry. "Who told you about that?" he demanded, his voice sharp.

Hoggart reddened and covered his momentary confusion by lifting the glass to his mouth and drinking. "Mrs. Dyson telephoned me," he said finally. "She was—naturally—worried about your sergeant's visit and her husband's peculiar behaviour."

Rogers had refused (with an astringent courtesy) to join the compulsive drinking and was glad he had. "It strikes me as exceedingly odd," he said, "that you haven't seen fit to mention this before. That you allowed me to believe you had no prior knowledge of Dyson's disappearance."

Hoggart swallowed but said nothing.

Rogers twisted his shoulders angrily but decided not to press the point further. "Had you spoken to her since he reported sick?"

Hoggart looked at him sideways. "No." He was curt.

"I wondered."

"You wondered what?"

"Why he should say he was sick with gastric trouble."

"I don't see your point."

"You should. It's a simple one. There was always the chance his wife would be speaking to you."

"M'm, yes." The glass was filled again. His expression was thoughtful. That of a man who has inadvertently put his foot within striking distance of a dangerous snake. "I see what you mean."

"But she didn't?"

"No. She didn't."

"I'm glad of that."

No reply.

Rogers continued. "While Dyson was baring his soul to you, did he mention anything about his own . . . anything about a woman?"

"No. Not definitely."

"Indefinitely, then?" If the air in the office was not cool, the atmosphere between the two men was.

"I had the feeling... you know?"

"No, I don't. Such as?"

Hoggart shifted his spare frame in the chair. "The innuendo was there. He talked about Anne not being... not being alone in what she was doing."

"What was the object of these discussions?"

"They weren't discussions. It was one-sided. I just listened."

"All right." There was impatience in the detective's voice. "As you will. What was the object of the monologue?"

"I don't honestly know. He wasn't asking for advice. He didn't really ask anything."

"Unburdening himself?"

"It could be. We're colleagues, if not friends. I imagine I would be a natural confidant."

"Wasn't he ever more communicative about this woman?"

He drew abstractedly at his cigarette, following it with a sip of wine. "No," he said as he swallowed. "It was all very indefinite."

"I'm sorry, Mr. Hoggart," Rogers said firmly, not sounding sorry at all, "but I'd like you to be a lot more specific about this."

The chin came up. "I can't manufacture a conversation."

"I wouldn't dam' well want you to," Rogers snapped. "What I want you to do is to give it wholly."

Hoggart coloured again. This time with anger. "I thought I had," he said stiffly.

"You say Dyson was confiding in you. All right. He didn't just waffle indeterminately. So what was he confiding in you about?"

"I said. About his wife."

"Well? It isn't a state secret, is it? Not under the existing circumstances?"

"She's a friend."

"So she might be." Rogers was brusque with him. "I still want to know."

"I remember only a few details. I have a poor memory."

"Not for chit-chat of this order, Mr. Hoggart, I'm quite sure."

The words came reluctantly, dragged out and proffered like miser's gold. "He said Anne was having intercourse with some man. At his home. Dyson's home, I mean. When he was at work."

"Did he have any proof? Or was it just suspicion?"

"I don't know. He was vague about this. But he said he'd tackled her about it."

"Oh? With what result?"

"She'd denied it."

"With any success?"

"None. Except that Anne refused to sleep in the same room with him again."

"Did he name the man?"

"No." The word came swiftly. "I'm sure he didn't know."

Casually. "I don't suppose you could essay a guess? Or, perhaps, your wife?"

He scrubbed his half consumed cigarette in the bowl with short, vicious strokes. He had two angry patches high on his cheeks. "No," he said in a low, hardly controlled voice. "I wouldn't. Neither would my wife. I think it's an impertinence."

"I'm indifferent to what you think it, Mr. Hoggart," Rogers said cheerfully. "It's a valid question. Your relationship with Mrs. Dyson must give you some knowledge of her friends."

"I assure you not in the category referred to by you."

"Did Dyson say what he was going to do about it?"

Hoggart looked at him in surprise. "What do you mean?"

"Come off it. I made myself perfectly clear."

There was silence for a time, then. "Yes, I'm sorry. He once said he'd kill the man. When he'd found out who he was, naturally."

13

The town seemed to cower under the brazen heat of the afternoon. The roads deliquesced to a black treacle and large cracks splintered the dusty earth.

Joanne thought he looked pale and worn when he was driven into the station yard. He was glad to see her and offered no objection when she held his arm. Even for the short distance he had to walk to the office, he limped badly and leaned heavily on his stick.

"You're overdoing it, George," she reproved him.

He grunted, not answering.

She smiled sweetly. "Would you prefer me to push you down the stairs, you ungrateful pig?"

"Don't get touchy," he muttered, "and don't nag me either. There's nothing wrong with me and I'm not overdoing anything."

"Apart from looking like a bloodless albino, I didn't think there was."

"I cut myself shaving." He led the way into his office and pushed a chair towards her. "Mine's the pleasure, but why?"

"I'm not working this afternoon and I thought you'd like some transport." She was trim in a tangerine rayon dress with a lemon yellow straw hat sitting on her neat hair. "A change from those hobnailed truck drivers you use."

"Nice of you, Joanne, but I'm in office for the rest of the afternoon." He regarded her with affection.

"Can I do anything else?"

"You can make tea for us."

"In the canteen?"

"If they don't object to your trying to run the place. They're not partial to bossy females."

The telephone indicator purred twice and he answered it. It was Hagbourne. The Citroën had been found by a searching detective. Dyson had left it in the Hatts Wharf municipal car park. Surrounded by hundreds of other cars, it had possessed an almost successful anonymity. Hagbourne, visiting the park immediately, had examined the car; opening the door with a twisting of bent wire, searching deftly and unsuccessfully for the gun. There was nothing of significance in it. An A.A. guide, a black rubber torch, a yellow duster, a ball pen and a door key. He had resecured the car and left the detective to keep observation on it. Dyson might, conceivably, return for it although neither Hagbourne nor Rogers would have bet money on the possibility.

As the afternoon grew older, cars were driven from the park and not replaced. After a while, the Citroën was an indigo-blue shark basking in a scattered shoal of lesser fish and the likelihood of Dyson's return was a mathematical improbability.

The four men sat on the window-seat benches with glasses of iced lager before them. They were shirt-sleeved and their trousers stuck to the leather on which they sat. There were spreading damp patches under their armpits. Although the windows of the bar were wide open, no air moved and they perspired freely. Each had the sheen of sweat on his forehead and upper lip; each dripped moisture from the throat down into the pulled-open collar of his shirt.

On a metal stand to one side was a long tank of exotic fish. Ignoring the bright green submarine forests of plants before them, they nuzzled the surface of the water in their search for oxygen.

Although the evening had barely begun, the barman was irritable with the effort of moving from one end of the bar to the other; prickling with sweat from lifting bottles and pulling levers.

Rogers had limped his way into Lingard's car and they had stopped, en route for his flat, to replenish the expended moisture of their dehydrated bodies. Coltart and Hagbourne were already there and it had been pleasant and convenient to form a quorum for a chewing-over of the day's garnering of information.

Rogers, pipe in mouth and tobacco smoke hovering above his head like a pungent familiar, was putting some of the facts into perspective. "First," he said, "Quandom has grouped the blood on the bandaging. It's different from that on the knife. That's likely to surprise none of us. There isn't much doubt Dyson's our man." He pulled at an ear. "It would help if we knew what he's our man for."

Coltart's eyes were the deep translucent green of bottle glass. "I'll put my money on murder," he rumbled in his deep voice. "It's so simple, it hurts."

"You can fit that in with the injuries?"

The pale freckled forehead wrinkled. "I think so. He's right handed—we now know that. At least," he said as an aside, "everybody but Hagbourne does. So he cuts his left hand during the struggle." He looked inquiringly at Rogers. "Is that how you see it?"

"It could be. It doesn't sound so wrong to me that I'd quarrel about it. But I've got what I think is a more tenable theory." He looked at Lingard. "What about you, David?"

"I could be completely wrong, but so far as *evidence* is concerned, we've nothing to connect the two." He was drawing circles in spilled beer on the polished surface of the table. "A cut hand. Obvious concealment about its origin. Out the back door like a scalded cat when Coltart knocks on the front. It adds up to something. But not necessarily stabbing an unknown female for unknown reasons."

Rogers addressed Hagbourne. "You?" he said.

"I think old birdbrain," he nodded pleasantly at Coltart, "has a point in connecting the two. Certainly it's unlikely that there's any tie-up over the Stronach death. One thing of interest, though. Might not the reluctance to see a doctor stem from being one of Stronach's patients? If, for example, he *is* connected and the doctor would recognize it from the existence of the injury." He blinked his eyes in exasperation at the complexity of his thesis and shook his head. "No. That doesn't fit either. Nothing fits without the corpus."

Rogers drew complacently at his pipe. "Have none of

you considered defensive wounds? Had they been on a woman I've no doubt you would."

"Of course!" Hagbourne was mortified. "It sticks out like a sore thumb."

"Are you saying somebody attacked Dyson? Not the other way around?" Coltart grumbled, his forehead creasing again.

"It's the obvious corollary, isn't it?"

"It is?" Lingard was thinking fast. "Then why all the to-ing and fro-ing? Dodging the quacks and fleeing the law?"

Rogers grunted, a coating of self-satisfaction on him. "Like Coltart said; it's so simple it hurts. We have a man and we have a woman. She attacks him with a knife and he defends himself. Thus the defensive gashes. Her right hand would be wielding the weapon; his left defending." He looked at the three men in turn. "So he does everything he can to conceal the wounds. *Why?*"

"Because he killed her," Hagbourne said promptly.

"That's right. With the knife he took from her so painfully."

"He could plead self-defence then?" Lingard offered.

"Against a woman?" Rogers snorted. "And to go to such lengths to conceal the crime? I don't think he'd get very far."

"What about the blood grouping?" This from Coltart.

"Not too difficult to explain. In the first instance the blade would have his blood on it. After he'd used it on her . . . well, it would be hers all the way. His would have been wiped from it when it penetrated the clothing and skin."

"I'll go along with that," Coltart said, "but why should she want to cut his liver out?"

"A thousand reasons," Rogers replied carelessly. "Haven't you ever been loved by a passionate woman?"

"You must be confusing him with someone else," Hagbourne said dryly, "or lowering the tastes of womanhood to a depth hitherto unknown." Coltart blandly allowed his insulting pleasantry to pass unremarked. It was a common enough coin of their very close friendship.

"We might," Rogers observed, "assume her to have been very possessive. In which case, any statement to her by Dyson that he was intending to kiss her goodbye might goad her into knife-waving. Or, a carelessly conceived pregnancy would provoke talk of marriage on her part and, perhaps, some understandable reluctance on his. Indeed, any woman can find more than enough reasons to have you justifiably butchered a dozen times over."

Lingard smiled, slightly off centre. "I said I might be completely wrong," he said lightly. "It looks as if I am."

"It's only a theory, David," Rogers warned. "It won't stand up to anyone leaning too heavily on it. We'll know when Dyson's picked up. If he ever is."

"You think he might blow his own head off?"

"It's been done often enough. Otherwise, why the gun?"

"He could want to shoot someone," murmured Hagbourne. "Someone like old Casanova Coltart over there. Seems to me he paints too glowing a picture of the delectable Mrs. D. to be wholly disinterested."

Rogers laughed. "I must admit that from his report she sounded too nice, too wholesome, to be true."

The green eyes glinted, not altogether with good humour, but he said nothing.

"Dyson's supposed to have alleged she was being subjected to a course of extra-marital exercises," Rogers continued.

"I don't believe it, sir." Coltart was stiffly formal.

Rogers was amused although he did not show it. "All right. Don't get stodgy about it. There are always two interpretations of gossip and I often get the wrong one." He turned to Lingard. "You've got all the men we can spare out looking for him?"

"Yes. Unless he's gone to ground in a private house we can't miss him. Mind, we've no guarantee he hasn't skipped the town."

"So?"

"Well, I've covered the railway stations and bus termini more or less permanently."

"Copies of his photograph to hotels?"

"We've flooded the place. Some of them think we're going it a bit over a mere missing person."

"It's all we can say."

"Apart from that," Lingard murmured, "it's been *laissez faire* in bottom gear all the way."

"Seen Stronach yet?"

"No. He's either out or not disposed to answer the telephone. I suspect the latter."

Rogers flicked his thumb and finger at the barman and, catching his attention, held up four fingers. "We've got to sometime. The sooner the less painful. For us, I mean. It's a fair bet he's dodging the issue." He showed his teeth. "If, indeed, there *is* an issue to dodge."

"I've still that buzzing in my subconscious. It tells me we haven't finished with him yet."

When the frosted bottles arrived, Rogers put a ten-shilling note on the tray. There was a silence while they filled their glasses. "It's all got to break some time," he comforted himself. "When it does, no doubt the pieces will slot into place. Equally doubtless, we'll have a murder on our hands. Still," he said cheerfully, "it appears the solution will all be nicely cut and dried for us while we wait events."

"Reverting to Dyson," Coltart said. "He seems a dangerous man to be in possession of a gun."

"I agree with you." For a moment Rogers looked bleak. "Whichever way it goes—homicidal or suicidal—he's going to mean trouble."

"His won't be the first comminuted brain we've had to scrape off the ceiling," Hagbourne commented.

"Remember the old chap who woodpeckered his skull open?" It was a deliberate manoeuvre to discard Dyson from their considerations.

Lingard was interested. "New to me, George," he said.

"He was rising on seventy-five and lived on his own. A stringy old bird without a lot to live for. When we found him he'd been dead a day or so. He had sat himself on a kitchen chair and tapped away with a ball-pane hammer at the top of his head. It had gone through what little hair he had, then the flesh and, finally, the bone. By then his brain was poking out of a circular three-inch hole in his skull. As neat a trepanning job as I've ever seen."

"Bless my soul," Lingard swallowed. "Do you have to? It's making my toes curl."

Rogers stared at him politely. "Oh, that didn't kill him although I've no doubt he had the mother and father of all headaches. What he finally did was to get his razor, sit down in the chair again and cut his throat open to the backbone. Which did the trick." He drank deeply of his beer and mopped his forehead and neck with a handkerchief.

"A bit prolonged," Hagbourne grimaced. "I prefer the surgeon I once dealt with. He went to bed with a bottle of brandy and a scalpel. Sliced his ankles and wrists very professionally. The paradoxical point was that he'd carefully dipped the scalpel in a sterilizing fluid first. The empty brandy bottle and the container were on the table at the side of his bed."

Coltart came in with his harsh voice. "I remember one I prefer to your crudities. It happened when I was a young constable. My Station Inspector received a letter from a local woman saying she was going to kill herself." He was silent for a moment. "I shall never forget the ending of her letter. The words had a kind of poetry. She wrote, 'You will, I pray, find me dead.' She lived outside the town and I remember it was autumn and misty. She was the first dead woman I had seen. She was old but very lovely and she looked almost happy. As if she'd met a lost friend. She had cleaned and tidied the house, put the bottles out for the milkman and laid out small piles of coins for the little bills she owed. Then she swallowed the tablets and went to bed. Her only regret seemed to be that she was being a nuisance in dying."

Rogers blew down the stem of his pipe and tapped the bowl of the hard heel of his palm. "I suppose it's a truism," he said at last, "that Death knocks quickly at the door where he isn't wanted. Otherwise, he has to be searched for." He looked at his watch. "Can you give me transport to my flat, David?" he asked. "I think I'll rest my leg for an hour or two."

Delivered at the flat by Lingard, he found Joanne preparing him a meal. After the heat of the streets the room was cool.

"Christ," he grunted to her, "but I've had a rough day." He took off his jacket and loosened his tie. The back of his shirt was grey with perspiration and sticking to him. "I'm having a shower, plaster cast and all."

She was brown-skinned and trim in a white linen dress. "Won't it dissolve or something?"

"*I* will if I don't have a shower."

"I suppose you'll be too tired for the party?"

"The par...?" He was surprised until he remembered. Then he slapped his forehead. "Oh God, Joanne, I *am* sorry. Is it tonight?"

"You don't have to come." She covered her disappointment with a smile. "It's nothing special. A few of my hooligan friends in for a gin and pâté on toast. I think they use my parties as a medium for changing partners anyway. You wouldn't be eligible for that, darling."

"You mean I'm not on the transfer list? You're keeping me on a pretty tight snaffle, aren't you?" He smiled maliciously. "I think I'll come after all. There might be a potential divorcee there. I've always had an ambition to be cited as a co-respondent."

"Over my stretched-out body," she said. "I'll call for you in two hours." Her small hand was cool in his. "Please be pretty for me," she coaxed.

When Joanne tapped at his door, Rogers was trim and neatly groomed in a graphite grey suit, a formal white shirt and an aura of soap and lotions.

The party had slipped into a noisy first gear before his arrival and he happily propped himself against the small bar, a tumbler in one tanned fist, a thin green cigar smoking between his teeth. Immobilized by his leg, he amused himself passively as a spectator, speculating on the reshuffling of marital and sexual relationships the gin and heady warmth would provoke.

Deep dusk had merged into dark night and orderly strings and patterns of amber street lights were visible through the open windows. The moon, large and butter yellow, hung low in a cyanosed sky. Wisps of industrial smoke stained its pelucidity and across the dark vault was a faint powdering of emerging stars. The air was freshening although the blocks of concrete and brick, the bitumen and paced streets, still gave off a stored warmth like the cooling carcase of a living being.

The woman approached Rogers drunkenly, a slopping glass in her hand. She was sun-tanned to a chocolate

brown. Her hair was a black glossy cap over the narrow
attractive face. Her lips were thin, the teeth behind them
small and very white, her tongue pointed and serpent-
like. The protuberant eyes had the brown shine of treacle.

She was slim in a white brocaded dress and had the
wide hips and flat stomach which draw the immediate
attention of men.

"George, you slippery bastard," she drawled, the gin
she had drunk blurring the articulation of the consonants.
"Do you still belong to Jo?"

He smiled, not answering.

She pouted and twisted a finger behind the knot of
his tie. "Say something nice, poppet. Say she's a selfish
bitch to keep you all to herself."

"I'm no use to anyone at the moment, Barbara," he
said easily. "I can't leap out of a bedroom window with the
agility demanded."

"But you would otherwise, darling?"

"Wild horses wouldn't stop me," he lied with a straight
face. "How did your holiday go?"

"Marvellous!" she said, showing her nice teeth and
squeezing together her blued eyelids. "Let me tell you
about my Spanish dancer." A knowing, please-be-outraged
look was on her brown face. She drank from her glass and
moved nearer, pinning him with the backs of his thighs
against the hard edge of the bar. "We went to this night-
club in Ibiza." Her tongue flickered at him. "There was
this Flamenco dancer stamping his high-heeled shoes on
the boards and clapping his hands. I was lapping him up
with the yummy champagne you get with your ticket. He
must have got the message for this *gorgeous* hunk of
Spanish bull sneered down his nose at me. *You* know," she
said slurringly, "how you men do it. Anyway, he was up
above us on a raised stage thing and he was *massive*,
sweetheart. Huge shoulders and everything under that
ducky costume of his."

Her mobile and wicked face was inches from his. For
all her drinking and smoking, he noticed her breath was
completely odourless. "I was flat on my back on the beach
next day," she went on, "when along came this dancer
hunk. "Señorita," he screamed from half way up the
beach. So I waved to him; all flashing teeth and shocking

pink bikini, darling." Her cerise mouth inverted itself in mock dismay. "When he was near enough to sneak a view down my bosom, I looked up at him. *Darling!* I nearly died. He was about five feet nothing and the poor little dear just didn't have it. He must have stuffed himself up with cotton wool!"

He laughed, his brown eyes creasing to slits. "Stop trying to crawl up inside my shirt," he said. "I make no pretensions to physical abnormality of any kind."

She scrubbed herself drunkenly against him and said, a little contemptuously, "I could make you come running any time I wanted to."

"Having fun, George?" Joanne had materialized at his side.

"Yes, I was," he said, closing one eye at her. "Barbara was explaining the hierarchical structure of the Spanish bishopric."

She stared unwinkingly at the drunken woman. "In a pig's ear she was," she said smoothly. She moved across and caught hold of her arm, propelling her away from Rogers. "Come on, sweetie," he heard her whisper. "You should be more careful. When he's had a drink or two, George has no taste at all."

When she returned she stood on tiptoe and kissed the tip of his nose. "You slobbering, lecherous bastard," she said amiably, "she's old enough to be your mother."

"She didn't act like it," he grinned. "And stop kidding yourself, Kelly. She can't give you more than a couple of years. She just happens to have had a lot more of the right kind of experience."

Her narrow heel stamped down on his instep. "Have another drink, darling," she said, "and behave yourself."

The telephone made itself heard through a lull in the shrieking conversation and thumping melody from a record player. "For you, George," Joanne shouted through the bedlam, handing him the handset. "It's David."

He pressed the instrument hard to his ear, trying to exclude the clamour pressing in on him. "Yes, David," he said.

"George," Lingard said urgently. "Mrs. Dyson's just bought it. Shot at through the window of her bedroom."

"Oh Christ! Dead?"

"I don't know. She's on her way to the hospital."

"When did it happen?"

"Only minutes ago. I haven't been there yet."

"Right." Rogers's voice was hard and staccato. "Send one of the sergeants to the house. Coltart if he's about. And a scenes of crime man. Put a guard on it. 'Red file' the circulation about Dyson and add to it the shooting. Go to the hospital straight away and send a car for me. I'll meet you there. Anything else?"

"No. I'll get on with it."

Rogers replaced the handset. His face was set, his eyebrows a black bar of anger. He limped across to Joanne. "I'm sorry," he said, "but it's trouble and I'm on my way."

Somewhere in the background, within the tangle of moving, laughing bodies, the hungry, sun-tanned woman was wall-papering herself to the front of another man.

14

Lingard was waiting near the main door of the hospital when Rogers climbed out from the patrol car bringing him. He was illuminated by the orange loop of light thrown down from the sodium-vapour lamp above his head. Night-drunken moths rapped their thick bodies against the brilliant glass bowl. Underneath, in a pool of black shadow, a tiny bright-eyed mouse sat, crunching like so many sticks of celery those insects that dropped stupefied from the hot light above.

Now that night had fully come there was a gentle nudging of a cooler wind, imparting a slight turbulence to the drifts of dust in the gutters, lifting almost imperceptibly the discarded paper rubbish littering the streets.

The two men walked together, shouldering through the overlapping inner doors of thick transparent plastic sheet into a complex of painted brick passages. In them were waiting rubber-wheeled trolleys and huge wickerwork baskets of soiled linen. Red-lettered notice-boards pointed wooden fingers to the openings of other square tunnels. Overall, there was a smell of warm rubber, polish and suffering bodies. The passages echoed quietly with a faint faraway undertone of things being done and words being said; the movements and whisperings of distant, menacing and nightmarish creatures.

Mrs. Dyson's black hair was tousled and her face pale. Her eyes, Rogers noticed, although red-rimmed, were a clear hazel and bright with an oil-slick sheen. Her mouth, its bottom lip full and moist, was a pouting softness. A doctor in a white coat was at her side, busily swabbing with a pungent solution the upper part of one of her arms. This was peppered with tiny red holes, some of them still bleeding. This corner of the casualty ward was isolated by surrounding green canvas screens.

"I'm not interfering, doctor?" Rogers asked.

A shake of the head as the deft brown fingers worked on the pale arm. She was lying on a leather couch, closely wrapped in a blue cotton sheet. There were small circular blotches of blood on it. The lower part of her body was covered by a grey and scarlet blanket.

He produced his warrant card and held it open in front of her face. "Can you talk to me?"

"Yes." She looked at the doctor. "Could I have a cigarette, please?"

The doctor, a dark-skinned young man with gentle chocolate eyes and sunken cheeks, nodded.

Rogers reached into his pocket and withdrew a small yellow box. He shook a cigarette out and put it between her parted lips, then held a lighted match to the end of it. She closed her eyes and inhaled deeply. "Thank you," she said softly.

"Tell me what happened, Mrs. Dyson," he said.

He had, while they threaded the labyrinth of gloomy corridors, received a hurried report from Lingard on the finding of her and the extent of her injuries. Her assailant had fired into the bedroom from a range of fifty yards or so. The window had been partly open and those pellets not deflected or decelerated by hitting the glass and curtaining had bounced from the ceiling and walls to pierce the soft flesh of Mrs. Dyson. The small lead balls had entered the muscle of the right upper deltoid and, to a lesser extent, the thinner skin over her shoulder blade. She was not seriously injured and the shock to her not severe.

"I was getting ready for bed," she said. "I hadn't heard from my husband and after Mr. Coltart left I didn't know what to do. So I went to mother's. I took my son and left him there. I came back at about nine o'clock, expecting—I suppose—to see that he had returned." She breathed in deeply at her cigarette. "Anyway, he hadn't. I had intended to stay with mother but decided against it. I telephoned and told her. I ate some cake and drank some milk and locked up. I turned all the lights out and went upstairs. Then I undressed and walked into the bathroom. I cleaned my teeth and took a shower." Her voice was soft and melodious and held them interested in her domestic trivialities. "When I'd finished showering, I didn't bother..." She lowered her eyelids, making a prurience of the unuttered words. "It was so hot, you know... I'm afraid I was shameless. I sat at my dressing-table, brushing my hair... well, just as I came out of the shower."

She put the little finger of her free hand on to the tip of her tongue and removed a flake of tobacco. Doing it, she pulled the sheet aside, revealing that beneath it she was naked. Her flesh was beautifully opalescent with a smooth nacreous gloss to it. Her black hair was a vivid contrast.

The two men exchanged glances, their expressions unrevealing. Neither could decide whether the artless movement was deliberate or not although it seemed fortuitously contrived to illustrate the point she was making. The doctor pulled the sheet across the exposed body with professional impersonality, smiling briefly but saying nothing.

Rogers swallowed. "Were the curtains drawn?" he asked.

"They were open. As were the windows. To let in what cool air there was."

"Would you be visible from the road outside?"

She lowered her eyelids again. "I'm afraid... the

upper part of me might have been. I didn't think . . . the
neighbours don't really . . . not in the Crescent."

"They do everywhere, Mrs. Dyson," he said flatly.

She smiled gently. "It was wicked of me . . ."

"I'm sorry I interrupted." He did not sound it. "Please
go on. You were brushing your hair."

"Yes, I do that every night. Brush my hair. Not . . ."
She again smiled, apologetically this time. "It probably
sounds silly to you."

"Not really."

"I brush it a hundred times. It keeps it glossy." She
pulled at it ruefully. "Not like this, though."

"It looks very nice," he said gravely. "What time were
you doing this brushing?"

"Oh!" She thought for a moment, her forefinger pulling at her lower lip. "Ten-thirty as near as I can guess."

He pushed back the cuff of his shirt sleeve and
checked with his watch. He appeared to be satisfied. "Go
on."

"Well, I was brushing away and counting . . . thinking
about what was happening to Bill, when . . . bang! . . . glass
showered all over me and I heard a shot. At the same time
I felt something hitting into my arm." She stopped while
Rogers and Lingard made sympathetic noises. "It didn't
hurt," she continued. "Not then. It felt numb. Then I fell
off the stool." She looked at them, her shining eyes wide.
"It was *him*, wasn't it? It was Bill who shot me?"

"We don't know. Not for sure . . ."

She cut him short. "He must be insane." She inhaled
at her cigarette and a sprinkle of ash dropped on to the
sheet. "All those drugs he used to take." As if to herself,
she whispered, "Why? Why?"

"What drugs, Mrs. Dyson?"

She looked blank for a second. "Not that kind," she
said quickly. "They weren't wrong . . . you know . . . criminal.
They were prescribed for him by our doctor. Phenobarbi-
tones. But he used to eat them like sweets. So very many,"
she finished sadly.

"Why were they prescribed?"

The doctor was listening intently to the questioning
although he said nothing. Occasionally he would direct a

faintly puzzled look at his patient as if he could not wholly understand her.

"His nerves, I suppose," she answered him. "He couldn't sleep. He used to scream and wake up perspiring dreadfully. He could be horribly touchy about little things. Things that didn't matter."

"What was his condition without them?"

"He would be restless . . . not being able to settle down to anything. He would prowl around like . . . like a caged lion, cracking his knuckles."

"Can we go back? What happened after you fell off the stool?"

"I lay there . . . on the carpet . . . for a long time. Waiting for something else to happen. I couldn't hear anyone outside . . . no moving or anything." She shuddered. "I was expecting him to unlock the door and come in. To kill me." She looked at him imploringly. "I don't want to die, Mr. Rogers."

He tapped his teeth with his cold pipe. "I'm sure you don't," he said sententiously. It seemed inadequate but the only thing to say.

"Well," she continued, not very comforted. "I crawled downstairs." Surprisingly, she giggled. "I was . . . I was naked as the day I was born and on all fours like a frog. I just had to get out of the light in the bedroom and get help."

She handed the cigarette stub to Rogers. "Would you mind awfully?" He took it, dropped it and put his foot on it, grinding it into the rubber tiling. The doctor frowned at Mrs. Dyson's shoulder but remained silent.

"Anyway," she went on, "I got down to the hall . . . still too frightened to stand up . . . and waited. I knew I was bleeding. I could feel it running down my back and arm and on to the carpet. I began to tremble . . . I don't think I could then have stood had I wished."

The doctor had now finished attending to the arm and he straightened himself up. "I want to deal with the patient's back now, gentlemen, if you'd excuse me for a few minutes."

Outside the ward, Rogers and Lingard paced the length of the corridor. Each, by different means, was now able to satisfy his bottled-up need for tobacco: the one, burning it in fierce clouds of blue smoke; the other, absorbing the soothing narcotic through the membranes of his sinuses.

"What do you think, David?" Rogers asked.

"I don't know. Not yet. But I do know what ails Coltart." He looked at Rogers. "For a plump little hausfrau she exudes a hell of a lot more sex than perspiration."

Rogers shook his head. "No," he said with conviction. "Not with Coltart. Not in a million light-years. Sympathy, yes. Pity, perhaps. But not *that!*"

"Come off it, George," he protested. "He's activated by the same glands as we lesser mortals."

"So he might be," Rogers said with authority this time, "but he still wouldn't be interested in Mrs. Dyson. She's a married woman and he's the most sexually moral man I've known." His voice sharpened still further. "Get off his back, David. He's a man deserving your respect."

Lingard was hurt and showed it. "I'm sorry," he said shortly.

Rogers poked a finger into his arm. "Don't take it so seriously," he smiled. "I happen to know him better than you." He steered away from the subject of Coltart. "What about Dyson?"

"No signs of him. The Red File on him has produced nothing. He's probably scuttled back to wherever he crawled from."

"We're a little better off than we were before."

"Oh, how?"

"We know he's homicidal."

"But his own wife!" Lingard was outraged.

"Why not? Particularly if Hoggart is right."

"Then why not before? Why wait?"

"The situation. Perhaps it's changed."

Lingard thought about this. "He could have misunderstood Coltart's visit. Thought his wife had shopped him, possibly."

"A distinct possibility. He needn't know it was a routine check. Mm," he mused, "it could be."

"Or he's unequivocally insane."

"I could settle for that, too." He pulled at his pipe. "But it isn't going to finish with her"—he jerked his thumb in the direction of the ward—"is it?"

"Not?" Lingard was puzzled.

"Hoggart said Dyson threatened to kill his wife's lover. If she's got one."

"And if he identifies him."

"Which he may have done already."

Lingard smiled. "I can see she's in for an embarrassing five minutes."

Rogers puffed smoke as they turned together at the end of the corridor. "I've got to ask her and she's got to name him." he said. "By the way," his eyes were glinting with humour, "what was your opinion of the sheet business?"

"You mean showing us her tits?"

"It seemed deliberate to me." He laughed. "A not unwelcome diversion."

"Did you read it?"

"No. It seemed quite the wrong time."

"It did?"

"Well, who would think about sex with an arm full of pellets?"

"A distraction? A smoke screen to circumvent an awkward question?"

"If it was, I got left behind. I don't see the point."

Lingard looked knowledgeable. "Who does with women?"

Returning to the ward, they saw that Mrs. Dyson was propped up on pillows, her eyes closed. The doctor spoke to them away from the screened-off corner. "Do not be too long, please." His long brown fingers were folding his stethoscope. "She is to go to the theatre soon."

Rogers was startled. "Has something gone wrong?"

"No, of course not." He was a little impatient. "We have to remove the pellets. A very tedious and necessary operation. Please try not to upset her."

They smelled the antiseptic as they approached the couch and she opened her eyes. "All right?" Rogers smiled.

She moved a weary hand. "I feel tired."

"We shan't keep you long," he encouraged. "You were telling me you were in the hall. Did you then telephone?"

"Could I have another cigarette, please?" Exhaling the smoke down her nostrils, she answered him. "I reached up and pulled it off the table. It hit me as it fell." She pulled a face. "That was the last straw and I started to cry. Then I got hold of myself and dialled nine-nine-nine."

"By touch?"

She nodded, screwing her eyes against the smoke from the cigarette between her lips. "Yes. It was dark but I had no difficulty."

"And then?"

"I called out 'Police' a couple of times and fainted. At least, I think I did because I only vaguely remember the policeman and another man wrapping me up in the sheet."

"That must have been an embarrassment to you?" Lingard interposed, his voice neutral.

She smiled, putting a shade of suffering to it. "I don't think those things matter when one is in trouble." He was plainly being reproved.

Rogers intervened quickly. "I'm sure they don't," he soothed. "Was there anything else?"

"No," she replied, almost regretfully. "But I'm still terribly confused. . . ."

"You know Mr. Hoggart, I understand?" He slid this one in smoothly, a knife into butter.

She glanced quickly at the ceiling and blinked. "Of course. He's a colleague of Bi . . . my husband's."

"You also knew him socially?"

There was a long silence while she drew in jerkily at her cigarette. "Yes."

"A friend?"

"Casually so. More of my husband's. We dine occasionally. He can be helpful to Bill."

"First-name friends?"

Another silence. "Yes." She did not elaborate on this.

"You've spoken to him about your husband? About him toddling off?" He was watching her intently.

"No." She was frowning and no longer friendly.

"I'm a little confused," he explained disarmingly. "I gathered you'd telephoned him."

"No."

"Not? Not immediately after Sergeant Coltart left you? Not telling him about the gun?"

"Oh, *then!*" she exclaimed. "Of course! How utterly stupid of me." Her smile was warmly apologetic. "It went completely out of my mind." She widened her eyes at him. "Do please forgive me."

"It's quite all right," he answered genially. "We can all have our little lapses. I wondered," he said, attacking from a different direction, "if you could suggest why your husband shot at you?"

She looked from side to side as if seeking a way of escape. "He must be insane," she said at last, her eyes asking them to accept this. Again there was the apparently clumsy movement of her arm and the falling apart of the sheet. She giggled, "Oh dear, I am sorry." She made no attempt to cover herself but looked at Rogers with calculating eyes.

He leaned forward and flicked the sheet back over her, admitting to himself a desire to know—on some less public occasion—her soft white body. Preferring women lean and fined down to a sinewy hardness as he did, she nevertheless attracted him. He shifted his plastered leg and scowled. "You'll catch something or other," he said irritably.

In the background, Lingard coughed gently, an edge of laughter to it. There was little doubt that she had put her interrogator out of his stride.

"Let's go back to movies, Mrs. Dyson," he continued firmly. "Assume he isn't insane. Now what's the reason?"

"There can't be one. I'm his wife."

"Might not he be jealous of someone?" He left it naked as it stood, calculating its effect on her.

Her reaction seemed excessive. She put a clenched fist to her mouth and moaned, "Oh no! Oh no! It isn't true."

"What isn't tr . . ." He glared around him in irritation. The doctor had materialized from behind the screens.

"I'm sorry, inspector," he said, "but Mrs. Dyson is tired."

Rogers showed his teeth and stood his ground. "Be a good chap," he said, "and give me just a minute or so longer. Someone," he said portentously, "might get killed." He turned back to her. "What isn't true? That he was jealous of him?"

"There isn't anyone to be jealous of."

His voice was hard. "Your husband believes there is and, believing, says he intends to do something about it. Perhaps something like shooting him." He waited. She was pushing her knuckles between her teeth. "Who is he, Mrs. Dyson? *Who is he?*"

She moaned again and the doctor once more intervened. "Gentlemen," he protested, "I really must insist..."

Rogers shrugged. "I'm sorry, doctor. Thank you for your help. You've been more than kind." He spoke to her. "Think about it," he said sharply. "A man's life may be at stake."

Without speaking, she humped herself around; her back to him, her eyes closed and her face ugly.

Coltart was a broad, solid mass in the shadow of the obscuring porch. Behind him, from each window of the house, shone a rectangle of poured-out light.

Rogers had left Lingard at the station to check on the progress of the intensified search for Dyson. Despite the increasing discomfort of his aching leg, he persisted with his involvement in the inquiry. It put a raw edge to his temper and he was prone to lashing out in sudden irritation. Outside the office he found it necessary to make a conscious effort to observe the minimum social graces. Paradoxically, this resulted in a more than usual politeness, although a politeness which was only a thin film away from an uncontrollable eruption.

Now, irritable and tired and making no effort to conceal it, he growled at Coltart. "Well? How far have we got?"

"Nowhere," Coltart replied. "Not yet." He looked at him warily. "How is Mrs. Dyson?" He said it diffidently.

"She's all right," Rogers replied shortly. "Don't worry yourself about her."

"No news of her husband?"

"Lingard's sorting that end out. But, so far, not."

"Does she know?" Coltart opened the door and stood aside. Rogers entered and he followed him. "I mean, that it's her husband."

"She does." He gave the big sergeant a run-down on the interview.

The carpet inside was smeared with blood, as was the ivory telephone handset standing on it. Rogers followed the staining up the stairs and into a bedroom. One pane of glass in the broad window was shattered to a jagged star. Fragmented glass littered the carpeted floor like spilled sugar. The silk cover on the bed was crumpled and untidy.

On its shining kingfisher-blue surface were small dark blotches. The ceiling above the bed was scored and pitted in a dozen places and a flour of plaster had drifted on to the cover and carpet.

A stool with a white fur seat was overturned near the dressing-table from which bottles, jars and tubes had been pushed to the floor. The room was heavy with the scent of a heady perfume and Rogers saw again—a vividly remembered picture in his mind's eye—the pale carnality of the user's body.

There was more blood near the door and already, he noted, it was darkening. A cigarette had burned to grey ash on the scalloped edge of a glass bowl on a bedside table. In the bowl were several crushed ends. Two of them were oval and had gold tips.

Coltart pointed to a handbag, partly under the bed. Some of its contents had been spilled. Rogers nodded. "Check it for me," he said. "I can't get down with this dam' leg of mine."

There was nothing of interest; nothing particularly evocative of the owner. A small pad of toilet tissues, a packet of cigarettes and a slim gold-plated lighter, a confusion of cosmetics, a handkerchief embroidered with the letters AD and a metal ring of keys. Coltart scooped them back into the bag with his large hands and tossed it on to the bed.

From the bedroom, Rogers went into the bathroom; noting the towels, touching the soap with his finger, pushing at the bath mat with the toe of his shoe. Then he ran his hand down the inside of the shower curtain. He was silent; not puzzled but as if seeking confirmation of a known fact. When he came out he was humming to himself, his face that of a man who could write large cheques without suffering a massive angina.

"I hope I'm not treading on your toes, sergeant," he said, "but Mrs. Dyson's a bloody liar."

Coltart's pale face flushed. "I don't think I'm as naïve about her as you imagine," he said, his voice harsh with annoyance. "I never thought the bi... that she was any different." He made a disparaging noise in the back of his nose.

"As a generalization," Rogers observed, "I agree with you."

"So what has she lied about?"

"Naked she might have been," he said, "but taking a shower she certainly wasn't. Hoggart was also being entertained, although," he admitted, "there's no putting a time to it. But being in the bedroom suggests he wasn't enrolling her as a deaconess."

"The facts are enough for me."

"Of course they are. They admit of no other inference. I've no doubt Dyson knew what she was up to and who with. He probably saw the light in the bedroom and shot blindly. Just for the hell of it. Winging his wife with pellets bouncing off the window-glass was possibly a bonus."

Coltart thought this one out. "She was wounded in the back," he commented. "An oddity, considering what they were doing."

Rogers snorted. "Your thinking is far too orthodox in these matters, sergeant." He grinned suddenly. "You should watch more television. I wonder," he continued reflectively, "how many pellets friend Hoggart picked up. And where?"

The air outside was perceptibly cooler and formless masses of dark cloud were piling above them, slowly obscuring the incandescent dusting of stars, threatening the floating moon with extinction.

Coltart had been thoughtful. "He ran for it, then?" he rumbled at last.

"Wouldn't you?" Rogers said patiently. "Apart from dropping dead *in situ*, being shot stark naked must amount to a first degree embarrassment in the most permissive neighbourhoods. I'll give him credit for judging she was in no real danger. After which, there was no pressing need for him to stay. I presume he grabbed his underwear and socks and went over the back fence."

"You'll be seeing him?"

"Not tonight," Rogers said. "I'll let him sweat blood until the morning. In the meantime," he directed Coltart, "put a man outside his house. If Hoggart sees him, so much the better."

"You think Dyson might have another go?"

"I'd look a bloody fool if he did and I hadn't done anything about it."

"What about the wife?"

"Mrs. Dyson?"

Coltart nodded his head.

"Already done. I've had a policewoman report to the ward sister's office." He looked at the sergeant from the corners of his eyes, wanting to mollify him. "You're doing well, Eddie. Just find Dyson. That's all I'm asking. The rest will fall into place." He sounded a lot more confident than he felt.

When the car drew up at the kerb he limped across and manoeuvred himself into the passenger seat, wrenching his knee as he did so. He barked irritably at the poker-faced driver who was committing nothing more than the unpardonable sin of being there.

15

In his flat, dragging his trousers down over his legs, Rogers sat on the edge of his bed, drained of energy and almost too tired to complete his undressing. His eyes were a raw grittiness, his bones a dull ache of weariness. It was an almost certain aggravation that the telephone bell should explode into his tiredness.

It was Coltart. "A dead man in Housman Park," he said. "Found by P.c. Pelly on patrol. A brief message to say it's murder. No more."

"Do we know who it is?" He was slurring his words with weariness.

"No. Just what I've told you."

"How was he killed?"

Coltart was patient. "He didn't say."

"He didn't say much at all." Rogers was nasty.

"He passed the message on. He's still with the body."

"You've sent the photographer?"

"Yes. Also a message for Mr. Lingard."

"Radio link?"

"A car is up there."

"Lighting?"

"In the car."

"Murder box?"

"I'll bring it with me."

"Doctor?"

"Waiting for you to say."

"All right. Archie Rees. And notify the coroner."

"Will do."

"Pick me up in the car," Rogers ordered. He had now thrown his weariness off, his reawakened mind already reaching out, reviewing the established procedures and techniques of a murder investigation. At least, he thought sardonically, I have a body. A beautiful, solid, investigable corpse.

The indestructible and apparently tireless Coltart was with him in a few minutes and once more Rogers fitted himself painfully into the car. As he did so, a drift of light rain began to spot the windscreen.

Death and mutilation had failed to obliterate the handsome flashiness Drazek possessed in life. One of his eyes—now a milky-blue opacity—rested on his cheek. In its place was a bloody and ragged hole. The remaining eye, gleaming dully, stared expressionlessly through a partially closed lid. Beneath the upthrust chin was a circular black wound, big enough to put a finger into and from which issued a congealing stream of blood. This had collected in a liquid darkness beneath the crispness of his stiff collar.

His open mouth had dribbled a bloody saliva into one ear. His teeth, red stains fouling their whiteness, were bared in a rictus of terror. Like a thin white slug on his cheek, his scar raised one corner of the upper lip in a horrible parody of a smile. The disarranged clothing was smeared and muddied.

A sheet of transparent polythene had been erected, tent-like, on a metal frame over the head and shoulders, protecting them from further interference by the elements. Outside the tent, the lower part of the body was covered with silver beads of rain.

In the hot, white glare of the flood lamps clustered men and surrounding bushes stood out from the encroaching night in photographic detail. The deep shadows they cast retreated and advanced across the grass-covered wasteland as the lamps were moved and, nearer, gave the face of the dead man the pretence of a mobility it no longer possessed.

Rogers limped across and pressed the cold cheek briefly with the pad of one finger. The flesh was rubbery and without resilience, the dimple made by his nail remaining. Lingard and Coltart were close by, walking slowly with their heads down like contemplative monks, scrutinizing the immediate area. A twenty feet perimeter of white tape had been pegged down around the body, a path to it being similarly marked and carpeted with a tarpaulin.

The slamming of a car door signalled the arrival of Dr. Rees, carrying his small leather bag of tools. He accepted the inconvenience of his call-out and the responsibilities of his office with a Welsh insouciance. Without speaking, only raising his eyebrows at Rogers in mock concern, he knelt by Drazek, peering under the canopy of shadowing material.

Rogers called Lingard over to him. "Take one of the men with you," he said, "and do an immediate check on Stronach." He said it in an undertone, not letting Rees hear.

"Lift him?" Lingard asked.

"Christ, David," he muttered impatiently, "play it off the cuff. You know as much as I do... at the moment, dam' all."

"It can't be anyone else." He said it defensively, realizing his error in asking for a blank cheque.

"You don't have to tell me," Rogers growled, "but we want some evidence first. All the knowing in the world won't prove it's him. Check on his movements. That sort of thing. Have a go at him if you've got to. Scream if you get into difficulties."

Crouching awkwardly beside Rees, Rogers directed a beam of light to the throat and chest of the supine body. Rees prodded tentatively at the torn orbital socket with a silver probe, moving the eyeball on its retaining ligament. Coltart joined them, squatting in the wet grass on his massive hams. Rees grunted his acknowledgement and continued probing. He pushed at the small puncture in the stiff throat, his expression one of puzzlement.

"A weapon similar in shape to a pencil, George," he said at last. "Entered the eye socket and appears to have lacerated the brain. Throat wound similar. The amount of blood suggests a perforation of the artery. He thrashed around a bit. Not," he added pensively, "that it took him long to die."

"A steel poker, Archie?"

"Something like that."

"A fencing foil? One with a button on?"

Rees smiled. "That's about it. Yes, it could very well be."

"Dead how long?"

Rees flexed the arms and legs. "Two hours? Don't tie me down to it. Not much more."

Rogers looked at his watch. "About eleven?"

"Yes. I'll be more definite when I get him to the mortuary."

Drazek had been stumbled over by a patrolling constable who stood now, a tall helmeted figure, outside the periphery of floodlit grass. He had passed from the orange splashes of sodium lighting, through the moving shadows cast by wind-tossed trees and into the quiet black gulfs between lamps, striding slowly the geometrically-patterned footpaths and asphalted tracks flanked neatly by lime and ash trees, bordered by gardens of standard rose trees, clumps of feathery pampas grass and golden rod swaying in the earth-smelling wind.

In the centre, a sinister ink blot from which radiated the spokes of yellow street lamps, was the blackness of Housman Park. A dank and gloomy jungle of whispering silences broken only by the screaming of owls, the scraping of moving branches and the muted growling of distant traffic: a suitable theatre for the butchery of Drazek.

And there he had been found, flat on his back; his petrified hands vainly supplicating, his tortured face looking fixedly at the weeping sky above.

It seemed to Rogers an over-severe penalty to pay for pandering to the physical and emotional needs of a neglected wife. He remembered the murderous glare he had detected in Stronach's eyes; the pale shadow of potential violence behind the bland and pink moon-faced respectability. He wondered uneasily whether he had somehow failed in not warning Drazek. But Christ! he thought, I'd have deserved the ridicule I would have invited and got. Reading (like a character in a third-rate film) murder in the eyes of an irreproachably respectable medical man. He cleared his throat and Rees looked at him with amusement.

"Unpleasant thoughts, George?" he asked.

Rogers screwed out a confident smile. "Not a bit of it," he prevaricated. "I've just made a vow not to covet other men's wives."

"Is that what *he* did?" He aimed his probe at Drazek.

"Yes. Whether it got him killed I'm not yet sure."

"But you obviously think it a possibility?"

Rogers nodded.

"Ignore me if I'm being too nosy, George." He was unbuttoning the shirt, sliding his hand down over the rib cage. "Is this anything to do with Bridget's case?"

"Could be. What do you know about Dr. Stronach?"

Rees had finished his preliminary examination and he stood, turning down his rolled-up cuffs. "Very dangerous man to say the wrong thing to. Or," he added warningly, "about."

"Someone's got to say it to him, Archie," he said easily. "Is this how you medics sort out your emotional problems?" He nodded to a waiting photographer who unfolded and erected his tripod to one side of the body. The man then removed the sheltering polythene in order to commit to a black and white record the grotesquerie of the dead face, grimacing as his sleeve fouled itself against the bloody eye socket in doing so.

"We wouldn't do it with rare poisons and artificially induced embolisms, that's certain," Rees replied. "On the other hand, neither do I think a doctor would do it this way."

"No?" Rogers head was tilted to one side. "And why not?"

Rees made a gesture of distaste. "A bit crude, George," he protested. "Even for us butchers."

"Roused passions *are* crude and often demand crude reprisals."

"A point well made and taken. I accept that we have our share of violence."

"Now fit the hat on Stronach."

"Christ, George, have a heart." He was cleaning his hands with pieces of spirit-soaked cotton wool.

"No, Archie," he said flatly. "No falling back on ethics or whatever you call them . . . it won't wash. No more than it would with me were he a policeman."

"I'm not taking a stand on anything like that. I just don't think I can help." His face was anxious. "I know him. Of course I do. But not so well that my opinion is going to be worth anything."

"You said he was a dangerous man."

Rees shrugged. "I should watch my tongue with you around," he said wryly. "Out of context but still an apt riposte. All right, so he's morose and easily irritated. He's not very sociable and prefers working alone."

"Potentiality for violence?"

"I'm a pathologist," he said irascibly, "not a bloody psychiatrist." The reflection of an explosion from the photographer's electronic flash illuminated his lean Celtic face for a micro-second.

"I know, Archie," Rogers said soothingly. "I'm not asking you to be."

A stubborn shake of the head. "Sorry, George. I'm no good at guessing."

"All right," he said mildly, "I only wondered whether you would confirm an opinion."

"I honestly wouldn't like to say." Rees changed the subject. "I suppose you're waiting for me to give you the cause of death?"

"It isn't scarlet fever?"

"———to you!" It wasn't Welsh but unadorned Anglo-Saxon scatology. Rees laughed with Rogers. The thought of the coming post-mortem examination was a warming one. Happiness for him was a scalpel and an unknown cause of death. "I'll know better," he said, "when I unzip him. It must have been a toss-up, though."

"Between?"

"Between dying from laceration of his brain and

haemorrhaging from the carotid." He indicated the curdled blood beneath the head. "Arterial, without question."

"Quick?"

Rees nodded. "Very much so."

"Not," he banged a fist into the open palm of his other hand, "like this?"

"No. A few moments. Enough to have him flounder around a bit."

"Retaliation?"

"Almost certainly not, although it depends on which injury was first."

"Say the eye."

He pursed his lips. "Doubtful."

"Don't commit yourself, Archie," he said sarcastically. "What about the throat?"

"Much more likely," he conceded, ignoring his friend's jibe. "He *could* have got one in himself."

"And in quick succession he'd get nothing in?"

Rees leaned over Drazek and, turning each of the stiff hands over, wagged his head. "No skinning. Nothing to indicate a fist fight."

"Well, Drazek—whatever his faults—wasn't the type to stand up like a paralysed rabbit and do nothing about being poked in the eye with whatever it was." He rasped his throat in irritation. "I can only imagine he let his arrogance put him off guard. But, dammit," he grumbled, "say it was an iron rod, a javelin, a rapier... any other kind of a weapon. He *must* have been on his guard. It just isn't up Drazek's street that he's going to let himself be stuck like a pig. Not him. Particularly not if the man doing it was Stronach. He only had to *see* Stronach to realize he wasn't going to be presented with the Croix de Guerre and palms."

"Perhaps his assailant"—the detective noted with amusement that Rees was determined in his neutrality—"had the weapon hidden. Wouldn't that make a difference? Wouldn't Drazek then be confident of his ability to resist an ordinary assault?"

Coltart approached Rogers. He was a huge black silhouette against the yellow dazzle of the flood lamps. His features were a pale blob, the expression undiscernible in the shadowed darkness. "No weapon," he grumbled in disgust. "No footmarks. Not a trace of anything. Nothing."

Rogers, knowing the capabilities of the formidable sergeant, could accept that the area around the body was as devoid of evidential marks and material as a swept floor. "All right, sergeant," he acknowledged, "keep it roped off for daylight."

"Can we move the body?"

Rogers looked at Rees. "Finished here, Archie?"

Rees nodded and two men, signalled by Coltart, carried forward a shallow coffin-shaped wooden tray. The body was fitted into a transparent plastic envelope and lifted into the waiting shell. It was painted a dull black and was less than a foot deep. Only Drazek's nose remained visible above the edge as it was humped into the waiting van.

It was still raining and moisture beaded the clothing of the silently busy men. It began to darken the dryness where Drazek's body had lain. From the sleeping town under the dark bowl of the night came faintly the noises of shunting trains and the occasional muted clangour from the late-working mills.

Rogers turned to Coltart. "Start a check on Drazek's movements this evening, will you?" he directed. "From the time he left his work until he was last seen." He looked towards the moving van. "From his suit it looks as if he'd had an evening out with one of his married girl-friends. I don't think he would otherwise get out of his overalls."

As Coltart turned and left, Rees spoke. "I take it you would like the examination tonight, George?"

"I'd be grateful."

"In about half-an-hour?"

"Can you delay it for an hour?" he asked him. "I must see how Lingard's progressing."

"Of course. No bother." He snapped shut the fastening of his bag and turned towards his car. "The best of luck, George."

"I'll need it," he acknowledged. "Yesterday I had a weapon with no body. Tonight, I've a body and no weapon."

Having tried unsuccessfully to contact Lingard by radio, Rogers ordered his driver to take him direct to High

Moor. The rain was increasing in intensity although, as if to compensate, there was a welcome chill in the atmosphere. The lights of the speeding car tunnelled twin holes of white brilliance into the darkness held between the parallel rows of blank-faced and shuttered stores, the curtained and sleep-silent terraces.

Lingard's car was in the driveway of Stronach's house. There were no signs of activity and the windows overlooking the front lawns and shining wet gravel were dark. As Rogers's car braked to a standstill, its dark blue nose dipping forward and the back rising, the slim raincoated detective climbed from his car and approached.

"A hell of a lot of masterly inactivity," Rogers observed drily, leaving his own vehicle and joining him. "What's happened? Or not happened?"

"Come off it, George," Lingard retorted with spirit. "Your leg's undermining your sense of proportion. You haven't yet heard what I have to say."

Rogers looked at him in surprise and then laughed loudly, his eyes creasing in good humour. "So tell me what epoch-making development has occurred."

"None." Lingard now looked a little sheepish, keeping his voice low and glancing at the upper windows. "The bastard's gone back to bed."

"Back!"

"I knocked at the door. Sounded like doom in this moribund road. A woman answered. Her sister, at a guess. She lives here with him. Fat, like the worthy doctor. Same nasty arrogant glitter in her eye and very formidable indeed. He came down then; dressing-gown, slippers and puce complexion. 'What the hell do you want?' he said." Lingard shielded his snuffbox from the falling rain, pinched some comforting grains and sniffed them into his nostrils. "I said I'd come from seeing Drazek dead. Clobbered by a person or persons unknown and thought he'd care to assist the police in their inquiries." He gave a short mirthless bark of laughter. "He was like a bloody schizophrenic chameleon. First he went the colour of a fish's belly. Then a beautiful plum purple, shading finally to his customary puce. Even his sister blenched and held on to the wall. Then he gobbled a bit and told me to shove off. Not," he said lightly, "in those exact words but to that effect. I started to argue and quote from Magna Carta but he was so obviously intent on bundling us out that I did the discretion bit." He gestured towards the car in the drive. "The radio's gone sick on me—hiccups or something—and I couldn't contact you. So I sent Vowden to telephone. Then the lights went out and here I am." He grinned, his teeth white in the darkness, but not so much at ease as he had wished to be. "Sorry, George. You warned me, I suppose. I didn't have much to go on and short of using violence on his fat person I had no option."

"It's all right, David," Rogers said, suppressing a desire to laugh. "You'll cope with characters like Stronach one day and think nothing of it." He chose his words carefully, not wishing to offend his junior. "I won't mention experience because it isn't precisely what I mean. It's not a narrow enough definition. It's the sum of having dealt with worse men, bloodier-minded men, than Stronach. Prickly bastards who have to be approached in different ways, using different kinds of tin openers to get under their skins. But which ever way it is, you've got to dominate them. If you don't, they'll dominate you. There's no neutrality in clashing personalities. Nor in investigating crime." His eyes were hard and, for a moment, his mouth grim, "I've never allowed another man to dominate me. Neither with his will nor with his muscles. I've fought any that tried. On the level they wanted it; mental or physical. The important thing is to be well-bolted together by self-confidence. And to possess a mind without doubts about the rightness and necessity of our job. The world's a jungle, David, and don't you forget it. Without us it would be a chaos running in blood." He smiled suddenly. "I won't say 'watch me' but I'll lay odds Stronach will at least be listening to us within a very few minutes."

"You appreciate you've probably more information than I have," Lingard said pointedly.

"Not a lot, David. Nor does it matter." He clamped his teeth hard on the mouthpiece of his pipe. "I'm not being critical so don't take umbrage."

He swung on his heel, scoring a depression in the gravel of the drive, and pushed hard with his thumb at the white bell-tit at the side of the door.

Deep inside the brooding house a bell vibrated

metallically and a dog barked. Then a long silence. Rogers bared his teeth at the door and seized the ring of the lion-headed brassknocker in his fist. His banging reverberated along the sleeping road and sent the dog into a paroxysm of baying. An upper window suddenly rattled open and a pale full moon of a face glared down at the two men. Until she spoke, Rogers had thought the figure that of Stronach.

"Go away," she hissed, her voice venomous, "or I'll call the police."

"We are the police, madam," Rogers called up to her sternly, "and we wish to speak to Doctor Stronach on a matter of the utmost importance. Be good enough to call him for me."

"Come back in the morning, damn you." The window slammed down and the dog renewed his howling.

"She's lost Stronach the moral advantage he had," Rogers observed complacently. "She departed from the accepted norm of outraged citizenry in damning us."

"And that helps?" Lingard queried.

"If it gives her a feeling of guilt, it does." Rogers pursed his lips and whistled softly a passage from *The Pirates of Penzance*. He grasped the knocker and hammered it balefully. "Mrs. Kitcher also threatened to set the police on us," he said ruminatively. "I wonder what it is about us that invites such maledictions."

A light snapped on in the room from which the woman had spoken to them, being followed almost immediately by a reflected glow through the crack under the outside door. A bolt slid sharply along, was slammed in its socket and the door opened.

She was bulky in a vivid-green silk robe from underneath which her slippers sported large yellow pompons, overblown chrysanthemums of fine wool. Her hair, the light brown of dried grass, was drawn and held tight to each side of her shiny face by thin blue ribbons. She was younger than her brother and, Rogers thought, wore the look of a woman deserted by luck and a couple of husbands. Her flesh was sagging along the line of the jawbone and she possessed the spuriously healthy bloom of a large woman. A man would take a great risk in hefting her on to his lap and Rogers, so far as he was concerned, didn't think it a likely eventuality.

One strong-fingered hand was clenched around the collar of the Afghan hound, now showing its irritation with deep chesty growls. It was obviously in no position to launch an attack. The woman's arm appeared capable of holding back a struggling rhinoceros.

When she spoke, her breath was an amalgam of sweet sherry and peppermint toothpaste. "I'll set the dog on to you," she said angrily, "if you don't stop this silly business."

He was curt with her. "Do that and I promise you that you'll be charged with assaulting a police officer."

She floundered, tried to say something wounding and failed. She flushed with mortification and tried again. "My brother isn't well. He's in bed and I won't have you disturb him."

Rogers produced his warrant card and held it out to her. "Read it," he commanded. "I want you to understand we are not selling vacuum cleaners—or whatever other nonsense you might dream up."

Her small grey eyes went from his face to the card. "I know already who you are." She showed clearly she wished to be rid of them.

"I'm making sure you do," he said shortly. "Now listen to me. We are investigating the murder of a man Drazek." Her lips tightened at the mention of the name. "I think Doctor Stronach can help us. Tonight. Not when you or he think it most convenient."

She glanced over her shoulder and hesitated, pulling the restive dog closer to her side. "I'll ask him," she said and stepped backwards. She endeavoured to close the door between them but Rogers's foot, solidly against its base, held it immovable.

"We'd better wait inside," he said urbanely. "The neighbours are beginning to peek." He entered the hall and Lingard followed him.

Although her lips were compressed to a pink thinness and her eyes hated them, she said nothing, departing through the door at the end of the hall, pulling the dog along with her. She returned almost immediately without the Afghan and mounted the stairs, holding up the amplitude of her robe like the flounces of a crinoline. From behind and below she had the hindquarters of a carthorse.

The two men stood stolidly, their faces held expressionless with official rigidity. When the yellow pompons had vanished round the bend in the stairs, Rogers stepped swiftly over to the crossed foils displayed on the wall. Easing them partially away from their base he inspected the fine wiring holding them together and then the surface of the leather-padded grips. He wiped the pad of his right forefinger on his handkerchief, looked at it and drew it carefully along the length of one blade. He examined the finger, wiped it again on his handkerchief and repeated the process on the remaining foil. He removed a small folding lens from his pocket and, through it, studied the blunted ends of the two blades.

Lingard looked at him, apparently incurious, although his eyes were absorbing every fact, each movement. "Not with those," he observed. "Too flexible."

Rogers scowled and shook his head. He looked closely at the coat stand, noting the bowler and the deerstalker hats, the crumpled brown trilby with the stained band; the fawn tweed coat and the stiff-skirted tan mackintosh; the assortment of walking sticks and the hanging leather dog leads. He silently pushed the coats to one side, checking against his original observation. He rubbed his hands together and said, "Ah!" to himself.

Lingard said, "It's missing." He beamed at Rogers.

"You noticed?" The older man was surprised.

"Christ, George! I'm no Watson to your Holmes, you know. Sometimes," he said tartly, "I'm way ahead."

Rogers grunted. It was difficult to define the mood prompting it.

She descended the stairs, walking lightly for one carrying the weight of flesh she did, finding them motionless in the positions in which she had left them. "My brother cannot get up," she said stiffly. "He is not feeling well but will see you." She said it as if she thought her brother a witless moron.

"Not well?" Rogers meant it to sound sardonic and disbelieving. Which it did. "This was sudden, wasn't it?"

She stared at him with antipathy, her pale eyes

protuberent in doing so. "If he had any sense at all he would refuse to see you."

"Are you his guardian?" The woman was nettling them both. "If he says he will see us, please show us up and don't waste our time being obstructive."

She swivelled around, her foot lifting out of her slipper as she did so. Her face was a furious red. "A solicitor," she gobbled. "He's sent for a solicitor."

Rogers was unimpressed. "I'll discuss it with him."

They followed her up the stairs, past an open door framing a shower curtain and a glass shelf of jars of bath crystals. It smelled damply warm and perfumed. There was a condensation on its mirror-lined walls. She rapped softly on the adjacent door, leading to a room overlooking the rear of the house. Stronach's voice answered. "Come in," it said irritably.

Rogers followed the broad back of the woman through the door. She was fierce-eyed and angry. "I'm sorry, Leslie," she panted, "but you oughtn't to see them."

Stronach was a stranded pink porpoise on a tumbled shore of white linen, his blue eyes brooding at the two detectives. He was well enough in appearance and, until disturbed, had been writing on a small notepad. His bedroom was booklined and heavily curtained. There were two easy chairs bulging beneath flowered cretonne. A bed-high earthenware amphora, overflowing with a pink and green tangle of ivyleafed geraniums, stood slim on an iron support in one corner. Three fat lamps with jade drum-shaped shades cast small islands of light on the plain apricot carpet. One of these threw brilliance on the white hair and pink flesh of Stronach.

He had been smoking and a cigarette, resting in an ash tray on a small table at the side of his bed, was spiralling grey smoke to the ceiling. Near it was a tumbler of water and a few pink tablets.

"Good morning," Rogers said briskly. "I'm sorry you couldn't come down to see us."

Stronach put the notepad under his pillow. "What do you want?" His eyes were challenging but within, Rogers saw, lurked a tiny black spider of fear. Although he spoke strongly, his thick throat jerked as he did so. He inclined his head at Lingard. "I thought I'd made it clear to him," he said.

"Clear but not final," Rogers answered.

"I'm to be subjected to interrogation then?"

"How dam' right you are," Rogers replied aggressively. "Are you above being questioned?"

"I am not required to answer."

"We know that," he said witheringly, "although it might well be a matter for comment elsewhere. It may also suggest you have something to hide."

Stronach looked at his sister. "When you hear Purslove knock," he ordered, "show him up, will you?"

"Your solicitor, I assume?"

"Yes." He was pulling up the drawbridge, preparing to fight all the way. The woman crossed to the side of his bed and sat down. She was more apprehensive than her brother. The two were remarkably alike in feature and build.

"You thought you'd need one?"

"I think I'd better wait until he is here before I say any more."

"Do you want us to conduct the interview here?" Rogers embraced the bedroom with an unfavourable regard.

Stronach inclined his head. "If you insist on seeing me against my will, yes."

"I'd prefer it to be downstairs," Rogers said coldly. He thought there was something defenceless about a man in bed. Or something royal. He was not proposing to subject himself to either inhibition. "A man cannot evade being asked proper questions merely by denying the investigating officer access to himself. You need not answer my questions unless you wish to do so but I have the right—and the duty—to ask them."

"You forced your way in."

"Rubbish," Rogers snorted. "If you think we did, no doubt Purslove will not be backward in advising you of your redress. Personally, I think you are talking nonsense." He paused. "You've already been told by Inspector Lingard of the reason for our inquiry. Are you now prepared to tell him where you spent last evening?"

"I do not wish to answer any questions unless my solicitor is present." He said this in a monotone.

"As you wish," Rogers said. "I'm happy to wait for him."

It was a quiet watch-ticking wait of only a few minutes before the sharp smacking of the door knocker was heard.

Purslove was a pot-bellied and shabby man with a narrow face peering out from behind heavy slab-sided spectacles. His sandy-grey hair was unruly, his neck-tie crooked and his white collar crumpled. His lips and ears were mauve and he breathed in short rasping puffs. He walked with a slight stoop and smelled strongly of stale cigarettes and iodoform. He looked at Rogers and Lingard without friendliness. He was given a chair by Stronach's sister.

When he had recovered his breath he said to Rogers, "I would like a word in private with my client."

Rogers, maintaining a stiff formality with this man whom he neither liked nor respected, turned and, without speaking, left the room with Lingard.

Downstairs, pacing the confining hall, they waited. From above, they could hear the low rumble of Stronach's voice, the mellifluousness of Purslove's and the occasional tart querulousness of the woman's. Neither man spoke but waited in companionable silence, Rogers reflectively blowing pipe smoke to the curlicued ceiling, Lingard sniffing softly. Occasionally Rogers banged the plaster on his leg with the heel of his palm to relieve the irritation.

When they heard the bedroom door open they moved to the foot of the stairs, stopping when they saw a dressing-gowned and pyjama'd Stronach, preceded by Purslove, descending. The sister was not with them.

"My client," the solicitor said, pulling at his heavy moustache, "recognizes fully your right to seek an interview with him and is prepared to listen to you." He stood to one side and Stronach, silent and flint-faced, led the way to his study.

"The slippery bastard's only conceding the inevitable," Rogers said in an undertone to Lingard.

In the study, Purslove was brisk. "Sit down, gentlemen," he said, his smile wintry. "It's late and I'm sure none of us wishes to prolong the interview." He looked at Rogers inquiringly.

Easing his leg to a comfortable position, Rogers waved

a hand towards his assistant. "Inspector Lingard sought the interview."

Purslove directed his exposed dentures towards Lingard who smiled blandly back. Adjusting his shirt cuffs and hitching his tweed trousers at the knees he made himself ready. Despite his previous exposure to the rain and his inability to change, he was still neat and well-pressed.

He looked at Stronach, seated magisterially at his desk. He addressed himself to him, his voice toneless and deliberately without expression. "A man Drazek was found dead tonight in Housman Park." He kept his blue eyes fixed on the fat man. "He was murdered. Spiked through the eye and throat." Somewhere at the back of the house the dog barked. Nobody spoke, all waited. Longard continued. "Drazek was a friend of your late wife, doctor. I hope I need not elaborate on the logic of our visit: nor the reason why I am asking you to account for your movements last evening."

Purslove stirred in his chair and rustled the papers he held. "You need not do so, Stronach," he said. "In fact, I advise you not to."

Stronach swivelled his pudding of a face towards the solicitor. "Shut up, Purslove. I don't mind playing chess with the inspector."

Rogers intervened, his head thrust forward, his eyebrows a hard black bar over the angry eyes. "There's a man in the mortuary, doctor, with one eyeball on his cheek and a hole in his neck. I don't suppose *he* would call that a game of chess. Nor," he said with emphasis, "do I." His voice was admonitory. "Don't treat murder as a game, doctor. A man's dead and we are charged with the responsibility of seeking his killer."

Purslove looked reproachfully at Stronach but said nothing. The fat doctor grunted his disdain, although a flush of colour was discernible on his cheeks.

Lingard continued. "I'm waiting for Doctor Stronach to say he wasn't in Housman Park."

"I have already advised my client not to . . ."

Lingard cut him short. "When I ask Doctor Stronach a question I expect him either to answer it or to refuse. Not to have you do his talking for him."

Two splotches of pink dappled Purslove's sallow face.

"How dare you," he snapped. "How dare you say that to me."

"I do so deliberately," Lingard said sternly. "Advise him if you will. Don't talk for him as if he were a deaf mute." He turned to Stronach. "Doctor," he said, his words like catapulted pebbles. "Were you in Housman Park last evening?"

Stronach looked at the solicitor who once more bristled. "I protest at your attitude, inspector. This will not go unreported."

Lingard ignored him. "Well, doctor?"

Stronach compressed his lips. "No," he said flatly. "I was not."

"Were you out at all?"

"If I was, I have no intention of discussing it."

"Ask *me* where I spent the evening, doctor," Lingard said pleasantly, "and I'll tell you." His manner was engaging. "I haven't anything to hide, you see."

He waited. Purslove was fidgetting with his spectacles; Stronach sat passively, a contained look on his face. Neither rose to Lingard's mild baiting. "I mean," he continued, "if you spent the evening at home, or at your club, it isn't much of a secret to keep, is it?"

"My client wishes to reserve any statement as to his whereabouts for the appropriate authority," Purslove interjected.

Lingard's attitude was that he did not exist. He pinned Stronach with inquisitorial eyes. "Do you know the dead man?"

A pause. "I believe he might be a patient of mine."

"When did you last see him?"

"I cannot recall seeing him at all." He said this carefully.

Lingard was persistent. "Although he was a patient?"

"He could be on my books for years and never need so much as an aspirin." He said it contemptuously.

He was, Lingard observed, still treating the interview as a game of chess, moving his pieces of information with studied calculation. All right, he said to himself, if that's how you want it, see what you can do with my attacking queen. "Did you know," he said levelly, "he was associating with your wife?"

The others could almost hear the inward tension building up to straining sinews, bulging eyes and the slow creep of shocked lividity to Stonach's face. For a few moments his mouth gaped soundlessly and spittle ran down over his slightly bristled chin. Then he fought back within himself, his self-control as hard as adamantine. He shuddered a few times and spread his fat fingers on the maroon cloth of his lap as an index of his recovery. When he had stilled their palsy he reached sideways for the decanter of whisky and a glass. Before pouring himself an undiluted drink of the alcohol, he wiped his chin with a handkerchief. The whisky brought colour back to his flesh and he coughed at its harshness. Then he looked at Lingard, his face composed but with raw murder in his eyes.

"No, I did not," he articulated carefully. "Nor do I believe he was."

Purslove had removed his spectacles and was breathing on the lenses and rubbing them with a green silk handkerchief. "Unsupported, your statement could be slander," he said nastily.

Lingard turned on him. "Some of this must be laid at your door, Purslove. It gives me no pleasure to pursue this line of inquiry but your advice to Doctor Stronach precludes a more reasonable approach."

The solitor tightened his lips and blinked his eyelids. He looked warningly at Stronach but did not answer Lingard.

The detective stared at the doctor. There was pity in his expression. "I'm afraid you'll have to accept it as a fact of life," he said. "Unpalatable as it may be. I am not convinced that you did not suspect it. I'm sorry to bring it up but it *is* relevant to the deaths of both your wife and Drazek."

"I do not believe it." Stronach was stubborn in his loyalty.

Lingard shrugged. "That must be a matter for you to rationalize. It may be referred to at the inquest if the coroner thinks fit."

Purslove stepped in. "I'm sure the coroner will not require the evidence of any supposed association," he said soothingly, making an obvious effort to be pleasant. He smiled by stretching his lips. "We can rely on the discretion of the police in this."

"As I said, it will not be given unless it is relevant." Lingard was not to be cozened. He addressed himself to the doctor again. "Do you wish to say anything further?"

"No!" His refusal was explosive.

The hitherto silent Rogers snorted and, when Lingard had closed his notebook, rose. "If you've finished, David," he said.

"Our inquiries will continue," Lingard said to Stronach. He stood. "It may be necessary to see you again."

"In my presence," Purslove added.

Lingard turned his head and looked at him with unfriendly eyes. "If I want to see Doctor Stronach, I'll see him. I need no authority from you." He addressed Stronach. "Would you be good enough to see us to the door, doctor?"

Stronach, taken by surprise, pushed himself back from his desk and left the study, followed by the two detectives. The solicitor brought up the rear.

In the hall, Lingard caught Rogers's eye and his own asked a question. Rogers nodded. Approaching the coat stand they halted and removed their raincoats from it.

"One other matter, doctor," Rogers said, his voice casual. "Would you care to tell us where your umbrella is?"

The silence that followed was comparative only. It was a silence of muted sounds from the road outside; the purring of distant cars and the hissing of rubber treads on wet surfaces. It was the silence of the restless padding and whimpering of the Afghan hound in the room beyond; it was the unidentifiable creaking from upstairs and the shuffling movements from the woman in her room. It was the silence of a quiet clearing of the throat by a puzzled Purslove, the brittle scraping of the raincoat held by Lingard and the slight noise of Rogers's shoe tracing invisible arabesques on the olive carpet as he waited for Stronach's reply.

When it came it was anticlimactic. Although Stronach's face appeared composed, Rogers thought he could discern behind the mask a dark shadow of alarm. "I don't honestly know," he said. "I think I must have mislaid it." He did not ask the reason for the inquiry and this, to the two detectives, was more revealing than anything he had hitherto said or not said.

Rogers regarded him with dark eyes for a long time. Then, having obviously come to a well-considered decision, said shortly, "Goodnight, gentlemen." He swivelled quickly on his good leg and followed Lingard out through the door into the quiet waiting night.

16

With Rogers as a passenger, Lingard drove to the hospital, leaving Vowden—a silent dark figure in the shadows of High Moor—to record as best he could the activities of Stronach's disturbed household.

Rogers was chewing at his pain-killing tablets, cursing occasionally at the sensitivity of his leg to the bumping of the car. "I'll stay with Archie," he said to Lingard, "while he does the autopsy. I'd like you to check the park and Stronach's possible route. We've got to find that umbrella."

"Are you sold on it being the weapon?"

"I'm as sure as I'll ever be. Aren't you?"

Lingard smiled lopsidedly. "I had it all worked out, George. The means. The motive."

"Apart from his motive, his intent seems clear enough," Rogers observed. "Drazek was a man who had rogered his wife. Only the choice of a weapon seems fortuitous."

"Perhaps he meant only to savage him with his bare hands," Lingard suggested. "He was man enough to do it."

"He could be. An act of revenge?"

"Or loss of face?" Lingard suggested.

"Yes." A lot more violence-provoking than people imagine."

"Stronach might have thought Drazek had caused her death." Lingard trod viciously on the broke pedal as a cat streaked, brush-tailed, across the road in front of them and into the darkness of shrubbery. The car slid sideways, the tyres squealing like an anguished pig. Rogers swore vividly as his knee grated painfully.

When Lingard had wrestled the car under control, he was vinegary with him. "Christ, David, take it a bit easier, will you. You're not driving that bloody great Bentley of yours." He relaxed and returned to the subject of Stronach. "In the face of the post-mortem results he shouldn't be in any doubt. He's a medical man after all. Although," he admitted, "it would be natural for his emotions to cloud his judgement."

"He never batted an eyelid when you asked him about the umbrella." Lingard was changing rapidly and expertly through the gears, his eyes intent on the road before him.

"Perhaps the most significant reaction to the interview," Rogers said.

"God, yes. An innocent man—an unknowing man—would have said *something*."

"I'm expecting Archie to confirm the use of an umbrella." He sounded wholly confident. "By the way," he inquired, "what time did it start to rain?"

Releasing one hand from the steering wheel, Lingard pulled out his watch. It was an engraved silver fob, attached by means of a thin chain to a button on the waist-band of his trousers. He pressed a button on its rim and three tiny notes of a chiming bell sounded. "Say, about twelve-thirty?" he suggested.

Rogers nodded. "It started as I got into Coltart's car. Drazek must have died before then."

"The grass was dry under the body," Lingard reminded him.

"I know. It still gives Stronach a pretty wide field of time to manoeuvre in." He rattled his pipe stem between his teeth. "You noticed the coats were bone-dry?"

"Yes, I did. But conceivably there could have been another elsewhere."

"I suspect he wore no raincoat at all. Why should he? Even the prospect of rain needs nothing more than the carrying of an umbrella. I'm only surprised he didn't have a second one in the stand."

"I suppose that's the one thing he couldn't anticipate.

Or substitute at the last moment," Lingard said. "Nor could he foresee we had noticed he possessed one."

"Did you get a look at the heating?"

"Oil-fired. In the garage."

"So he can't easily burn the evidence." Rogers pressed his sound leg hard on the floorboards as the headlights reflected the moving twin emeralds of a cat's eyes. "Watch it, David," he rasped. "My bloody leg can't stand much more of your harebrained driving. Anyway," he went on, "the odds are that he disposed of the umbrella on his way home."

Lingard decelerated as he approached the entrance to the hospital forecourt, allowing the car to run silently to the main doors. "This good enough, George?"

"If you see Coltart, tell him where I am," he said. "He's out checking on Drazek." He limped over to the lake of light outside the doors, his swarthy face split by a grin. "If I see Bridget, I'll say you asked after her."

Lingard's answer was the snatching and squealing of his tyres as he took off into the darkness.

When Rogers opened the door to the mortuary, pushing aside the blue plastic curtains, Rees was already scissoring open Drazek's underclothing. Bridget Hunter, her serious eyes dark in the intensity of the reflected light, was helping him.

"You don't object, George?" Rees asked. "Bridget thought she could help. It's not every day we get one like our friend."

"By no means," Rogers said, eyeing her high-breasted body. "I would wish all pathologists had her attributes."

She looked at him levelly, not smiling. Her eyes had a disturbing glint in them and were the colour of a blackbird's beak. Her regard raised the hairs on the nape of his neck. "Don't flatter me pointlessly, George," she said. "It can be very dangerous." She meant every word she said.

He held her gaze for a few moments, licked his lips and walked over to Rees. "When he's ready, Archie," he said, "will you see how the ferrule of an umbrella would fit the injuries?"

Rees pulled out from under the body the last of the clothing. The limbs were stiff and awkward and made wooden thumping sounds when let drop on to the slab,

"I'll tell you now," he said. "Barring the unexpected, it will."

With Drazek naked, he fitted the disfigured head on to a wooden neck block and again reached for his scissors. Like a gourmet selecting a ripe grape he clipped the thread holding the eyeball, allowing it to drop into a glass phial held ready by Bridget. There, without a brain to give it expression, it stared uncomprehendingly from the shelf on which she placed it.

Selecting a scalpel from the small case held by Bridget before him, Rees pinched up a fold of flesh from under the chin and put the point of the blade on it. With the verve of a painter executing a familiar brush stoke, he drew the scalpel in one firm and unhurried sweep from the throat to the genitals, avoiding the navel with a practised twist of his wrist. When it was done the bisecting wound was a vast mouth of red tissue and yellow fat.

Concentrating on the throat and orbital socket, Rees and Bridget probed and dissected, talking their observations and conclusions into a miniature tape recorder propped at the foot of the slab.

Rogers, leaning his tired body against a wall, smoked his pipe thoughtfully, occasionally regarding Bridget with an amused expression. But, primarily, his thinking processes were strictly professional. Divided, they ran on parallel tracks; one leading to Dyson, the other to Stronach.

The rain had ceased to fall and the moon was sailing serene in a cobalt sea of ragged black islands. Far to the east, silhouetting the looming bulk of the moors, was the oyster-grey lightening of the false dawn. From somewhere within the park, a thrush fluted its waking-up noises.

Lingard, his raincoat thrown cape-like over his shoulders, was quartering the scene of Drazek's death. Using a portable floodlamp, he was applying his concentration to the flower beds and borders near by. He was searching for an umbrella, possibly thrust point downwards in the soil: a sombre spike of black cloth and wire, flowering into a horn blossom and concealing itself in a shrub or clump of blooms.

Six other detectives were similarly occupied in different parts of the sealed-off ground, their lights bobbing and disappearing in the darkness, insubstantial will-o'-the-wisps. Around the periphery of the scene, uniformed constables paced in the shadows like ponderous black storks, prepared to deny access to the idle and curious who would arrive with the coming of daylight.

Although the area would be searched again, Lingard was satisfied now in eliminating the park as a place of concealment. He was endeavouring to think as Stronach would with the blood of Drazek fresh on his hands. He heard from the dark mass of foliage above him the muted piping of the early-waking thrush. It provoked in his mind the small Bewick woodcut of a spotted thrust pulling a taut worm from the security of its tunnel in the soil. He halted suddenly, biting his lower lip and trying to recapture the misty thought that had entered his mind. Then it solidified and, retracing his path with quick and anxious steps, he returned to the place where Drazek had died.

On his knees—his folded raincoat between their trousered neatness and the wet ground—he scrutinized the turf methodically. The light from behind the shoulders of the moors was a spreading roseate pearl and the darkness dissolving into dawn before he found what he was looking for.

In the close-shaved turf, partially obliterated by a scuffing foot, were a number of small holes. The ferrule of an umbrella, jabbed into the ground, could produce similar holes. It would, Lingard thought, be a natural enough means of cleansing it of blood. Clearing the entrance to one hole of grass and mud, he folded his handkerchief over a ball pen and inserted it slowly and carefully until it reached the bottom. Twisting his crude swab in the hole, he withdrew it with equal care and examined it under the light of his lamp. He made a sharp sound of satisfaction in the back of his throat when, within the chocolate-brown smear of wet soil, he saw a smudge of red.

He called over a detective and ordered the covering and preservation of the holes. Then he walked from the park; apparently aimlessly but, in fact, projecting himself again into the mind of Stronach. He scrutinized the roofs of buildings as well as the areas and gardens abutting them. He noted bus stops, taxi ranks, alley-ways, walled gardens, public lavatories and private clubs. He saw and remembered accessible fall-pipes, manhole covers and the rubble and confusion of roadworks. He passed down into the town, breathing the clean fresh air left by the retreating night. A few isolated travellers were abroad, clumping hump-shouldered to the toil claiming their coming day. Threads of smoke were beginning to rise from chimneys and down in the basin of the town the buses were growling their early morning warm-up.

Lingard's chin was bristled with a golden nap of hair and his eyes were bloodshot and gritty with lack of sleep. The thought of scalding coffee, black and without sugar, was a constant companion.

He entered the labyrinth of cobbled streets and passed over the canal bridge, wincing as he thought of the anonymity of the black water, then reassured when he remembered that umbrellas float. All these places would be searched later that morning, systematically and meticulously, by teams of men seemingly endowed with second sight and eyes in their fingertips. Under the control of the cynical super-efficient Hagbourne they would retrieve the dross and debris of a careless, extravagant society. Possibly—with luck—one of them would whoop with success and produce from its place of concealment an umbrella with a boar's tusk handle.

And on the wickedly-pointed ferrule, Lingard anticipated, despite all the precautionary plunging of it into the soil, would be traces of human blood.

Drazek's.

Drazek was a hollow trough of flesh, far removed from the boisterous, lusting human being he had once been, when Coltart clumped into the mortuary. The sergeant glanced with disinterest at the body, creasing his face in greeting at Rees and Bridget and turned his back on them. He looked utterly spent and as he spoke to Rogers he rasped the back of his freckled fist on the bristles of his chin. There were lines of fatigue under his small green eyes.

Rogers had found a chair and was sprawled in it, his suffering leg supported stiffly on a low shelf. He removed his pipe from between his teeth and yawned, stretching movement back into the stiffness of his shoulders. "Tell me in telegrammatic prose," he said good-humouredly. "I'm in no mood for a saga."

"I've seen his wife," the large detective growled. "She took it pretty badly at first. Woke up all the kids and had a good howl."

He had explained to her as best he could, how her husband had died; softening it, endowing it with a daylight ordinariness, taking from it the raw horror of lacerated tissue and spilled blood.

After her initial weeping she had gradually contained her emotion, slapping the children to submission and putting them back to bed.

She had, when the tears dried, spoken to Coltart willingly enough. She had seemed to need a confidant. Her husband's lechering was no secret and she had accepted it with the resignation of a woman with five young children and no alternative means of providing for them.

She was a tall woman with heavy shoulders and buttocks. She was also pot-bellied with a pregnancy. Her black hair was as disordered as a used wire pot-scrubber. Disturbed from sleep, one side of her face was flushed. The flesh had retained much of its youthful smoothness although there was a pink scribbling of exposed capillaries under the throat. Her mouth, disfigured by the loss of teeth, had still the pouting weakness that had betrayed her into repeated motherhood.

She had pulled a shabby brown coat over her nightdress and put a pair of day shoes on her feet. Her legs were hairy and Coltart noticed the dark shadow of dirt in the hollows of the anklebones. She smoked a cigarette without removing it from between her lips, coughing with the hard-edged bark of the addict.

A neighbouring housewife, called in by Coltart, sat in the room with them, making occasional clucking noises of sympathy.

Her husband had, she said, returned from his work the previous evening and changed into his best suit, not staying for the meal she had prepared for him. This, Coltart noticed, was still on the crowded kitchen table. A plate piled high with crusted potatoes, dried-up beans and congealed lumps of pale meat set amongst unwashed crockery and a jumble of milk bottles and cereal packets.

He had shuddered his distaste at the scene of domestic dirt and disorder. The gritty tarred-paper linoleum with its accumulation of food debris around its edges: the pimpled, blotched woodwork of the cheap furniture and the items of limp, casually-washed clothing on the string line stretched across the room, all underlined her sluttishness. The ash-filled grate, dead since some nameless day in early spring, was littered with stained and screwed-up paper, cigarette ends, tangles of her hair and metal bottle caps. The empty bottles from which they had been removed were stacked skittlelike beneath the table. At the one narrow window was a torn and dingy lace curtain. The glass was smeared with the rubbings of small filthy hands and through it, dimly illuminated by the light from within, he could see the constricting closeness of lime-washed brick walls and dismal sheds.

She had shown a brief pride in her husband's prowess with other women. "Course," she said, "you 'ad to 'and it to the bleeder. 'E could do anything with those silly fancy women 'e knocked around with." She looked outraged. "The cows *paid* 'im. They must a' been bleeding mad." A short mirthless laugh "Jesus! *I'd* a' paid 'im! I never 'ad any bloody option. Not when he'd 'ad a skinful, I 'adn't."

"You knew the last woman he was going out with?"

"The one 'oo was dead? The one 'e was nicked for?"

"Yes. You know her name?"

"No." She had been grim about it. "But I knew 'er scent. 'E used to come 'ome stinking like a polecat with it. That and gin. That's 'ow I always knew." Her pride had risen to the surface again. "But 'e always wanted me anyway. 'E 'ad to 'ave me whatever." She pulled the old coat around herself in a scornful gesture.

Then she said, "What's going to 'appen to the kids?" and he had mumbled something about relatives and a widow's pension, tailing off into embarrassment. He had thankfully handed her over to the neighbour, removing himself quickly from the oppressive atmosphere of a woman's sorrow.

Afterwards, Coltart said, he had hammered up the landlord of The Bessemer Arms. The latter had been considerably less than co-operative but the big sergeant had been brusque and imperative, requiring clear answers to his questions. When he got them, none of them helped. Drazek had not visited the premises the previous evening and the prickly little landlord had not seen him.

To Rogers, Coltart was apologetic. Murder or not, there was a distinct limit to the number of unoffending citizens he could prise from their beds. Until daylight, there was little chance of tracing the movements of the dead man. It was his opinion, he said, that Drazek was in the park either to do a Peeping Tom on couples or to pick up a dog-walker.

Rogers was inclined to agree. Both men had, in their turn, patrolled by dark the town's parks. They were familiar with the phenomena of the dog-walkers; strolling casually or walking briskly, weaving silent patterns around the lamplighted periphery of the gloomy jungle of damp grass and weeping shrubbery.

There were those who made a ritual of their dog's needs, chewing glumly over the day's monotonies as they did so. But there were others to whom it was an escape, a release from the yawning boredom of over-familiar faces and from bodies as stale as old newspapers. So then there was a departure from the staid pattern of walking to a conspiratorial commingling of tweed skirts and flat shoes with prosperous horn-rimmed spectacles and medicated mouthwashes; a whining of bored dogs with grinning mouths and imploring tails.

Also, in the whispering blackness of the parks, middle-aged women used their snuffling, leaking pets to escape for an hour or two from indifferent husbands, seeking chance solace in their boredom. To men like Drazek, they were a fertile field for exploitation. To the women, these easy-speaking and virile men were separated from their bridge playing and dinner parties by a gulf wide enough not to pose any later problem of embarrassing recognition.

"Might he not be meeting a woman there?" Rogers suggested.

"He could. He had a clean collar on for it," Coltart said. "But I'm more inclined to him being freelance for the evening."

"And being followed by Stronach?"

"Yes."

Rogers considered this. "He'd have to be on his own before Stronach would tackle him," he said finally. "It could mean he hadn't been with a woman or, having been, had left her."

He got up from his chair and limped across to Rees. "Just a thought, Archie," he said. "Would you mind checking for lipstick marks on him? And alcohol in the stomach."

Rees nodded to Bridget who moistened a dab of cotton wool with a spirit and began swabbing the pale mouth with small scrubbing motions.

Rogers indicated the scarred face. "Injuries and excisions excepted," he said to her, "is he someone women would be attracted to?"

Having completed her task, he stood back and looked at Drazek. "A serious question, George?"

"Yes. Choose the likeliest age group."

She moved over towards the bench and inspected the cotton wool under a low-power hand-lens. "Nothing on here," she said. "He couldn't have had a successful evening or she didn't use it."

"There's alcohol in his stomach," Rees intervened. "Gin from the smell of it. But not a lot."

Bridget returned to the body but her eyes were on Rogers. "At my age, I wouldn't." She put a finger on the scar and pulled it sideways, making the mouth grimace. "A cicatrix like this would be off-putting. To a teenager, it might seem a protest against something or other and she'd be attracted on that score." Her eyes were holding Rogers, allowing him to look deep into her if he chose. "Knowing about Mrs. Stronach as I do it might be presumed to colour my judgement. On the other hand, it may only confirm it." Her eyes dropped to the dead face. "This is a man for the middle-aged romantic. This," she ran her finger down the length of the scar, "would be the excuse for initial sympathy. Then it would provoke excitement."

"A badge of rakish masculinity?" Rogers suggested.

"Something like that," she agreed. "Add a soupçon of sweat and a hairy chest and it would titillate them for sure." She pushed the stiff mouth to its original position. "It's not easy for me to see a man from the viewpoint of a younger or older woman. I only know for certain those whom I prefer."

"But you don't disquality him from being a comfort to the Mrs. Stronachs of High Moor?"

"Not when they want comforting, George," she said.

Rees straightened his back and walked to the sink. He stripped off his rubber apron, his overalls and yellow gloves in that order, nudging on the long-handled tap and soaping himself to a germ-free sterility.

"An umbrella it could be," he said briskly. "Among a couple of dozen similarly shapen weapons."

"But you'd accept an umbrella did it," Rogers pressed him, "if you had your arm twisted hard enough?"

Rees laughed. "I would that," he said. "Just at the threat of it."

17

A scalding shower, a shave and a change of linen produced in Rogers a marked enough appetite for breakfast. At The Bar Grill he joined Lingard who, despite the morning's promise of continued heat, wore a waistcoat; a figured silk confection in spinach green with polished jade buttons.

The fragrant black coffee produced in them a feeling of well-being and tranquillity; a confidence and optimism for the day's tasks ahead of them. Through the leaded lozenges of the window, the morning sun cast bars of golden daylight on to their table, splashing gloss on the linen and reflecting points of brightness from the silver coffee service.

Making his leg comfortable, Rogers remarked that it was about time the sawbones responsible for plastering him up to the eyebrows saw fit to remove it. "I'm getting considerably fed up with being perambulated around like an old woman," he complained fractiously. "No disrespect intended, David, but you drive like a paranoic schizoid. I'll be happier," he finished ambiguously, "avoiding my own accidents."

Rogers's own car was humped and compound-lensed,
a shiny red beetle of a car. Typically, he was hypercritical
of its performance, demanding the impossible from it,
expecting it always to function unfalteringly at maximum
power with a subdued hum of ordered and flawless eupho-
ria. Unlocated squeaks and incurable rattles provoked in
him quite inexcusable outbursts of irritation.

And he was thus with his department. His men were
out now, unflagging in their efforts, combing the route
indicated by Lingard, searching for Stronach's umbrella.
Stronach himself had not been forgotten. The man reliev-
ing Vowden was even then watching the house from the
anonymity of a plain van. So far, the place was a brooding
blankness; the only daytime activity being the snatching in
of the milk by an unidentified arm. Purslove had been
noted leaving the house an hour after the two detectives;
hump-shouldered and choking away at a cigarette. His
grey car had been parked outside another's house and this
was characteristic of the man's deviousness.

Over the packing away of the peppered ham and
eggs, they discussed the search. "I think, David," Rogers
was saying, "we are more likely to find it by applied logic
than by physical effort."

"If he hasn't completely destroyed it."

Rogers sucked at his teeth. "We have to accept he
hasn't. Otherwise we might just as well go home to bed."

"Why don't I shut up?" Lingard murmured to himself. To Rogers, he said, "We know he didn't use his car.
Are we equally satisfied he didn't walk?" He reached
across the table for the Worcester sauce.

"I wouldn't think he's the type to walk far. He didn't
drive his car for obvious reasons. What about a taxi?"

"Already being checked but, so far, no record or
knowledge." He frowned at his plate, wondering if he had
not been overgenerous with the sauce.

"Assume he did," Rogers said. "He could conceal it
somewhere inside."

"Under the rear seat?" Lingard looked doubtful. "Even
the most lumpish of them check there. I understand it's
better than having a one-armed bandit in the back. None
the less," he promised, "I'll have every taxi scrupulously
searched this morning."

"Thinking like Stronach, though, I'd judge it a reasonably safe place. And it doesn't have to go go under the seat. There must be other places. Still, we'll soon know," Rogers said philosophically. "What about the buses?"

"Assuming Drazek was killed between ten and eleven, they'd be running." He looked doubtful. "Can you see Stronach buying a shilling return and being squeezed in between a load of fish and chips; being puked on by the occasional drunk?"

"Look at it from his point of view, David," Rogers argued, cutting his ham vigorously. "He knows that to take a taxi is to invite identification. Even not knowing him, who could forget a man with his build and appearance?"

"The same arguments could apply to him taking a bus," Lingard objected.

"Not really. You said yourself there would be a load on, including drunks. Sitting—probably on the upper deck—he would be as anonymous as the conductor was busy."

"So where could he conceal the umbrella?"

"He wouldn't. Or needn't," Rogers corrected himself. "Why not just leave it there? To a casual inspection it's an umbrella. No blood. Nothing. It's going to be either commandeered by a dishonest passenger or handed in at the depot as found property." He forked a fragment of ham into an egg yolk and then into his mouth. "In the first event, there is nothing more concealing than a guilty conscience. It would probably mean goodbye to the umbrella. In the second, it's one item in a hundred or so others. Due to be sold by auction several months too late for us to do anything about it."

"I'll add the depot to my growing list of commitments," Lingard said wryly. "Incidentally, I noticed a pub or two en route." He pushed his empty plate away and refilled his coffee cup.

Rogers cocked a black eyebrow. "That's a possibility, David," he said approvingly. "Elaborate."

"Assume our obese friend did his dirty work before eleven," he said. "He could visit any public house in the area for a whisky. What easier than to lose his umbrella in the bar? Or to leave it in the entrance? Most of them have an umbrella or coat stand." He held up his hand, palm outwards in mock protest at Rogers who held his cup motionless in surprise. "Don't say it, George," he laughed. "I'll have them checked. Also," he added, "the clubs he'd have to pass. You wouldn't have to be overly bold to step inside on some excuse and leave your umbrella in the foyer."

"See what I mean," Rogers exclaimed complacently, "about brains versus brawn?" He grunted. "I expect we will both be comfounded in the end by one of the chaps finding it stuffed up the rear end of a mechanical digger. It's a racing certainty that unless we *do* find it, there's no case against Stronach." He changed the subject. "We mustn't run the risk of forgetting Dyson. Although I'm beginning to think the knife must be something of a red herring."

"Or a white elephant?"

"Damn it, David. We *must* have heard of an unnatural death by now."

"I'd have thought so," Lingard agreed. "We've covered every conceivable line of inquiry. Even some inconceivable ones." He brushed snuff grains from his tie with a maroon silk handkerchief.

"I forgot to show this to you," Rogers said. He suddenly heaved with laughter and produced a folded paper from his pocket. "A report from Quandom. Belated but worth reading." His brown eyes sparkled as he handed it over and watched Lingard reading it.

The blond man finished scanning the paper and then laughed with him. "Coloured aspirins and dried foxglove leaves!" he said. "He couldn't be *that* stupid!"

"He could," Rogers assured him. "And he was. The only genuine thing about it was the hemp seeds. You can buy them anywhere as bird seed." He laughed again. "He was getting high only in his imagination. And paying two shillings for a dyed aspirin and five for a mixture of compost and canary seeds into the bargain."

"So no offence?"

"Not unless we charge the supplier with false pretences." He took the report back from Lingard, replacing it in his pocket. "I think we can accept that young Otter is now a changed man. Circumstances and his father have seen to that." He dismissed him. "I've arranged to see Hoggart this morning. In my office."

"Another cheese and wine party?"

"Not so that you would notice. This time," Rogers promised, "I don't think I shall be quite so polite." He looked pointedly at his assistant's plate. "Now that you've finished stuffing yourself, perhaps you'll motor me back to the office."

"Do you want me to strap you in?" Lingard asked with exaggerated concern. "Or would you rather I crawled along in second gear?"

Rogers reached the station only minutes before the arrival of an oleaginous Hoggart. With the anxious man sitting opposite him and drawing hard at the inevitable cigarette, the swarthy detective assembled and advanced his strategical questions.

"I'm still digging away, Mr. Hoggart," he opened cheerfully, "and there are a few minor oddments left to be cleared."

"And I'm only too anxious to assist, Mr. Rogers," he assured him. He exposed his dentures in a show of good citizenship.

"Thank you. I knew I could rely on you," Rogers said, as insincerely as he judged Hoggart to be. "How is Mrs. Dyson?" Hoggart rubbed his hands together. They made a tiny, dry rasping noise. "Very well. Very well indeed."

"Better than when you saw her at Spye Green Crescent last night?"

A complex of different emotions patterned his face, finally suffusing it to a bright pink. He was a man who coloured easily. He lowered his eyes to the backs of his hands and cleared his throat. Then he grinned with an assumption of a frankness his eyes belied. "I'm sorry. I should have told you before. I was going to," he said. "I would have but...you know. It wouldn't have done Mrs. Dyson any good."

"Or you?"

His laugh at this was hollow. "There was nothing...it was all quite innocent...."

Rogers, without taking his eyes from Hoggart, filled the bowl of his pipe with shreds of tobacco, letting the unspeaking silence discompose the man opposite. Through his office window drifted the noise of a town getting into first gear; the preliminary sub-notes of awakening industry. When he had got his pipe burning smoothly he returned to the attack.

"Did you remain long enough to help her?" he asked.

"I waited while she telephoned. There wasn't really anything——"

"Just blood and things," Rogers said remotely. "A wounded woman who might have bled to death. Or been shot at again."

He was pink once more. "She said she was all right. Really, Mr. Rogers," he protested, "you make me sound——"

The detective was bland. "I do?" I thought the circumstances did that." He put a second match to the tobacco in his pipe, still pinning the man with his steady gaze. "So then you ran for it?"

"I didn't run . . . I went. Under the circumstances——"

"You mean the innocent ones?" Rogers said, not disguising his sarcasm. "You left her injured because you had nothing to conceal?"

Hoggart bit his lip. "It's not what things are, Mr. Rogers, but what they seem to be."

"As, for example, two gold-tipped cigarette ends in the bedroom?" After waiting abortively for an answer to this, he smacked his pipe down hard on the blotting-pad. "Do you want me to go on? Proving your association detail by detail?"

The translucent skin was a candlewax sallowness and the eyes hated Rogers. "I don't mind what you do," he said in a strangled effort at speaking with confidence.

"*You* are the man Dyson was looking for," Rogers said flatly. "His chummy little confidant. You had it all fixed up neatly, didn't you? No doubt encouraging him to take time off from work to do it." He hawked his disgust. "The poor bloody fool."

The colourless lips moved soundlessly and the vibrating, smoke-stained fingers shredded a cigarette to a paper-and-tobacco ruin. He shook his head, not answering.

Rogers was openly contemptuous. "As you wish. If necessary, I could prove it easily enough." He referred to a written note on his desk. "I saw you arrive in a grey Jaguar?" He quoted its registration number.

"Yes."

His crooked finger tapped hard on the piece of paper. "It has been observed on a number of occasions outside Mrs. Dyson's house." He paused, hardening his voice for emphasis. "In the daytime." He noted the widening of the pupils as he made his point.

Hoggart levered himself up from his chair and moved like a stunned man to the open window. He gripped the sill with bony, whitened knuckles, taking deep lungfuls of the morning freshness. After a while the slim shoulders dropped and he turned round to face his interrogator. His face was composed, his colour nearly normal. "I'm sorry," he said. "I've been a fool but if it's not too late I'd like to help." He resumed his seat and lit himself a cigarette.

Rogers watched him, saying nothing. He puffed contemplatively at his pipe.

"It's true," Hoggart said, "that Anne and I are . . . were lovers." He swallowed several times in embarrassment. "It started so simply . . . casually, not intentionally. I called one evening . . . some weeks ago now . . . to collect a file of papers from Dyson. I knew Anne already. Our families had dined together." He lowered his eyes. "Dyson was out and she came down from the bathroom in a towel robe thing. She asked me in and somehow she never got around to getting properly dressed. You could say what happened was accidental." He flushed as he saw a smirk on Rogers's face. "I'm sorry it amuses you," he said shortly.

It was Rogers's turn to be discomfited. "I'm sorry, Mr. Hoggart," he said. "Forgive me. But I took leave to doubt that what happened was accidental." He was thinking of Mrs. Dyson's exposure of herself in the hospital. "Please go on."

"I was going to say that I suppose if it hadn't been me it would have been somebody else." He put the gold tip of the cigarette between his lips and drew deeply at it. For a moment he looked complacent. "A rewarding experience, Mr. Rogers, when you are knocking on fifty."

"I'll let you know one day," Rogers muttered to

himself. Aloud, he said, "Why were you doing afternoon matinées?"

A slim hand arched itself, seeking understanding. "With Dyson at work . . . you understand?"

"I would be singularly obtuse not to," Rogers commented. "Right, Mr. Hoggart." His voice hardened again. "Who was Dyson knocking off? It's about time you told me."

The slim man flinched. "That I *don't* know. Honestly. I knew he was seeing a woman. But no more."

"How?"

"He told me. Ambiguously, not directly," he said. "Anne told me as well."

"She knew?"

"Only as any woman knows when her husband is sleeping in another's bed." Hoggart pulled at one of his ear lobes. "Something in his expression . . . a lack of interest in her as a woman. I don't suppose I need to spell it for you?"

"Not really." Rogers allowed himself a dig at the man. "I take it your own wife must be similarly percipient? About you?"

Hoggart looked at him long without expression. "If she does, I wouldn't know. Or," he said roughly, "care."

Rogers smiled tightly. "All right. Tell me about Dyson's mistress. Have you any idea of her identity at all? Whether she's married? Single? Living locally?"

He was tapping his fingers on the desk, anxious to be away. "I had the distinct impression she was married."

"He didn't say so?"

"No. Nor did I want him to. His confidences were becoming distasteful . . . embarrassing."

"Anything else?"

"She lives in the town . . . high up, I believe."

"You mean High Moor?"

He shook his head positively. "No. The building was tall. A top flat . . . something like that. It wasn't what he actually said but the inferences I got."

"Has he a desk or table?" Rogers asked.

"A desk. And I've looked in it already. There's nothing but his experimental calculations. Stuff like that."

"Did you see him last night?"

"God, no!" Hoggart was visibly disturbed. "The first

thing I knew was this dreadful bang and poor Anne screaming."

"Didn't you look out of the window?"

Hoggart stubbed his cigarette end into an ash tray. "I'm not too much of a coward, Mr. Rogers," he said firmly, "but then neither am I a bloody fool. I was . . . I was naked for a start and not overly ambitious to have my face blown off." He hesitated. "It needs the proper clothing and a righteous mind to be courageous, Mr. Rogers." For the first time the detective responded to his smile.

"I see no bandaging," he said. "Didn't you pick up a puncture or two?"

"Surprisingly, no." He withdrew another cigarette from his case and lit it. He ravished tobacco rather than smoked it.

"Mrs. Dyson received her pellets in the back." He said it woodenly, making it more of an accusation than a comment.

Hoggart cleared his throat and sucked his cheeks in at the cigarette. He lowered his eyelids and said nothing.

"Was the bedroom light on?" Rogers asked.

The eyelids came up. "She had a thing about . . . about being in the dark. Not being able to see." He smiled ever so slightly. "It was like perf . . . being in an aquarium."

"So it was on?"

"Yes."

"You don't know who fired at you?"

Astonishment creased his face. "Of course I do. It was Dyson."

"We might infer it was," Rogers corrected him. "But we can't be certain. It would have to be proved." He paused. "Assuming it was, doesn't that give you something to worry about?"

"I'm sorry. I don't understand."

"You told me yourself Dyson was proposing to shoot the man sleeping with his wife." Rogers scowled at him. "Last night's shot might have been an attempt to do it."

The dark eyebrows lifted. "You think he knows?"

"How the hell would I know," Rogers snapped. "He wasn't shooting at Halley's Comet, that's certain."

"You think Dyson would do that to *me*?"

"Don't look to me for assurances," Rogers growled. "It

so happens I think he would. Business colleagues and lodgers are among the world's most popular targets for cuckolded husbands. Anyway, I thought sufficiently seriously about your chances to put a guard on your house during the night."

"You did?" Hoggart was startled, his mouth a ring of dismay. "Oh, God!"

"Damn it. You can't be *that* bloody naïve," the detective said in exasperation. "It's an occupational risk." He did not wait for a reply. "He could be quite mad, you know. You said yourself he was cracking up."

"I said it was a possibility." Hoggart appeared uncomfortable.

"You think your association with his wife might have provoked it?"

"That's a damn' nasty thing to say." The thin man was nettled and the red patches were back on his cheeks.

"It is and it needed saying." The detective was manifestly indifferent to Hoggart's opinion. "It'll be even nastier if Dyson does something bloody-minded with that gun of his."

18

Although the day was still yawning, Hagbourne's operations room was already a bustling of activity. The walls were papered with street plans of the town and these, resembling gigantic freckled amoebae, were blotched with coloured pins and flags. These latter were the ciphered syntheses recording that this street or that road had been visited: that its constituent parts had been unravelled, sorted and documented; sucked clean of available material and the results fed into the paper-hungry gut of Hagbourne's intelligence section. Here, hard-smoking men evaluated the information cluttering their desks, either discarding if of no value or referring it to Hagbourne. He in his turn refined it, reduced it to digestible chunks and fed it to

Rogers. On his instructions the protein of it was passed to investigative teams for further inquiry or clarification. Nothing viable was permitted to escape. In the process the unit acquired a mass of unconnected but interesting data concerning the habits, practices and customs of the town's citizenry; a fair proportion of it being bizarre beyond daylight belief.

It was from such a precipitate of matter that Hagbourne pieced together the almost daily visits of the grey Jaguar to the Dyson house. His men had found time to produce to the chemist a photograph of the missing engineer. The little man had nodded his rosy head admiringly and said, "That's him. That's him for sure," as if they had miraculously conjured the photograph from the outer reaches of the universe.

The knife had been photographed and reproduced in its hundreds. No person was so unimportant or so lofty in the social structure that he or she had not been shown a photograph, been questioned and had the answer recorded in one of the busy green notebooks. The blood-stained knife itself had been shown to Mrs. Dyson from whom there had been no reaction or recognition. Nor had an invited search shown that it was one with the pattern of knives kept in her kitchen.

The unit would, subject to the main tasks of finding and identifying the amorphousness that was the unknown woman and the elusiveness that was a tusk-handled umbrella, undertake innumerable checks, uncovering its multitude of irrelevancies in the so doing.

The otherwise unoccupied members of the department, combining with their uniformed colleagues, were inspecting hotels, boarding houses and lodgings; searching empty houses and vacant buildings, combing the moors behind the town for the vanished Dyson.

And the town, having swallowed its initial outrage, went on doing what it had to do to live.

Coltart, freed from the discipline of administration had, with a small team of men, subjected the cab drivers, each in his turn, to a search of his vehicle and the inquisition of a list of questions. It was he who had uncovered the first sighting of Drazek.

The driver, the subject of his questioning, was a squat

man with a fleshy nose simulating a misshapen and pitted potato. He wore, despite the growing warmth of the sun, a heavy overcoat. His voice, a gravelled hoarseness, was further muffled by being forced between the teeth biting firmly on the stem of his large curved pipe. Occasionally he removed it and blew grey smoke against the glass screen in front of him. The upper part of his clothing was peppered with tobacco ash and dandruff. Beneath the shiny peak of his cap his eyes possessed the drooping and pink-pouched sadness of a bereaved bloodhound. He admitted to being called Skinner.

"I saw this man Drazek last night," he told Coltart in his grating voice. "About ten. I was waiting outside the park for a fare."

"You know him?" The huge detective was propped against the car, the sun warm on his back. Around him, flowing past the cab rank like water lipping a rock, was the thickening stream of the day's traffic.

"I know him all right," he replied grimly.

"He was on his own?" Coltart asked.

"Not *him*. He had a judy with him."

"You know her?" Coltart beamed at Skinner in encouragement.

The fleshy face expressed regret. "No. She was in the shadows anyway. He was on the outside. I couldn't mistake *him*." It was obvious he did not count Drazek among his friends.

"They went into the park?"

"Yes."

Coltart snickered. "Any indications of intent?"

"No." Skinner was definite. "The smarmy bastard was conning her about something but not touching her."

"Describe her."

"Can't do. Apart from her being on the inside, I didn't take any notice of her."

"Busy hating him, were you?" Coltart said, chancing a guess. It wasn't difficult to read the man. "What's he done to you?"

Skinner twisted his head in remembered impotence. "The bastard sorted me out once," he admitted thickly. "I'm not bitching about that but when I was down on the cobbles he put the boot in. I was off the rank for over a month."

"You complained to the police?" Coltart was wholly cynical, his green eyes humourous.

Skinner grunted and pushed himself deeper into his seat, not answering this strictly rhetorical question.

"You had another go?" the sergeant suggested.

"A bloody clairvoyant aren't you, mate?" The cab driver looked at him askance. "I did have another go and got another lacing. Not just him. His mates joined in and played football with me." He spat a fragment of tobacco out of the open window. "Since then I've left him alone."

"Until the time comes when you meet him in the dark? You in the cab and him walking in the road?"

The eyes swivelling around in their pouches towards him were unresponsive to his humour. "Accidents like that happen every day."

Coltart sniffed. "They won't happen to Drazek, chum."

"Say you don't know," Skinner rumbled. "If it isn't me it'll be someone else. There's always a someone else for bastards like him."

"You're on the ball there. There *has* been a someone else."

"Christ!" Skinner breathed the word like a prayer. "So that's all the fuss. My bloody big mouth." He looked at Coltart. "Is he dead?"

"Like you said, your bloody big mouth. He's dead all right."

He was hesitant. "Not like I said?"

"No. And lucky for you it wasn't." He grinned maliciously at him. "He was stabbed to death in the park. Just after you say you saw him."

Skinner smiled feebly and swallowed. "You're a great kidder, sergeant," he said at last.

"You never saw him again?"

"No. My fare came out almost immediately."

"From the park?"

"No. A house opposite."

"I'll have his name and address, please."

Skinner looked hurt. "Don't you trust me?"

"Trust you!" Coltart was incredulous. "Even were you

my grandfather—and God knows the thought appalls me—
I wouldn't trust you to give me the right time."

Both men laughed. It was the sort of laughter that
had an edge of affection to it.

There were two matters awaiting Rogers's attention
after he had ushered a gently sweating Hoggart out into
the sunlit yard and into the blast-furnace interior of his
parked Jaguar.

The detective watching Stronach's house had called in
by radio, reporting the fat doctor leaving and motoring in
the direction of the hospital. He was following him in the
van and would remain within earshot of his exhaust,
subject to an Act of God or Rogers's instructions to the
contrary.

More interesting, a Miss Fiona Stronach had telephoned, leaving a request for Rogers to contact her when
free.

Waiting for his call to her to be put through, he
discussed Coltart's recently acquired information with
Lingard. "I want to know who Drazek's latest lady-love is,
David," he said. "Go and see that baggy barman friend of
yours. Any woman he's been seen with, we'll check on
her."

"It might be a good line," Lingard agreed. "She could
have seen something. Or someone."

"He didn't lose much time, did he?" Rogers said
derisively. "I mean, after Mrs. Stronach dropped out of his
life. I thought you said he was giving up such diversions?"

"The man was a——"

The telephone purred shrilly, interrupting him. Rog-
ers lifted the handset and grunted his acknowledgement.
It was a woman's voice and it was frozen with dislike.
"This is Miss Stronach," it said.

"You wanted me?" He was offhand with her.

"That is Mr. Rogers?"

"Yes." Rogers looked at Lingard and gestured at the
extension telephone.

"I wish to see you."

"Here?"

"I would rather it here."

"When, Miss Stronach?"

"My brother is out. Can you come now?"

"In half-an-hour?"

"That will do." She paused. "On your own, Mr. Rogers."

"On my own?" he echoed blankly.

"Not him. Not the other one."

Rogers looked at his colleague and frowned his perplexity. "You mean Inspector Lingard? Why not?"

"Just not." Her voice was a finality.

He shrugged. "I'll call on you in thirty minutes." As an afterthought, he asked, "Can I assume Mr. Purslove will be there?"

"No you cannot," she said flatly.

"I'll see you, Miss Stronach," he answered.

Both replaced their handsets, neither formalizing the disconnection with words.

Rogers looked at Lingard and laughed. "There's one female who isn't bowled over by your charm."

"I'm too armoured in conceit to care," he said. "But I'm human enough to want to know why."

"I'll ask her when I see her," Rogers promised. "Only God and her brother can know what she wants. But it might provide the opening we need."

Lingard slid a well-creased trousered leg over the shiny leather seat of the tall stool. The bar of The Falcon was a dim and shadowed cavern and he watched with interest his friend preparing him a Pernod.

Over his shoulder, the barman said, "A bit early for your kind of masochism, isn't it?"

"I caught a touch of dipsomania in a public bar. A distressing illness but the medicine's palatable." Lingard slid his ivory box from his pocket and put it on the dark polished wood of the bar counter. Illuminated by the only bar of sunlight spearing into the room, it glowed with a pale fire. He opened it, a thin smile on his tight face, savouring the perfume of the fragrant powder before inhaling its grains. "I still have an interest in Drazek," he said idly.

The bald-headed man put the glass of cloudy Pernod in front of the detective and pushed a bowl of cashew nuts nearer to him. "I'm told he's flat on his back and short of breath." He levered the metal cap from a bottle with a sharp hiss and poured himself a glass of lager. "The bastard didn't outlive his Doris by very long, did he?"

"Violence begets violence," Lingard murmured aphoristically. "I don't suppose he came in last night?"

"Drazek? I haven't seen him since you came in. I would," he said reproachfully, "have told you."

"Of course you would," Lingard soothed him. "Cast your mind back, will you? Did you ever see him with a woman other than Mrs. Stronach?"

The barman thought. He drank some lager to assist the process. It left him with a moustache of white froth. "Yes, I did. Quite some time ago."

"The pre-Doris era?"

"Yes. They didn't overlap."

"You know her?"

"I *remember* her. Not very clearly." He pulled his mouth in apology. "I see so many women in here. They all begin to look the same after a while. Like bottles in a crate."

He had finished his lager and was polishing beer tankards with a warmed towel. The glass glittered with cut-crystal richness in the dimness of the bar. Helpful as he tried to be, he could not complete the effort of recall. She had been archetypal of the well-dressed, middle-aged women using (or being used by) men like Drazek. His memory, befogged and cluttered with the impressions of a myriad chattering faces, could produce only the retrieved recollection that on one occasion she and Drazek had been photographed.

The photographer had been a tolerated nuisance in this discreet bar, flash-lighting the drinkers and touting for their custom. Neither Drazek nor the woman with him had solicited his attentions and a brawl had been avoided only by the ejection of the photographer from the bar. He had never returned.

The barman remembered him. That is, he recalled he was about twenty years—or could he be, perhaps, thirty? —wore silver-wire spectacles, had a mop of bushy black hair and drank beer shandies. No solicitation by Lingard or the purchase for him of another lager, could draw from the library of his recollection anything more detailed than this.

The detective finished his Pernod, brushed non-existent dust from his clothing with the flat of his hand and left. The buildings outside were reflecting the heat of a brassy sun and it was a scorching day.

Although the instruction, "look for and find one bushy-haired photographer wearing silver spectacles," had a certain naked simplicity, it roused no wild excitation in Hagbourne's overburdened office. Taking men off other equally pressing tasks, he detailed them anew, returning to his graphs and street plans with stoical purpose.

If he kicked the metal paper bin from the door end of the office to crash into the far wall, it was not in exasperation but because he had smoked too many cigarettes and eaten too many made-up meals rendered palatable only by strong sauces.

Rogers, who had given the instructions, was in no more equable mood. Before he kept his appointment, he drank two whiskies and ate twice his allowable ration of tablets. Despite the gloomy prognostications on the tablet bottle he felt better, although the world of his mind seemed misted with light cotton wool.

Miss Stronach was no lightweight slip of femininity. Nor did she act as if she was. Preceding Rogers to the living room, she was wholly mistress of herself, moving with a heavy grace. "Please sit down Mr. Rogers." She indicated a conifer-green chesterfield at his side.

He sat obediently and waited while she fitted herself precisely into a chair opposite, holding her skirt tightly over her thighs as she did so. It was done in a manner suggesting that—given the opportunity—Rogers would leer at any chance exposure.

Having more leisure to observe her than on his previous visit, he did so. Although as large as he remembered, she was more graceful, less bulky than expected. Her legs were slim and shapely. Her biscuit-brown hair was lightened with blonde streaks and had not the severity indicated on his first viewing. It framed a face more wilful than shrewish. Below her no-nonsense nose was the faint shadow of hairs incompletely concealed by a tan paste of makeup. When she looked down at her lap, the false eyelashes newly gummed to her blued lids were dark crescents over the slate eyes. Behind the smooth red enamel of her mouth he imagined her teeth, rat-trap sharp and ready to bite.

The would-be rampant flesh of her body was confined within bounds by tight girdling. Overall, she gave off a heavy carnal perfume. She was, he guessed, firmly established between forty and whatever additional years she thought she might get away with.

Her dress was simple and had the richness of expensive materials. A large man with large appetites and the capacity to ignore the danger signals in her face would consider her a not unattractive mistress. Rogers thought that marriage might be something else altogether, for none had yet hazarded it.

She folded her hands on her lap and pointed an attacking nose at him. "I don't think my brother would approve of my seeing you," she said with directness. "He is in many ways a proud man."

"I am a proud man too, Miss Stronach." Rogers was bland, relaxed in depths of the sofa. He could, he thought, sleep in it without too much encouragement. "So don't go breaking any confidences on my account."

"You misunderstand. I'm concerned only for my brother." She was clearly irritated. "He is too proud to answer questions."

"I don't know why he should be," he retorted. "But what questions in particular?"

"About where he was last evening."

His eyebrows went up. "Oh? Isn't this in Purslove's province?"

"The man's a . . ." She stopped herself. "I am perfectly able to decide for myself on this issue. Mr. Purslove is not *my* legal advisor."

"Well? What was it you wanted to say?" He had neither the energy nor desire to fence verbally with her and he was carelessly abrupt.

"My brother was indoors for the whole of last evening." Having said it, she looked at him challengingly. He was being dared to dispute it.

"He was?" He was light years from being impressed. "Are *you* going to corroborate it?"

"I can if the need arises."

He put the tips of his fingers together and squinted at them. "It is not unknown," he murmured, "for a family to rally round in the hour of need. Quite commendable, in fact. But it doesn't—on its own—carry a lot of weight. Not with me, it doesn't."

"It is none the less so." Her eyes were the grey of a stormy sea.

"You wish to make a written statement?"

"I haven't finished yet," she reproved him, frowning. "My brother also had a visitor last evening."

"Oh?" He stiffened in his seat. "What time?"

"He came at about nine and left after eleven."

The floor beneath his feet seemed suddenly to slide alarmingly and he had a feeling of dreadful insecurity. "Who was it?" he snapped.

"I don't know. I was in my room when the bell rang. I heard my brother answer the door and go with whoever it was to his study."

"A man or woman?"

"A man. My door was ajar and I heard him." Her hands, angular and blunt-fingered, rested on her thighs. "I did not recognize his voice."

"You heard him go?" The floor was more solid now, less like a treacherous bog.

Her head inclined, doubling the flesh beneath her chin. "I did. It was a short time after eleven."

"And you didn't see him? Not even then?" His innate scepticism was lifting itself from the canvas to which it had been knocked.

"I was in my bed." She made it sound like a maiden's sanctuary, coarsened by bringing it to Rogers's notice. "I would be hardly likely to."

"Not curious?"

She slipped her words. "My brother has many visitors, professional and social. I make it a rule to mind my own business." She glared at him with loathing. "I am not curious enough to spy on him."

"A pity you are not." He was openly disbelieving. "You might have something to tell me a bit more useful than the effort expended in telling me so. And," he said, pushing himself upright, "is your uncommunicative brother going to confirm this?" When there was no answer, he asked, "Is that all, Miss Stronach?"

"What else do you want, damn it?" she rasped at him.

"I want it from your brother," he said curtly. "And I want the name of his supposed visitor." He dragged his leg to the door, his face dark and forbidding. "Without that, it's a waste of your time and mine."

At the door he turned and his eyes took her in, examining her. There was a dampness of sweat breaking through the mask of paste on her face. She had not moved from her chair. "Just one thing," he asked. "What is your objection to Inspector Lingard?"

She held his regard long enough to allow him to recognize the quality of her resolution. "Goodbye, Mr. Rogers," she said and pressed her lips together. She made no move to see him out.

Shutting the door behind him and getting into the waiting car, he felt baffled. "What the hell was all *that* about?" he asked of the hot blue sky.

There was no rationality about what happened between the two men. Neither saw it as a symptom of their physical and mental exhaustion, magnified to distortion by the lowering heat. There was a humidity in the clogging air that drained vitality from the fibres of a sweating body. They each wore a sensitive layer of irritability beneath an easily scratched skin.

Rogers was at his desk. He had removed his jacket and draped it over the back of his chair. The unfastened cuffs of his shirt hung untidily from his wrists. The black hairs of his forearms were gummed with perspiration. His mouth was acrid from the smoking of a hot pipe without pause. A throbbing ache pulsated a motor in his brain. He felt deliquescent as the sap of his flesh flowed from him. Occasionally he cursed as the paper on which he was writing stuck to the heel of his hand.

The swung-open halves of the window were the doors of a blue and gold oven. A tortoiseshell butterfly beat its wings against the glass and the sound of its flapping nagged Rogers's concentration.

Lingard, entering the office, was starched and immaculate. The only outward signs of stress were the scrawled fatigue lines beneath the eyes and the depression of the flesh of his cheeks. "I wondered if I could do anything down in town, George?" he said. "I'd like to use the occasion to call in at the hospital."

"Bridget?" The query was couched in a tone of voice that stiffened Lingard.

"Among other things," he said distinctly. "I take it you have no objection?"

Rogers was careless with his words. In honesty, he knew he should have backed down immediately. "I hope you're not getting emotionally involved, David." He spoke offhandedly, sliding his chair back and changing the position of his legs.

The slim detective turned pale. "Would it be your business if I was?"

Rogers had never seen Lingard angry before and, while regretting his tactlessness, he felt impelled to defend the ill-judged remark. "Only as a friend, David." He was tapping the butt of his pencil on his pad. It was a danger signal had the other chosen to recognize it. "I wouldn't like to see you make an idiot of yourself." As soon as the words were said he realized he had further inflamed the situation.

Lingard stalked up and down the width of the room, his face white, endeavouring to control unforgivable words poised ready to spill out of him. "You can justify that, I hope." His voice was scarified of expression.

"I don't see that I need to," Rogers replied shortly. "Don't be so bloody touchy about a general observation." His own choler was rising like a black flood.

The narrow face, still under control, was in front of him, suspended above the row of text and reference books on the desk. "Say what you mean," he grated.

The choler finally overflowed and Rogers slammed his fist down on the desk. At the same time he stood and thrust his enraged face close to Lingard's. "All right!" he yelled. "I will. The damned woman doesn't belong to you. She never has and never will." He was brutal in his exaggeration. "How am I to guess how you feel? She bloody nearly raped me in the mortuary."

Lingard inhaled deeply, forcing himself to hold down his fury. "That was a bloody-minded thing to say."

"I'm sorry I had to say it," rasped Rogers, now thoroughly upset, "but you would have it so." He sat down and brooded at his assistant. "I don't propose saying any more or listening to you say it. Enough's been said by both of us. I'm telling you to get out and to cool off."

Lingard's face was empty as he stared long at him. Then he turned away and stalked out of the office.

Wiping a hand across his forehead, Rogers scowled at the closed door and chewed on their quarrel.

19

Lingard, stamping brutally on the clutch of his green monster, drove from the yard on to the road dropping into the town.

Slamming the gear lever into position with careless precision, he manoeuvred the Bentley out of the clogging traffic and into the quieter side streets.

In the Spanish Bar he was a silent and preoccupied drinker. In quick succession he swallowed two brandies, his eyes unseeing, his replies to the garrulous barmaid monosyllabic. When the brandy had anaesthetized his disorder, he went out into the street.

Across the road from the hospital an open concreted square contained the traffic of the bus terminus. He entered an office signboarded "Lost Property." In the half-an-hour it took him to cut through a thicket of bureaucratic obstructionism and to impress on the Traffic Manager the need to relinquish his obsessive stewardship, he was in possession of a black silk umbrella with a mauve label tied to its boar's tusk handle. Thumbing importantly through pages of buff forms, the prissy clerk responsible for the delaying tactics produced at last what he unmistakably regarded as first cousin to *Codex Sinaiticus*. It said (in pencilled characters of extreme size and *naïveté* that the umbrella—together with a pair of tennis shoes and a Police "No Waiting" sign—had been found on the last bus of the preceding night by one Conductor Stapp, E. Lingard submissively obliged the Traffic Manager by signing for the umbrella, exempting him from any tort or claim arising from his own nihilistic act.

The recovery of the murder weapon restored Lingard's morale and he was within inches of being good-humoured as he gentled his misused Bentley up the hill to the station.

Rogers—regarding him curiously and seemingly satisfied with the result—listened with interest to what he had to say. He took the umbrella from him and examined the ferrule under his lens. "Nothing obvious—naturally," he commented.

"You'll ask Quandom to do a check straight away?"

"I've already advised him it'll be on its way." His expression was that of a fox scenting chicken. "I can hardly wait."

"I'm afraid you'll have to," Rogers said expressionlessly. "Purslove telephoned a few minutes back and said he was prepared to disclose Stronach's visitor." His mouth dropped down at the corners. "What's more, he named him."

Lingard's face was a canvas of changing expressions. "But he can't! It's blatant skulduggery by that conniving bastard Purslove!" In his agitation he spilled snuff down his tie and he swore viciously.

"I expect it is but it couldn't have come at a worse time. Fifty umbrellas aren't any good against an authenticated eighteen-carat alibi. Still," he said philosophically, "it's only academic at the moment. Were it all straightforward, you and I would be superfluous. All we'd need was an undertaker and a hole in the ground. Nevertheless," he finished mysteriously, "I have other irons in the fire."

"Who was the visitor?" Lingard was eager to be at him.

"A man called Andrews. He is supposed to have called on Stronach at nine and left at a very vaguely estimated time afterwards. I suppose it'll be adjustable to fit whatever circumstance Purslove thinks necessary. Anyway, Andrews called with a box of Ichneumon-flies. Whatever *they* are."

He referred to a written note. "He's a fellow member of the Entomological Society and wanted to discuss variations in wing venation. It seems it matters." He grimaced. "So Purslove told me in detail. I asked him why his client was so coy about it before. He said Stronach wanted to ask Andrews's permission first. That, in any case, he resented the tone of the questioning." He tossed the note down. "The usual spoiling tactics we can expect, although it can still leave Stronach with time to——"

The telephone bell rang and he answered it. As he listened to the excited, metallic voice from the other end so the colour went from his swarthiness and his eyes became haggard.

Despite the overriding demands an investigation of murder makes on a police force, there is no diminution in the more mundane tasks it is called upon to deal with or of the incidents to which it is required it shall direct its attention.

Domestic disputes, straying dogs and found cats, lost property and mislaid children, intolerable noises from neighbours, rebellious sons and wanton daughters, accusations, counter-accusations, potholes in roads and the obstruction of streets and the never ceasing complaints of hooliganism, damage to property, dumping of litter and the theft of anything and everything from a coin-sized milk token to a two-hundred-gallon iron tank of diesel fuel.

It was thus a matter of routine that Police Constable Smallbone, sitting astride his navy-blue motor cycle and thinking of lunch, should receive a radio message instructing him to go to the rear of the Low Moor industrial estate. A man—no description available—had been seen acting strangely near the river.

Smallbone kicked down on the starter and put the machine into gear before acknowledging the order. The rear wheel left the mark of its sudden acceleration in the softening tar of the road as the machine roared into fierce movement.

Smallbone's primary wish was to clear an obviously trifling matter expeditiously. His landlady ("The Bitch of Belsen" he called her privately), on the store of economy, switched the oven off thirty minutes before the times she had laid down for the eating of his meals. His lunch would be faintly warm if he arrived punctually, stone cold if he did not. There was no appeal and lodgings were difficult to get. he was not entirely free of revengeful malice. When the fuses popped or the cistern ran water, he denied any electrical or plumbing ability. He counted the tradesmen's bills received as a score against the unpalatability of his lukewarm meals and her flinty bitchiness.

The waste grassland behind the estate dropped steeply down to a small copse of stunted juniper trees and hazel bushes. By the river's edge were the close-packed green blades of iris, their purple and brown heads displayed to the brazen heavens. There was a clean smell of water mint and warm grass in the air. Small dragonflies, hovering blue and scarlet needles, hawked for insects above the water. The field across the river was a shimmering yellow and white of hot marigolds and ox-eye daisies. Far up in the blue quietness of the sky a kestrel hung, its unwinking amber eyes searching the ground beneath for an incautious mouse or beetle.

Smallbone, propping his machine against a fence post, was only peripherally conscious of the scene before him. He felt warm in his blue serge and his white crash helmet was heavy on his head. His whole attention was directed to the locating of the reported skulker. He made no attempt at concealment and he walked without stealth. The machine he rode had advertised his approach with its racketing engine.

He stood for a while within the shade of a juniper and waited. If the skulker was still in the vicinity he might be expected to break cover or make some noise indicating his position. In the meantime, Smallbone took a packet from his breast pocket and lit himself a cigarette. He was grateful for the opportunity. The shadow of the tree was an adequate concealment while he awaited the first move. He leaned his back against the rough bark and tuned his senses to the audible world around him.

He was a very young man and only a month or two outside his two-year probationary period. His eyes were blue and still unstained by the dishonesty and filth he would be required to investigate. His skin had the pinkness of youth. What hair could be seen beneath the rim of his helmet was flaxen. The moustache of which he was so proud was a soft growth of golden hairs, beaded with sweat from the warmth of the morning.

A blackbird, flinging itself swearing from a hazel bush, gave him the first indication of movement. He dropped his cigarette to the earth and put a boot on it, regretting its wasted pleasures. Walking silently, placing his feet carefully, he moved toward the bush. On rounding the perimeter of it he came face to face with the man standing in its overhanging foliage.

Smallbone recognized him at once from the description written in his notebook. Dyson was holding a shotgun waist high. His left hand was heavily bandaged. The hand holding the stock had a finger crooked around the trigger and the shiny barrel was aimed at the policeman's belly. Smallbone felt isolated in an inverted glass bowl. From a long way outside it he could hear the sound of the town's traffic and the fluting of birds. His perceptions, sharpened by a sudden onset of fearful apprehension, revealed Dyson to him with a photographic clarity.

The man's eyes were wobbling madly in an unhappy face. He was bristle-chinned and very pale. Despite the dappling of shadow over the upper part of him, Smallbone had no difficulty in seeing the recognizable cluster of tiny hairs on each of the lobes of Dyson's ears. Around his head zig-zagged small black flies. His trousers and jacket were creased and dusty, the collar of his shirt grubby. He had been lying down and was covered with fragments of dried grass and leaves.

The constable was the first to move. He forced a smile of confidence to his stiff face and held out his hand for the gun. "Don't make it worse for yourself, Mr. Dyson," he said with a dry mouth. "Give it to me."

"No." Dyson dragged the word out like a stubborn child, his eyes jiggling uncertainly.

Smallbone took a deep breath and moved nearer. "Come on," he urged. "Don't make me..."

The ball of massed shot hit him full in the navel, taking in with it a part of the cloth of his tunic and a silver button. The thunderous force of it at close range knocked him backwards into the deep nettles and cow parsley fringing the copse. The impact of his falling body liberated a drift of floating seeds and above him insects rose in disturbed swarms.

To his yet open eyes, the colour was bleaching from the foliage around him. He felt no pain, only an unceasing pressure on his stomach squeezing blackness upwards and through him. There was a high-pitched vibration in his ears. Behind him, from over the river, he thought he could hear a well-remembered voice calling his name. His eyes brimmed with tears and he started to sob.

As it got louder, blotting out the remaining light, he went to meet it.

The murder of the hapless Smallbone generated even larger ripples of activity by the stony-faced men who had been his comrades. Dyson was Death and he had to be found. Detectives pushed unceremoniously into the labyrinth of scabby lodging houses and fly-specked cafés, levering from their interiors the pallid light-shy men using them, subjecting each to a careful examination for the fugitive murderer. His name was dropped like a warning into the affairs of the fraudulent and shady and the continued presence of questing men disrupted the comfortable pattern of their dishonesties.

Inconspicuous and self-effacing men stood where crowds congregated, each watching hungrily for the face plastered by memory to the walls of his consciousness.

The photographed face, the faint smile of happier days on its monochrome lips, looked down amiably from cinema screens and police noticeboards. It was, despite the surface bonhomie, the face of Death.

Men, ill-spared from the incessant search, watched and guarded the homes of Hoggart and Mrs. Dyson. Men went without sleep to join the ant-busy seekers. They returned from the leave that seemed suddenly empty and of no purpose. Men—hitherto convinced that the ailments they suffered were crippling—surprised their doctors by reporting themselves fit and well.

Unsteady on his feet from lack of sleep, Rogers overrode the weariness that weighed down his eyelids and drove himself on, a man wading through the treacle of tangling, clogging obstacles. He would go on now until he succeeded or collapsed. Stronach and Purslove, fretting in

the wings of Rogers's particular stage, seemed of secondary importance at this moment.

And so the hours of the sultry afternoon were expended
in relentless unremitting efforts to track Dyson down. In
the end, Dyson's continued liberty forced Rogers to diver-
sify his efforts. Smallbone's death was, he argued, ancillary
to the original hunt for Dyson. While it added to its
importance it did not alter its terms of reference. The
murder of Drazek had lost nothing of its immediacy and
must still be a factor in the allocation of effort. With the
early momentum smoothing to a sustained and organized
endeavour, Rogers prepared to pull Lingard in from the
general field of operations; to redeploy him to the Drazek
investigation.

He was in the Operations Room checking progress
with Hagbourne when the slim detective entered. There
was a gaunt determination about him and his straw hair
seemed more shaggy than ever. He had slept as little as
had Rogers.

"I've sent for beef sandwiches," Rogers said. "Sit down
and help me eat them."

He shuddered. "No thanks. I need food about as
much as I need two umbilici." He sat himself opposite
Rogers. The camaraderie between them was as before. "If
you've got any I'd be grateful for coffee."

"That's coming as well. You've eaten?"

"No." He looked revolted at the suggestion. "I've
gone beyond it. What's on, George? A development?"

"I want you to get on with the Drazek job, David. To
see this Andrews chap and settle his end of it before we go
any further." He yawned hugely. "Christ, but I'm tired. I
shall sleep for a month after this. Push me into a bed with
half-a-dozen naked women and I'd still prefer the sleep."
He put a hand in his breast pocket and withdrew a slip of
paper. "Always forgetting things," he said. "Hagbourne's
chaps turned up your photographer with the bushy hair
and taste for beer shandies. Remarkably enough, he re-
members the incident and he's busy sorting out his nega-
tives. Said he would bring the print to the station as soon
as he was done." He looked at Lingard slyly. "Don't open,
it David," he said. "I want to be dramatic if I'm proved
right."

"You think it'll help?" Lingard himself didn't appear to think it would.

"Just an idle thought about it. Nothing more." Rogers pushed it to one side. "The important thing is either to nail Stronach or to clear him. It's the uncertainties that are wasting our time."

"And if his alibi doesn't hold up?"

"Bring him in." There was a finality in Rogers's voice. "He's had more than enough rope." He picked up the telephone and dialled a number. "We've forgotten the most important fact. Although," he prophesied, "it'll only be confirmatory." When Quandom answered, Rogers asked, "The umbrella, Bill? Any result yet?"

Lingard could hear the tinny-thin transmitted voice from where he sat. It said that the tests on the ferrule had given a positive reaction to blood. Not quite enough to group, he thought, but he was still trying. Being rather what they had anticipated, neither man uttered cries of approbation and Quandom was most obviously disappointed at their response.

After he had been soothed and the telephone replaced, Rogers laughed. "Poor Bill. I really should not anticipate his findings. It gives him nothing to work for."

The sandwiches, stacked in doughy wedges on a paper-covered metal tray, were placed on the desk by a constable. The coffee was steaming in a blue jug. Rogers poured it into the two cups provided and pushed one across the table to his assistant. There were no saucers. Lingard had forgotten his supposed revulsion against food and he took a sandwich, biting into it without apparent comprehension.

"It adds up to the fact that we have to undermine Stronach's so-called alibi, I suppose," Lingard ventured. "It isn't outraging probability that he could have killed Drazek and still have chuntered insectology with Andrews."

"You could be right, David, but be sure. Copper-bottomed sure. And put out a call for Coltart on your way, will you?" He was not yet disposed to expound to his assistant the alternative theory he had tentatively contrived; a structure as frail as cobwebs and tissue paper, based on little else but intuition and his built-in sense of the logic of facts. Although fundamentally opposed to the staking of even a nominal amount of money on the hazard of chance, he was in a mood to wager that events were compressing themselves to a flashpoint. He had sensed his way with a cat's-whisker presentiment through too many investigations requiring this delicacy of intuition not to recognize the smell of it now.

Andrews looked a little like an insect himself: a loosely articulated putty-coloured weevil with small black eyes and a peeled mushroom cap of hairless head. He wore spectacles which, turned towards Lingard, reflected the light of the evening sun and rendered his regard a shining blankness. He sat primly opposite the detective in the curtain-shadowed room, a wide plateau of mahogany table between them.

He was impatient with Lingard's questioning; with his polite but firm refusal to accept completely Andrews's timing of his visit to Stronach. Expressing his impatience, his voice was a high-pitched squeakiness. "If Dr. Stronach says it was from nine to eleven," he was saying, "then it must have been so."

"But do you know it was that period yourself?" Lingard insisted for the fourth time. "Accepting a statement as you are doing is a third-rate kind of support. It amounts to nothing."

"God, man," Andrews said testily. "I don't walk around examining my watch. I repeat. I had a bite of food—poached eggs, if you must know—here at about seven-thirty. Or was it eight. Anyway, I decided to call on Stronach and did so." His glasses were glinting at Lingard. "By car it took me ten minutes. Work *that* out," he finished shrewishly.

"You know very well I cannot. You've not supplied anything that can be sued as a point of reference." Lingard was becoming exasperated.

"Exactly!" The small man was triumphant. "That's exactly what I've been trying to impress on you. I don't live by the clock. I don't propose doing so. It's two hours adrift anyway."

"Two hours adrift?" Lingard looked at him blankly.

"Summer time," Andrews explained impatiently.

"Oh Lord," Lingard muttered. Aloud he said, "Can

you fix the time you left High Moor any better? Were the pubs turning out? Did you note the town hall clock? Things like that?" He was really a very patient man.

"I cannot and that's my dogmatic last word. I noticed none of those things. If you force me to guess it would be as indefinite as half-an-hour either side of ten o'clock. Or," he offered unhelpfully, "even longer. I'm sorry, my dear fellow, but I'm not a reliable witness of anything more bulky than a hover-fly."

"Which is why I have to try and pin you down by reference to other known circumstances. I don't wish to bore you with repetition but violent death still demands a thorough investigation."

"But not by me." Andrews was definite. "It doesn't interest me. It doesn't come within a thousand miles of the violence meted out by insects."

"Hardly of the same importance or moral consideration, Mr. Andrews?"

"Say that you don't know. You've only man's opinion that he's more important to God than a dungfly. I'm making the point that any argument involving human violence demanding the use of my intellect and emotions has no validity. Look," he interposed, stopping the detective as he opened his mouth to extricate himself from this unfruitful discussion, "for all I know this dead fellow might have deserved to die. If he did, why should I be expected to help you? And if my friend Stronach decided in his wisdom to do it—which I refuse to believe, anyway—then I expect he had thoroughly good grounds for doing so."

Lingard allowed this to go unopposed. "Tell me what you were talking to him about?"

The insect man waved a hand around the room in which they sat. On the walls were drawings of monstrous flies and beetles, their antennae and tarsi enlarged to formidable proportions. There were glass cases of pinned insects and polished wooden cabinets exuding the necrotic smell of paradichlorbenzene. A black and silver microscope stood under a dust protector of clear plastic. On the table a stuffed and varnished Surinam toad held a bristle of pensils in its mouth.

"The bits and pieces of all this," he said, smiling as if at some subtlety of humour. "The philosophy of the life and death of the genus *Aphidus*. The wing venation of the *Ichneumonoidea*. The feeding habits of *Creophilus maxillosus*." He laughed openly at Lingard's growing impatience. "Greenfly, the wing patterns of Chlacis-flies and a particular scavenger beetle," he explained. "Somehow they sound so very much more bizarre in Latin. But I want only to underline another point that riding a hobby-horse rarely permits the measurement of time."

Lingard surrendered to this illogicality. "I can't see your point," he said, "but I'll accept you aren't going to be able to help."

The odd little man beamed his glasses at him, pinning him down as he might an insect. "I thought you'd accept that eventually." He pushed a small lens across the table to him. "Have you ever considered there can exist an exciting, totally engrossing world less obvious than the giantism of mammals? No?" He cocked his head to one side. "Have you not looked at anything under magnification but hairs and fingerprints? Don't disdain it, inspector. It's a world where you'll find a weevil that mimics a seed that looks as if it has been bored into by another weevil. Work out the reasoning of *that* one if you can. A world where a garden slug with teeth like a shark tracks down and eats earthworms. And has a shield on its own tail as a protection against its cannibalistic brothers. Or you may prefer the woodlouse that carries its young in a marsupial pouch and eats the old and sickly of its tribe. A stone blind grub that searches for and finds its prey by touch. I always think of it as an eyeless tiger in a field of haltered lambs." He said all this in the manner of a tutor lecturing a difficult pupil.

"If you cull the globe, you're bound to come up with freakish abnormalities." He parodied Andrews's nomenclature. "We've more than our share of them in the genus *Homo sapiens*."

Andrews disregarded this. "All that I've mentioned, you'll find in your own garden, laddie." He said it with immense satisfaction. "You're only to get down on your knees and look."

Lingard stood. "When I've time, Mr. Andrews. At the moment I'm more engrossed in the minutiae of murder."

The insect man also stood and held out his hand.

Lingard shook it, receiving a fanciful impression that he was holding a bird's claw. "I make these observations only because I believe they are relevant to a proper understanding of Doctor Stronach."

Lingard regarded him with bafflement and a moiety of pity. He considered the man to be lost in a delirium of illogicality. With a face void of expression he said, "I'm sure they are. I'm sure they are."

To himself, as he left, he muttered, "If it's the last thing I do, I'll check to see if Stronach's got a marsupial pouch!"

20

Rogers's consciousness dropped swiftly and without warning into an abyss of timelessness and, lax at his desk, he slept for a few obliterative seconds. He swoke with a painful jerk, his pipe dropping from nerveless fingers and bouncing across the linoleum, when a freshly bathed Coltart entered the office. A brown suit strained across the bulk of the sergeant who was whistling his indifference to a sleepless two days.

Rogers was startled and awkward with a wit-scattered confusion. He scowled at Coltart's evident smugness in detecting him in a physical frailty. "I was thinking with my eyes closed," he explained, daring a contradiction. He yawned with a face-cracking grimace. "Thinking about food and sleep. But especially sleep."

Coltart read the dial of his watch. "Nearly eight," he reminded him. "I took a few minutes off for a cold shower and I could push a house over. You haven't eaten?"

"Too busy. Lingard's seen this chap. Andrews and he more or less alibis Stronach. Not wholly but sufficient to get him off the hook unless we can produce something extra. It means opening up a fresh approach." He stood and unhooked his jacket from the backrest of his chair, yawning again. He felt wretched. "I want you to see Mrs.

Dyson. Try and get more out of her than I did. About his associates, his habits, what he does with his spare time. The bastard's got to come up for air sometime and I want to nail him. Not mop up more blood and guts. And she's as vulnerable as ever a woman can be, despite..."

He stopped suddenly and Coltart saw the shadow of a dark thought pass across the landscape of his features. Then there followed the shock of realized apprehension. When he spoke his manner was preoccupied and the lines of strain and tension even more marked. "I think I've slipped up, Eddie," he said quietly. "Leave Mrs. Dyson for the time being and come with me. Straight away."

The sergeant regarded him oddly but said nothing. It was no time for questions and Rogers's face invited no confidences.

It was fractionally cooler in the yard than in the sweltering building they had just left. Rogers heaved himself into the passenger seat of his car and flipped a ring of keys to Coltart. "Cato Lane and hurry," he instructed. The sergeant's forehead creased and he muttered, "Oh Christ, no!"

Both men perspired steadily in the car, the heat of its thrashing engine augmenting the humid air scooped in like warm wool through the opened windows. Braking the car to a squealing halt before a flight of stone steps rising steeply to a blotched maroon door, Coltart looked at Rogers, his expression seeking confirmation. The older man nodded. "Come with me," he said shortly. He was chewing at his lower lip, his manner tensioned to steel wire. A black balloon of foreboding filled the cavity of his chest, restricting his breathing.

The lane in which they stood was a shabby and degraded backwater to the commercialized brightness of the town's shopping centre, only streets away from it. Here, boarded-up brownstone houses eroded quietly in the shadow of windowless, monolithic depositories. Where still viable, the houses were compartmented into living spaces for those forced by squeezing circumstances to exist in their gritty squalor. Few lived here by choice. Those who did sought to profit by the lane's outlawry in pursuing their dishonest or immoral occupations. The lane possessed an outcast's clannishness that unified every grubby little shop in its corrupted length into being an intermediary in the prostitution that flourished there and in a collective support of repressive and usurious extortion.

The lane was narrow and its winding extent was cluttered with the disorder of parked and abandoned cars. The buildings on either side seemed to press in towards each other. In the gulf beneath these lofty structures the roadway was shadowed and sultry from the stored heat of an earlier sun.

Opening the maroon door, Rogers stepped inside and forward into a gloomy tomcat-smelling hall. "Stay with me," he said, leading the way up the uncarpeted stairs. On each successive floor, firmly closed doors sealed from the others any expectation of a community spirit. Before they reached the top, Rogers was grunting with the effort of swinging his leg from stair to stair. Both men, clammy with perspiration, were wheezing their distress at the oppressive climb.

The door to her apartment possessed some pretensions to smartness. It had been decorated white recently enough not to show the prevailing scarring of fading and peeling paint. The number on it was shown in neat screwed-on metal figures. Rogers put a warning finger to his lips and pressed his ear to the woodwork, listening intently. There were muted sounds of movement and conversation below them but nothing from behind the door. He rapped softly on it with the knuckle of his forefinger.

There was no response although Rogers imagined a brooding watchfulness emanating from behind it. His fears were building a tension between himself and what was concealed by the rectangle of white wood. To him, there was a tangibility about it as real as a wisp of fog.

He grasped the handle of the door and twisted it gently, pushing against it as he did so and meeting the resistance of a spring lock. Searching in his wallet, he removed a small strip of mica. Sliding it carefully between the lock face and the socket, he levered the tongue back and swung the door inwards.

Where the green curtains diffused the inpouring light, the interior of the shabby room was virescent with the luminosity of a fish tank. The translucent green bathed the

walls and flooded with lividity the face of the woman lying
on the narrow disordered bed. The smell of death was a
cloying putrefaction. A buzzing of metallic blue flies rose
and circled in the heavy air.

Rogers flinched at the dreadful sight and his shoulders
sagged. His face, draining of colour as if by an opened tap,
was a chalk-white background for his tormented black
eyes.

Coltart, taking in the picture from behind the stricken
man, stepped in front of him, using his large body to
screen the sight of the dead woman from him. For such a
normally phlegmatic man he was distressed, his expression
one of deep concern for Rogers. "Leave it with me," he
urged. "I can do what has to be done."

Rogers shook his head blindly. "No. I shall be all
right. It was my neglect. We would have found her earlier
had I thought." He walked around Coltart to the window
and pulled the curtains apart. Sunlight flooded in clear and
unobstructed and the flies rose again with a shrill stridulation
of protest. With the window opened, the atmosphere
became less foetid. "I should have guessed," he muttered
to himself. "She was the last person I considered. She
should have been the first."

Eileen lay sideways on the tangled and blood-soaked
bed cover in a foetal position. Her blue dress was rucked
up and her thighs were exposed. This was, to Rogers, an
immodesty that even death could not excuse and he gently
twitched the dress down. The wound from which her life
had been spilled was a horror of congealed blood and
extruding tissue situated below the shoulder-blade. Her
even white teeth were bared and dry of saliva. The
expression on her features was set by death in rigid
surprise that this thing had happened. He was glad her
eyelids were closed.

The swollen stomach showed that she had not died
alone. To Rogers, this was the outrageously pathetic cli-
max. It suggested a reason for the awful butchery done to
her body. She had never been a meek woman and her
spirit had always been fiercely burning, her tongue often
hot in anger. He suffered now the sickness of jealousy at
the thought of the fathering, a yielding she had always
denied him.

Looking at her, sombre now rather than grieving, he could think only of the fat past with the sun on her sweet-smelling hair and of the tactile familiarity of the handsome body. There was an aching regret in him for the years wasted in the arid desert of their domestic disharmonies and for the agony he suffered in the soiling of their marriage by her promiscuousness.

He put a finger on the skin of her arm. It was chill and without elasticity. "At least a couple of days," he said tonelessly. He looked around the room. It contained—apart from the bed on which his wife had died—a table and two chairs, a tangerine settee and a white and gold wardrobe. A small cooker and a white enamelled sink occupied a curtained recess. Clothing and shoes were scattered around in sluttish disorder. A plastic-bristled broom had been thrown under the table. An empty gin bottle, two soiled tumblers and a wristlet watch rested on a bamboo table by the bed. On the floor near the door by which they had entered was a scattering of envelopes. To the far side of the room was another door. It was painted cream and attached to it was a ceramic tile bearing the words, "Have this one on me."

A black cat with a white chest was humped beneath the cooker, its green eyes watchful but not frightened. Rogers crouched before it and fondled its ears. He had never known Eileen to display any interest in or affection for animals. That she had done so, added to the nostalgia of her memory. "I'll have you," he promised the purring cat. "Don't go away, will you."

He moved towards the inner door. "I'll check this before we get organized," he said to Coltart who was writing in his notebook. "It looks like the bathroom."

He pushed open the door without thought. As it swung wide, the panel in front of his face disintegrated with an ear-splitting crack into splinters of flying wood and pellets clattered into the room behind him. He staggered backwards with a hoarse cry of pain and surprise and slumped on his knees to the floor. Blood welled from the side of his throat and began to stain the cloth of the left shoulder of his jacket. Coltart was at his side in one bound. "Are you all right? Christ! What happened?" He was yelling in his anxiety and his expression was a distortion between dismay and anger.

Rogers took a deep breath and fearfully explored the numbness of his neck and shoulder. He looked at the blood smeared on his fingers. Pellets had gouged ragged strips of flesh from his throat and ear. A number had penetrated the muscle of his upper arm. He managed a twisting of the mouth that could be interpreted as a smile. "Don't fret, sergeant," he said. "It happens to pigeons every day."

His face was bone-white but he pushed the solicitous Coltart away and scrambled upright, his eyes bright and deadly with determination. But he was seconds too slow. Before he could move again the huge sergeant, travelling like an armoured vehicle, had lunged forward and slammed the sole of his tremendous shoe into the splintered door, sending it thundering back, tearing it screechingly away from its hinges.

The bathroom, blue-grey with a haze of acrid gunpowder smoke, was empty. At one end was an open window. As Coltart reached it and thrust his head and shoulders through, Rogers was with him. "Watch it, for God's sake," he snapped. "The bloody man's trigger-happy." He jostled Coltart aside and squeezed himself into position. Both could now see Dyson.

The roof on which he was flattened was at right angles to the window from which he had reached it. It sloped precipitously and dangerously to the waiting gulf of the lane. Far below could be seen the toy-like cars in the roadway and the tiny foreshortened human ants threading along the footpaths. Dyson lay prone, his feet wedged precariously on the rim of the moss-grown guttering overhanging the sheerness of vertical brick wall. One hand clutched the shotgun; the other, a bloody bandage rendering it virtually useless, was pressed against the slates, providing a kind of traction that held him in position. He was looking directly at Rogers, his eyes white-rimmed and goggling. Then he screamed at him hysterically, his mouth a black O in the greyness of his face. "Leave me alone! Why don't you leave me alone!"

With a convulsive movement he jerked himself to his knees, the gun swinging across in a short arc to point at the detectives. His balance gone, he grabbed wildly for the smooth slates, dropping the gun in a convulsion of movement. It slid down the roof, checking itself on the guttering before bouncing butt over barrel into the abyss. When at last it hit the road it exploded, spraying the lane with flying shot, splintering the closed-in area with pattering echoes.

Dyson, poised in straining imbalance, screamed again, this time incoherently and in fear. From some deep reserve of strength he willed his feet to move away from the death waiting beneath him and for a brief moment they scrabbled without purchase against the sagging guttering, his arms windmilling to recover his balance. The madness had gone from his eyes and they were both horrified and appealing.

Rogers called to him, urgently. "Fall forward, Dyson. Forward on your face!"

But nothing could now stop the inexorable loss of stability, the shifting of the body's equilibrium. With his trunk twisting and his legs sliding sideways Dyson curved outwards, a dramatic straining figure against the pale blue of the dying sky. Then, gathering speed, he dropped swiftly and smoothly into the gulf towards the ground leaping up at him, wheeling over and over in a pathetic travesty of arm-waving flight.

His despairing scream shut off abruptly, drowned in the sound of the bone-shattering thud that reached their ears.

As they turned from the window, the burly sergeant was the first to speak. "The bitch could have done it quicker with cyanide," he growled harshly. "I hope she enjoys her widowhood."

Lingard guiding the rumbling green Bentley through the press of people, saw the shattered body bleeding on the cobblestones and pulled in to the kerb. A constable had covered Dyson with a borrowed blanket and was working to maintain a clear circle around him.

Rogers was limping heavily down the steps with Coltart preceding him. Blood was running from his throat into his white shirt, dyeing it a bright scarlet. An ugly patch of darker red stained the arm of his jacket.

As Lingard approached him, he was refusing the assistance of an ambulance, threatening Coltart for his continued insistence that one should be summoned. "Sit me in the car and shut up," he snapped ungratefully with all the privilege of the injured. "Don't slobber over me as if I'm going to drop dead."

Lingard nodded at Coltart and opened the door of the car. "Hop in, George, like a good chap. Don't make an exhibition of yourself by bleeding to death in public." His voice was authoritative and with Coltart's assistance he pushed him in. "A sawbones is on the way and I'm seeing that you stay put until he arrives."

Rogers sank back in the leather seat, felt his lacerated arm and stared dumbly at the blood fouling the whiteness of his shirt cuff and staining the gold band of his watch. He looked through the door towards the huddle of spectators surrounding the mangled body. "It's finished, David." He was as bleak as winter granite. "It was Eileen."

"I know. They filled me in at the station. I'm sorry, George." He was leaning in over the door, watching Rogers intently, assessing his condition.

"The murderous swine was using the flat as a funkhole." He made a rasping sound in his throat. "I blame myself for overlooking Eileen in the first place."

"It wouldn't have helped her," Lingard said gently.

"It might have saved Smallbone." His voice was savage, not allowing himself to be taken off the hook.

The other man had no honest answer for this and he let it pass. He pulled an envelope from his jacket. It was addressed to Rogers. "The photograph you wanted. I picked it up just before I left. Can I inflict it on you?"

"Open it for me, David. If I'm right, it's a photograph of our murderer . . . and it isn't Stronach," he warned him.

Lingard paused, his thumb hooked in the act of gouging open the envelope. His blond eyebrows were down. "You can't mean it. Dammit , man . . . it's *got* to be!"

The grey face sagged. "It hasn't, you know. But open the thing, for God's sake."

The thumb nail ripped a jagged tear through the paper and Lingard drew out the photograph from inside. He looked at it, his expression incredulous, unbelieving.

Rogers reached over and took it from him. His fingers left a smear of blood on it.

"Full marks, Rogers," he said aloud to himself when he saw it. The shiny print showed Drazek, half-way risen from his seat and holding a glass, snarling lopsidedly his displeasure at being photographed. The woman with him, her stiff-faced annoyance frozen for ever by the flash, was Fiona Stronach.

Rogers wiped his forehead with the back of a bloody hand. "Drazek served both the Stronach women in their turn. It stuck in my gullet that she wanted to see me. I was cynical enough to look for a reason and her show of family loyalty had enough holes in it to give me one. You know," he said, "if you stand back and really look at her you'll see it writ large. I could smell it on her. She's as ruttish as her sister-in-law was." He cleared his throat. "You shouldn't have any difficulty with either of them now. Stronach did his best to cover her. He's a very intelligent man and wouldn't need it spelled out. He probably knew she'd used his umbrella that night and guessed the rest. I should have had the nous to realize at the time there wasn't one for her. A little thought and it was obvious that she wasn't giving her brother an alibi at all. He didn't need one. But *she* did and she was tying it to him."

Lingard took a deep breath and came up smiling. Lopsidedly, but still a smile. "I've a horrible feeling in my stomach you're going to be right, George. I'll take it from there," he promised. He opened the door. "I can see the sawbones trotting this way with his bag of pills so I'll leave you."

"I'm ready." Rogers was, indeed, at the nadir of physical exhaustion. "What's left of me is going on sick leave and the department's all yours. At least," he amended with a touch of his old arrogance, "it is until I get back."

As Lingard turned to leave, he called him back. "Just one thing, David."

"Yes, George?"

He hesitated. "I'm not being maudlin...but would you see that the...the post mortem on her is restricted." He twisted his head away, looking towards the side of the car. If Lingard hadn't known him as he did he could have mistaken the redness of his lids to be caused by something other than fatigue. "I don't want any idle and nosy bastards looking at her as if she was a bloody peep show." He was both possessive and exculpatory. "She's not *anybody*. She's my wife."

He turned to Coltart. "Thanks for wetnursing me," he said. "You'll make a dam' good grandmother one day." It was the nearest he would ever get to showing his affection for the big man.

Closing his eyes, he shut the sultry blood-smelling violence of Cato Lane from his consciousness, forcing his thoughts to the bright promise of Joanne and the crisp-sheeted rest awaiting him.

He slept.

ABOUT THE AUTHOR

CATHERINE AIRD

For 15 years, Catherine Aird's mysteries have won praises for their brilliant plotting and style. Established alongside other successful English mystery ladies, she continues to thrill old and new mystery fans alike.

THE THRILLING AND MASTERFUL NOVELS OF ROSS MACDONALD

Winner of the Mystery Writers of America Grand Master Award, Ross Macdonald is acknowledged around the world as one of the greatest mystery writers of our time. *The New York Times* has called his books featuring private investigator Lew Archer "the finest series of detective novels ever written by an American."

Now, Bantam Books is reissuing Macdonald's finest work in handsome new paperback editions. Look for these books (a new title will be published every month) wherever paperbacks are sold or use the handy coupon below for ordering:

☐ THE GOODBYE LOOK (24192 * $2.95)
☐ THE FAR SIDE OF THE DOLLAR (24123 * $2.95)
☐ THE ZEBRA-STRIPED HEARSE (23996 * $2.95)
☐ MEET ME AT THE MORGUE (24033 * $2.95)
☐ THE WAY SOME PEOPLE DIE (23722 * $2.95)
☐ THE IVORY GRIN (23804 * $2.95)
☐ THE CHILL (24282 * $2.75)
☐ THE DROWNING POOL (24135 * $2.75)
☐ THE GALTON CASE (22621 * $2.75)
☐ THE FERGUSON AFFAIR (13449 * $2.75)
☐ THE THREE ROADS (22618 * $2.75)
☐ THE DARK TUNNEL (23514 * $2.95)
☐ TROUBLE FOLLOWS ME (23516 * $2.95)
☐ BLACK MONEY (23498 * $2.95)
☐ THE DOOMSTERS (23592 * $2.95)
☐ THE NAME IS ARCHER (23650 * $2.95)

Prices and availability subject to change without notice.

NERO WOLFE

He's not much to look at and he'll never win the hundred yard dash but for sheer genius at unraveling the tangled skeins of crime he has no peer. His outlandish adventures make for some of the best mystery reading in paperback. He's the hero of these superb suspense stories.

BY REX STOUT

SPECIAL MONEY SAVING OFFER

Now you can have an up-to-date listing of Bantam's hundreds of titles plus take advantage of our unique and exciting bonus book offer. A special offer which gives you the opportunity to purchase a Bantam book for only 50¢. Here's how!

By ordering any five books at the regular price per order, you can also choose any other single book listed (up to a $4.95 value) for just 50¢. Some restrictions do apply, but for further details why not send for Bantam's listing of titles today!

Just send us your name and address plus 50¢ to defray the postage and handling costs.

WHODUNIT?

Bantam did! By bringing you these masterful tales of murder, suspense and mystery!

☐	23498	**BLACK MONEY** by Ross MacDonald	$2.95
☐	22618	**THE THREE ROADS** by Ross MacDonald	$2.50
☐	23514	**THE DARK TUNNEL** by Ross MacDonald	$2.75
☐	13449	**THE FEGUSON AFFAIR** by Ross MacDonald	$2.75
☐	22831	**MISS SILVER COMES TO STAY** by Patricia Wentworth	$2.25
☐	24285	**SHE CAME BACK** by Patricia Wentworth	$2.50
☐	20666	**MIND OVER MURDER** by William Kienzle	$2.95
☐	24288	**DEATH IN FIVE BOXES** by Carter Dickson	$2.50
☐	24035	**THE SECRET ADVERSARY** by Agatha Christie	$2.95
☐	23273	**ROSARY MURDERS** by William Kienzle	$2.95

Prices and availability subject to change without notice.

Buy them at your local bookstore or use this handy coupon for ordering: